Thomas and Adeline

A Ghostly Mystery

ALSO BY JENNA LINDSEY

Quest for Evil: The Magic of the Key

The Traveler

Mickey & Nadika, An Adventure Across Time and Space

A Precarious Journey Into Magic

The Dragon's Breath

Thomas and Adeline

A Ghostly Mystery

Jenna Lindsey

 iUniverse®

Thomas and Adeline
A Ghostly Mystery

iUniverse books may be ordered through booksellers or by contacting:

iUniverse
1663 Liberty Drive
Bloomington, IN 47403
www.iuniverse.com
844-349-9409

Because of the dynamic nature of the Internet, any web addresses or links contained in this book may have changed since publication and may no longer be valid. The views expressed in this work are solely those of the author and do not necessarily reflect the views of the publisher, and the publisher hereby disclaims any responsibility for them.

Any people depicted in stock imagery provided by Getty Images are models, and such images are being used for illustrative purposes only. Certain stock imagery © Getty Images.

ISBN: 978-1-6632-1193-4 (sc)
ISBN: 978-1-6632-1192-7 (hc)
ISBN: 978-1-6632-1194-1 (e)

Library of Congress Control Number: 2020920835

Print information available on the last page.

iUniverse rev. date: 11/06/2020

For my husband, Jerry.

Acknowledgments

A very special thank you to Sarra Angharad who cheered me on even when I felt sad.

Here's to you, Sarra.

Prologue

Tom. His name was Thomas, but when he lived people always called him Tom even though he asked them to call him Thomas. Now that he had died, there was no one to call him anything at all. There was no one to call him to dinner or remind him that he needed a haircut. No one to argue with him or laugh at his sense of humor. And no one to call him Tom.

Thomas remembered the morning he had woken up and everything in his room had looked like pictures from a black and white movie. When he stood up he felt strange, as if he too were lacking color. Then he saw his body on the bed, head turned to the right, one hand grasping a pillow, and Thomas knew. He was dead. Briefly he had wondered why. After all, he was only forty-three. His longish hair was still black; his brown eyes had only a few laugh lines at their corners. His nose, though some had considered it big, had not become too long or bulbous at the end. And his mouth, even in death, was slightly upturned on the right side, as if Thomas were laughing at a joke too private to share.

For a long time, Thomas looked around the room and then the house, for a note, a memo, a book on what to do when you're dead. He hoped to find a clue of some kind that might explain not only how and why he died, but now what was apparently to be his ghostly existence. He found nothing.

For a short time, many people came and went. Thomas eavesdropped on a few conversations: the house would be rented out. It was fashionable among the upper class to rent a country house for the summer. "Although this stone monstrosity can hardly be called that," said the solicitor. "We will have to focus on its location, stressing the good fishing and the beautiful countryside."

The plan worked for a few times, but the patrons never stayed long. They left shrieking that the house was haunted. It wasn't Thomas's fault; it was the wind. Certainly the unreliability of the electricity and the persistence of the cold were partly to blame, but always the wind was the final argument for leaving. The wind didn't bother Thomas, but eventually the house was locked up and Thomas was alone. That bothered him.

Often he would stare out a window and look across the gentle curves of land that belied the steep cliffs upon which the house stood, tall and imposing, like a misplaced castle. When Thomas was a boy he had thought the house was a castle. Most of its rooms were huge with high ceilings and large fireplaces. Some parts of the house were five storeys high and many of the staircases had balustrades carved from stone and guarded by empty suits of armor. But there wasn't a moat, just the lake below the cliffs. And there wasn't a dungeon, just a basement with a billiard table, and none of the fireplaces concealed a secret door like the castles Thomas read about in books. It was just a house.

The house had been purchased by his great-great-grandfather: a man determined, a man misguided. He had sought to begin a dynasty and become like the wealthy aristocrats he admired and disdained. But acquiring wealth made him neglectful of his young wife. When she died in childbirth, he hired a governess to raise his only son while he concentrated on his work. "Worked himself to death," it was said.

The son would make more money and his son after him, and the next. Generation after generation stayed at the house at first, despite the eerie noises in empty rooms and the mists that obscured the moor when sunshine could be seen on the horizon. Eventually they set up a home in the city, and came to the house only for Christmas. Each son's wife complained it was too cold, too expensive to update, too far away from everything, and all of them hated the wind.

The wind would churn the lake into a frenzy of waves, rattle rain against the windows, wail down the chimneys, and make the front door shudder. The sons might have stayed but their wives convinced them to move to the city, closer to business and friends.

But Thomas's mother liked the house. She liked to walk near the cliffs and look at the lake and the mountain. Thomas liked the house too, and when he grew up and the house became his, he hired a butler and a cook on weekends so he could give parties for his friends who lived in the city. In this way, he hoped to find a wife; one who would like the house as much as he did.

He had yet to find such a woman before he died. So the house stood silent, but not empty, waiting for something to happen. Thomas waited too. Then one day, something happened.

Chapter One

The car lurched along the dirt road that led to the house. Its driver peered at the silhouette ahead; the rain obscured any possibility of a pleasant first impression. Annoyed that she had defied the innkeeper's advice, the driver slowed the car and steered through the mud toward her destination.

From the pictures she had seen of the house, she knew it was built on a precipice of rocky cliffs. A lake embraced it in a tight horseshoe shape. But the pictures had been taken in fair weather and now the lake, the house, and the cliffs upon which it stood, were almost invisible because of the rain and wind. She concentrated on the road. The single lane would become the driveway and end just in front of the house.

Two minutes more and she saw the huge house on her right, braked slowly and parked directly in front of the single large door. The rain was falling harder. She reached for her purse, regretting her decision to pack her umbrella. Her suitcases would have to wait. For now, she needed to get inside quickly because she was about to get very wet.

Shoving her right hand inside her purse, she gripped a large, thick metal key. Taking a deep breath, she opened the car door. Wind blew rain into her face and soaked her thoroughly before she reached the door to the house. She pushed the key into the keyhole and turned it, imagining she heard a creak above the noise of rain and wind.

The door opened a little and she squeezed inside, pushing the door shut before she leaned against it.

"Miss Parker?"

Adeline looked up. She peered into the darkness of the foyer. "Yes? Yes, I'm Adeline Parker." Clutching the key and her purse, she took a bold step forward as her eyes adjusted to the dim light. "And you are?"

A tall shadow separated itself from the gloom. "I'm Mrs. Folly, the housekeeper."

"Oh. Hello." *Housekeeper?* Feeling self-conscious, Adeline quickly looked down and wiped her shoes on what she hoped was a doormat. A living, talking human being was not at all what she had expected. She had thought to find layers of dust and furniture draped with sheets in this supposedly haunted house, not a housekeeper. Let alone one crisply dressed, with gray hair pulled into a tidy bun and pale green eyes shining in the candlelight.

A door on Adeline's left opened and a shorter figure stepped forward into the foyer. It was a man. In sharp contrast to Mrs. Folly, the man was younger and slightly scruffy looking. He doffed his cap to Adeline, revealing black hair and blue eyes "Evening, Miss. My name's Ham."

"Ham?"

"Short for Hamlet. My father was a keen reader."

"I see." Adeline was uncertain what, or whom, to expect next. "And you are?"

"The handyman, miss. General help as needed."

Mrs. Folly turned to Ham. "Have you the electricity working now?"

"I do, Mrs. Folly." He reached to flick a switch on the wall to demonstrate.

An elegant chandelier came to life. It illuminated the bottom steps of a grand double staircase and spotlighted the rich mahogany wood of a small table to Adeline's right. Beside the table was a delicately carved chair. An oval mirror hung on the wall above the furniture and she saw her bedraggled reflection. Her dark brown hair clung to her shoulders in wet tendrils, and her figure looked even smaller now that her jacket and jeans were wet. She peered at her reflection, her brown eyes critical. *I look like a vagabond.* Hardly a good first impression, but then, she had thought she'd be alone.

"Would you like me to get your luggage, miss?" Ham asked.

"Oh. Yes. Thank you, uh, Ham." Adeline took her car keys from her purse and gave them to Ham. "My luggage is in the trunk. Just three bags. But in this weather—"

"Not to worry, miss. I'm well used to it." Ham took the keys and headed out the door.

Mrs. Folly took a step forward. "I've made soup and kept it warm. In case you might be hungry."

"That would be lovely. Thank you, Mrs. Folly."

Mrs. Folly nodded and waved her right hand toward the dark interior of the house. "I'll take you to the kitchen, if you don't mind. The dining room is not a friendly place this time of night."

"The kitchen will be just fine." Adeline followed Mrs. Folly through a doorway under the staircase and along a poorly lit hallway. Doors and corridors branched off from the central hallway, dark but enticing, promising mystery and discovery. But that would have to wait until tomorrow and until Adeline had determined the circumstances of her hostess. The long, wide hallway seemed to run all the way to the back of the house; it was a silent walk.

"I wasn't expecting anyone," said Adeline, as they entered the large kitchen.

"No? Well when the house used to be rented, it was always the custom to welcome guests as properly as possible. The weather often affected the extent of our courtesy but not its sincerity. But the house

3

has finally been purchased—though I don't know by whom—the solicitor said to make it fit and so I've tried." Mrs. Folly pointed at a square table made of weathered oak. "Please sit down, Miss Parker. I'll get your soup."

Adeline pulled off her jacket and draped it on the back of a chair at the side of the table in front of her. She sat down and looked around. The kitchen was an odd mix of old architecture and new appliances. Pots and pans hung above a six burner gas stove but the sink was a single porcelain basin. There were mostly shelves above the counters and cupboards below, the doors unusually wide.

"The refrigerator is stocked," said Mrs. Folly as she set a bowl of soup in front of Adeline. "If you make a list, I'll bring what you wish next time I return."

"Return?"

"Yes, miss. I was told that my services would most likely be needed by the new owner." She paused then turned to a counter with a cutting board and a loaf of bread. "I used to come up every Thursday, but I never stay the night." She sliced a thick piece of bread and put it on a plate. "I never stay the night."

"I see. And Ham?"

"He'll not stay the night either. But he'll be back tomorrow. He's a cottage nearer the house than to town." Mrs. Folly returned to the table with the plate of bread. "I live in town," she said firmly.

"Well, I very much appreciate that you came such a distance just to make me welcome." Adeline started to eat her soup, aware of Mrs. Folly watching her.

"Will you be expecting your husband to join you?"

Adeline glanced up at Mrs. Folly then looked down at her bare ring finger. "You know who I am?"

"I know. You're Mrs. Sean Isenberg. Your husband is a very wealthy man. I saw your picture in the paper; you and your husband. The press said they expected you to divorce, but I don't have an ear for gossip."

Adeline set down her spoon, deciding to set Mrs. Folly straight right away. "My husband won't be joining me, Mrs. Folly. He's in the city. With his fiancée."

There was silence and Adeline looked up, meeting Mrs. Folly's gaze. She was relieved to see understanding instead of pity.

"Yes," said Mrs. Folly. "Isn't that the way of the bastards?" She turned away and started tidying up the bread. She waved the bread knife once before putting it away in a knife block. "I suppose you'll not be staying long then, just a reprieve, a rest, and then away?"

Feeling a familiar exasperation from years of people, especially her husband, expecting her to behave in a certain way and do as she was told, Adeline raised her voice a little. "Mrs. Folly."

"Yes?"

"I'm the person who bought this house. And I'll definitely be staying."

Mrs. Folly turned around. "Definitely? And alone?"

"Yes."

Again silence, then Mrs. Folly undid the apron about her waist. "I'd best be getting along home. There's a phone here and one in the front hall. But neither is working tonight. The service comes and goes depending on the wind."

"You mean the weather."

Mrs. Folly went to get her coat which hung on a peg near the back kitchen door. "The wind is the weather, Miss Parker. I'll say goodnight. Ham will have parked your car and taken your bags to your room. It's on the second floor." She paused. "Of course, all the rooms are yours now. But as I wasn't told what to expect, I prepared one room of my choice.

"Would you like me to show you the way?"

"No thank you." Adeline stood up. "I'm sure I can find it by myself."

"Very well. Then I'm off. My number is there," Mrs. Folly pointed at a small chalkboard on the wall near the door. "You can call me about the groceries when the phones are working. I was planning on returning to finish tidying up in three days, but perhaps you'll not be wanting my services. You can let me know, please."

"I will. But there's no need to tidy up more for right now. After all, it's just me. But I will call for groceries, Mrs. Folly or just make a trip into town myself."

The silence was not disapproving so much as a sort of disbelief.

"As you like. Goodnight, Miss Parker."

"Goodnight, Mrs. Folly."

Adeline watched Mrs. Folly leave. She waited until she heard the faint thud of the outer door then sat down and finished her soup. It had cooled but she was used to that and the bread was fresh, the butter too. The quiet of the room was a relief after her long trip and unexpected welcome. She got up from the table and took her bowl and plate to the sink, rinsed the dishes and then left them in the sink. She'd wash them in the morning. Right now, she wanted to find the room Mrs. Folly had chosen for her.

Leaving the kitchen, Adeline retraced her path down the main hallway to the foyer. The chandelier still shone. She checked the front door, making sure it was locked, then she turned her attention to the double staircase. It looked as if it had been designed not to impress but to intimidate. She was accustomed to such psychological manipulation.

A light brightened the landing. Fearless, Adeline chose the left side and walked up the broad stairs to the second floor. Dark wood and darker carpet ran right and left but straight ahead another light streaked the carpet and brightened the dark colors. She walked down the hallway, wondering briefly why the walls were bare of paintings. She went to the doorway with the light and looked inside.

The bedroom was not large, but it was inviting. The wallpaper was a delicate pattern of red roses scattered on a pale pink background. The dark carpet of the hallway ended at the doorway and became a soft cream color. The furniture was obviously new, but tasteful and elegant. Adeline felt welcome.

She walked into the room. A fireplace flanked by two armchairs stood opposite a four poster bed. Her luggage had been placed at the foot of the bed and, after peeking into the en suite, Adeline went to unpack her nightgown. She was about to undress when a noise in the hallway made her stand still and listen. There was silence, then the sound came again: a scratching, like fingers on glass.

Anxiety swept over Adeline. Before it could become fear, she reminded herself that this was her house, her home, and no else was here. She strode to the doorway, hesitated for a moment, and then looked into the hallway. To the left, all was quiet, but to her right, just a few feet away, the end of the hallway was marked by a wide window framed with long drapes. One of the drapes moved a little as the wind pushed it away.

Going to the window, Adeline snatched the drape aside to face her intruder. The tips of a tree's branches touched the glass and moved back and forth in the wind. Adeline closed the window and locked the latch, leaving the drape pulled to one side. Now all she heard was the pounding of her heart. She returned to her bedroom, shut the door and then impulsively turned the key in the keyhole. A satisfying click made her smile a little at her nervousness. She had never been alone before, not like this. All her life someone had looked after her. Now she was determined to look after herself.

She looked around the room, her room, at the pretty lampshade trimmed with beads on the bedside table, the fireplace with a brass screen, and the window seat directly across from the door. *It must face the front of the house.* Adeline went to it and, kneeling on her right knee, leaned forward, drew back one of the sheer curtains, and peered out into the darkness. She couldn't see anything clearly. There was no moon to light the lake, just the dark shape of part of the roof off to her right, sloping up and away. She would investigate tomorrow.

The long day caught her and she half-closed her eyes, listening to the silence. She stood up and left the window, moving quietly, accustomed to trying not to disturb anyone, to go about unnoticed. She took her nightgown and went to the en suite. Several minutes later, she returned and, after pulling back the feather duvet, climbed onto the big bed. For a moment, she felt lost, then the feeling passed as she relaxed into the bed's softness and the duvet's warmth. The pillows were feather, too, and one tickled Adeline's neck as she turned on her left side and faced the door.

I'm here. I'm really here. She sighed and closed her eyes unaware that she wasn't alone, that someone was looking after her.

Thomas waited a long time in one of the chairs by the fireplace. He had been following Adeline since her arrival, curious and now pleased that she had purchased his house. It needed someone with a sense of adventure, and when he followed her into the hallway he had been impressed by her bravery.

Of course, thought Thomas, *it was only the old tree. But she hadn't known that.*

He had often climbed the tree when he was a boy. It had been his secret staircase to the lawn below where he could watch the wind on the lake, the sunsets, too. Long past his bedtime, he would climb back up the tree and let himself in the window.

This room had been his once, before it had been renovated. He hadn't liked the changes until today when Adeline had seemed to like the room. It was hers now; his home, too. For some reason, this made him happy and he had stayed to luxuriate in the feeling.

Thomas stood up and smiled at the figure asleep in the bed. He felt a bit wistful and for a moment he let himself hope that Adeline would stay. *I think she could be happy here.*

He almost forgot himself and was about to wish her goodnight. *She may be adventurous and brave, but seeing me tonight would most definitely be a shock. Tomorrow will be much better and give me time to plan.*

Thomas took a step toward the door and disappeared.

Chapter Two

Adeline stretched her legs and wiggled her toes. The warmth of the duvet belied the cold air in the bedroom. She pulled the duvet up and then over her shoulders and looked at the fireplace. Even if it wasn't decorative, she had no idea how to make a fire. Maybe Ham would do it for her; better still, maybe he would teach her how to do it for herself.

Pleased with her decision, Adeline sat up, pulling the duvet with her as she crawled to the bottom of the bed. She had left her housecoat there. *Now where is it?* An unpleasant memory interrupted her search. Her husband had always chided her for misplacing things. *Ex-husband!* She reminded herself firmly. She looked at the floor; her housecoat was a clump of blue on the carpet. She must have kicked it in the night.

Reluctantly, Adeline threw off the duvet, grabbed her housecoat, and then dashed to the en suite. A shower warmed her up, but she dressed quickly. The lack of sunlight in the room told her it was probably raining. Pushing her feet into her slippers, she went to the window seat and drew the curtains apart. It was raining: a steady rain that spread itself against the picture window like Vaseline.

Adeline didn't mind. She glanced at the clock on the mantelpiece. It was almost ten. Mrs. Folly had said Ham would be back today but she hadn't said when. Adeline decided she had better have breakfast and then she could look around the house while she waited for Ham.

Crossing the room, she paused at the fireplace. A small light switch, almost invisible beside the painted brick, made her curious. She pushed the switch down. Nothing happened. She turned away and heard a rush of noise behind her. She looked back and then returned to the hearth. A fire was burning under and across the three small logs in the fireplace. She looked closely at the flames. "It's a gas fire. A gas fireplace. Of course. After all, the stove is gas. Well, at least I don't have to admit total helplessness to Ham."

Adeline turned the fireplace off. She had no intention of staying in her room with an entire mansion to explore. But breakfast first. Unlocking her bedroom door, she stepped into the hallway. In the dreary light that made its way through the rain and the window, the carpet looked rusty red with a gold pattern fading into the pile. She wondered how old it was as she walked to the staircase. She could afford to have it replaced, but that would despoil the beauty of the house. Its antiquity, not just its location, was one of the things that had appealed to her when she first saw its picture. Reaching the top of the main staircase, she noticed that she had forgotten to turn off the chandelier the night before. Another thing she had often been derided for. But not now. Still, the light was too bright despite the gray day and the rain.

When she reached the foyer, Adeline switched off the chandelier, found the hallway light and used that to brighten her path to the kitchen. After finishing her breakfast she went to the Great Room that was just off the foyer. It was completely empty of furniture but at its far end there was an enormous fireplace. Fascinated, she went to examine it. It was made of large stones and was big enough for her to stand inside. Its floor was bare of fake logs or ashes. From its size, she guessed it was a wood burning fireplace and the room had probably been originally designed to welcome and warm visitors after a cold journey on horseback.

Several loud knocks interrupted her inspection. She went to the front door and pulled. It didn't move. She pulled again, using both hands and the heavy door opened. "Good morning, Ham." Adeline noticed that the rain had lessened to a sprinkle.

"Morning, miss." Ham touched the brim of his cap. "I hope you had a restful night." His eyes looked worried.

"Very restful, thank you. Would you show me where you parked my car, please? I've a few things in the back seat."

"Certainly, miss. We'll have to take the road. It's too steep from the back door. And we'd best go right away before the rain picks up. Rained all night, it did. But I think the wind's tired at the moment."

"The wind is tired?" Adeline was searching a small closet. Finding an old pair of boots and a raincoat, she sat down on the carved chair that stood near the table. "I hope no one will mind if I borrow these for now," she remarked as she pulled on the boots. She stood up. They were a bit large but more comfortable than her still damp runners.

"Oh, no, miss. Not at all. Mrs. Folly always leaves a couple of spare coats and boots for anyone who might not be prepared for the wind. And rain," he added.

Pulling on the rain coat, Adeline smiled at Ham, and stepped past him into the cold morning air. The sprinkle of rain on her face felt refreshing. In the city, you hid from the rain, dashing from door to door usually with only a newspaper as a flimsy shield. But here, with the clouds shifting to allow a little sunlight, the rain felt natural, almost friendly.

Ham shut the door and then escorted Adeline along the front of the house. She could see its pinkish beige stonework and the curve of a tower on the west front corner. They passed it and walked to a narrow side road that was merely two lines of tire tracks running through the mud. They followed it.

The slope was as Ham described it: steep and treacherous, a person could easily slip and fall. She looked over her shoulder at the house. In the lighter rain, with sunlight lifting the clouds, she could see everything she had missed in her drive the night before: the green and yellow of countryside with short, dark green trees in the distance, and to the south, a grass and heather covered mountain. During the tiresome details of the purchase of the house, the mountain had been noted and marked as a hill. It was part of the property and Adeline had decided to call it a mountain; her mountain.

Behind her, to the west, she knew the grass was less than fifty yards from steep cliffs about thirty feet high. But from where she stood on the road, the land dipped along the east side of the house then stopped at the lake. The surface of the water looked serene, a shade of blue and teal like she had never seen or imagined.

The rain stopped and Adeline stopped walking as sunlight burst through the clouds and changed all the colors of the landscape from muted and weary to bright and warm.

"It's beautiful," she said.

"I'm glad you like it, miss. It's not for everyone. You have to love the wildness and not try to tame it." He walked ahead of Adeline and pointed. "That there's the barn, miss. That's where I parked your car. When it's raining hard, the mud becomes a living thing. It's sunk many a car's tires—terrible difficult to dig out—and I didn't want you to suffer the same fate."

Adeline joined Ham and they walked down the muddy lane together. She was glad of the height of the boots as her feet sank in the mud. "Why did no one ever pave the driveway or convert the barn into a garage, Ham? Are there horses?"

"No horses these days, miss. 'Cept for mine. She's waiting near the gate; won't come further. She doesn't like the footing," Ham said quickly. "As for the road, I heard they tried a few times, but nothing held up. I don't know about converting. Back when the family lived here, they were always contending with the house and the wind. Fighting it, you might say."

Ham reached the barn door and slid it back revealing Adeline's Mercedes. It was parked on some straw straight ahead of them. A few large stalls stood empty and several square windows were covered with wood shutters.

Going to her car, Adeline went to the back door on the driver's side and opened it. "Ham? Would you take these for me, please?"

"Yes, miss." Ham stepped forward and took each bag as Adeline pulled them out. "I did notice last night that you had bags and such in the back seat." Ham's voice sounded apologetic. "But I didn't want to disturb anything private or get it wet in the rain."

"I appreciate that, Ham." Adeline unloaded a tote bag, two shopping bags, and her umbrella. "There, I think that's everything. Oh, wait." She went around to the passenger door, opened it, and leaned inside. "My music," she explained as she pulled a portable CD player and a bag of CDs from the passenger seat.

"Ah. That'll liven up a room or two." Ham looked out the barn door. "We'd best be getting back. The rain is returning."

Adeline shut the car door and went to look outside. The world looked peaceful. She turned to Ham. "How can you tell?"

"The wind is stirring up the clouds. See the black on the west horizon? That's a storm coming in."

Adeline looked at the black clouds. They looked like an army marching to war. "All right, Ham. Let's go."

They exited the barn and Ham closed the door. He slid a bar in place. "That'll keep it safe."

"From thieves?"

"From the wind."

Adeline nodded. She was finding the wind to be like a distant relative: annoying even when they weren't present. As they walked back to the house, Adeline pointed to the lake. "Look!"

Ham came up beside her. "Geese. Wild ones. There'll be more. Ducks, too. If we're lucky, swans may come up this summer. There's a whole mess of wildlife about the lake, but most people who come up here don't notice. They're busy mucking about with their boats with motors. All you need is a nice boat with a sail to enjoy the water."

"Have you got one?"

"No, miss. That's too grand for me. I've a wee boat for a bit of fishing and that suits me fine."

Rain spattered their heads. "We'd better get inside," said Adeline. She couldn't hurry in the boots, but she managed get to the front door before the rain became a downpour. Like the night before, the heavy door was easier to push than to pull. Adeline laughed as she stepped inside the house. "That rain happened quickly. Is it like this a lot?"

Setting down the bags, Ham took off his cap and shook it free of raindrops. "Often enough. Until summer. Then it's grand. You'll see. If you'll be staying."

"I'll be staying."

Ham nodded. "I'll take these to your room."

He was about to pick up the bags when Adeline, sitting on the chair and pulling off the boots, raised her right hand. "Please don't, Ham. I have to sort through them later. I wanted to ask you about the Great Room's fireplace."

Ham looked at the open doors to the Great Room. "I only know a little about the fireplace. I do know there's access to the basement from the Great Room. That's where the utility room is."

"Oh? Nothing else downstairs?"

"There's a billiards room. And the last of the family to live here put in a television." Ham pointed straight up. "He hired someone to install a fancy antenna on the flagpole and put televisions in several of the rooms. I don't know where exactly."

"Well, I'll have fun finding them. But, I was just in the Great Room this morning—" Adeline reached into one of the bags and pulled out a pair of slip-on shoes—"and I didn't see a door anywhere. Except those, of course." She pointed to the large double doors across from where she sat.

"Oh. That's because the inside doors, the ones that take you from one room to the next, are hidden. One of the owners' wives wanted the rooms smaller. She hated the wind and it's said she thought fewer doors and smaller rooms would somehow make the wind more tolerable. So I was told. It was a long time ago.

"But I can show you the door to the basement, if you like."

"Yes, please. And the fireplace, Ham? It looks centuries old. It's a wood burning fireplace, isn't it?"

"Yes, miss. But no one's ever been successful keeping a fire going there."

Adeline stood up. "Let me guess. The wind puts it out."

"Yes, miss."

"And how old is the fireplace?" Adeline headed into the Great Room with Ham right behind her.

"Centuries, as you said, miss. The house was originally going to be a castle."

"You mean it never was a castle?"

"No. Lightning struck it before it was half built. A fierce bolt that came with a fiercer storm. The legend says that the wind blew so strong it made the lake a tower of waves that attacked the castle like battering rams. A knight had been granted the lands and his men were building a castle for his lady. But something happened and his lady was killed."

"That's so sad." Adeline stood in front of the fireplace, imagining the scene that Ham had just described. She turned away. "Where's the door?"

Ham walked across the room to the far right corner. "It's over here." He put his right hand against the flowered wallpaper and pushed. Part of the wallpaper separated from the rest showing the outline of a door. Ham pushed a second time and the door opened. "There you are. Shall I take you to see?"

This time Adeline chose not to be alone. "Yes, please." She followed Ham. The short hallway was neither dark nor dirty. It was painted and clean and led to painted wood stairs that went down a short flight to a landing, turned and went down seven steps further to the basement.

Ham flicked a light switch on the wall and three tiffany overhead lights lit a large, rectangular room with a warm green carpet. In the center of the room stood a billiard table. Small, round tables flanked by chairs dotted the length of the room and there was a bar at the far end with a wide mirror behind it. The mirror reflected a television screen on the wall opposite. The walls were finished with oak, uninterrupted by pictures or paintings. Not even a banner or a flag.

Ham led Adeline to a plank door at the far end of the room past the bar. Opening it, he stood back and allowed her to go first. The next room ran horizontal to the pub-like room they'd passed through, like the top of a 'T.' It was square and plain with a cement floor, but Adeline could tell it was kept clean; there wasn't a whiff of dust in the air.

"I look after almost everything here, so you've little need for worrying. Over here"—he walked to the left side of the door—"are the breaker switches, and all the tricksy cable stuff too. A guest made quite a fuss when his computer didn't get a good signal. Something like that.

"I can fix almost anything for you, miss. But I don't know a thing about computers."

"That's all right, Ham. I don't have one." Adeline looked around. "Is this all that's down here? I mean, the house is so large and this basement is so small."

"It's the rock, miss. Took over a year of digging in the rain and mud before the construction crews could clear enough space to drill into the rock. They made these two rooms just big enough for what they'd need at the time."

Adeline thought of the cliffs, eroded by wind and water perhaps, but still formidable and indomitable. "They certainly did a good job." Adeline looked around the room. "But where is the laundry room?"

"Not down here. There's a small one near the servants' quarters, not far from the kitchen. It's nothing fancy. Just four washing machines and two dryers. I check them regularly and they're working fine, miss."

Ham took a step toward the door. "Would you like me to show you where they're located and how to use them?"

"No, thank you. I'm looking forward to exploring the house. I'm sure I'll find the laundry room."

"'Course you can have your laundry done in town, if you like. There's a dry cleaner there. I can take it in for you." Ham seemed anxious to please. "If there's something special you need, Mrs. Folly's the one to ask. She's in charge of the house."

"Well, I'm in charge now, Ham. But I'll be sure to ask Mrs. Folly. Thank you for showing me the basement. And the hidden door."

"You're welcome, miss. Will you be needing me for anything today? I'd rather not keep my mare waiting in a storm."

"You don't have a car?"

"No, miss. I do have a truck. Good and sturdy, but a storm makes the mud treacherous. You were lucky not to get stuck yesterday."

"Yes, I was. Well, I can't think of anything I need today or even tomorrow. You and Mrs. Folly have provided for me so well."

"Thank you, miss."

Adeline thought for a minute. *A handyman could prove indispensable.* And she liked Ham's genial attitude. "If you're available, Ham, perhaps you'll stay on as handyman for me? We can work out the details later."

"You're the new owner then, miss?"

"Yes." Adeline waited for his objection. She was accustomed to her opinions being questioned.

"That'd be fine, miss. And Mrs. Folly too?"

Adeline hesitated. "For now, yes. I'll be speaking with her later."

"That's grand, miss. Just grand." Ham gave her a big smile and they left the utility room. As they crossed the pub room, Adeline thought she saw a movement by the bar. She stopped and turned, half expecting Mrs. Folly or another house employee she had yet to meet. But there was no one there and the large mirror behind the bar reflected only the room and its contents.

"Something wrong, miss?" Ham, just two strides ahead of Adeline, returned to her side. He followed her stare.

"No. I—I was just admiring the room. That's all." Adeline gave Ham a slight smile and then walked to the door. She stopped when she realized Ham wasn't right behind her. When she turned to face the room she saw Ham touch the front of his cap with his right index finger, as if he were acknowledging something. Or someone?

"Are you coming, Ham?"

He turned and joined Adeline at the doorway. "Right, miss. I'll just turn off the light." He flicked a switch beside the door and they left the room together.

Behind them, the light turned on again.

Chapter Three

All morning Thomas followed Adeline as she roamed about the house. He kept a discreet distance, feeling a bit deceitful that he didn't reveal his presence. He was waiting for the right moment, certain an opportunity would present itself. He had his story ready. It wasn't exactly the truth and could later be construed as a lie, but it did stick close to the facts. He hoped that would count in his favor, for Thomas felt almost love struck by Adeline and her thoughtful investigation of his house.

She would open a door, stand very still, and seem to breathe in the atmosphere of the room. Next, she would enter slowly and move quietly about the room, touching the occasional object 'dart or piece of furniture. In the Music Room, she didn't show interest in the old piano or the violin, but she did look at the empty space above the fireplace for a long time.

Thomas heard her say, "There was a painting there once; possibly a portrait." She had turned in a slow circle, looking at the walls. "But where is the painting now? Where are any paintings?"

She went to the room's only window. It was smudged with dirt, offering no view. Thomas stepped quietly away from the corner where he stood, expecting her to give up and leave, but she turned around instead, eyes narrowing accusingly at the wall opposite the window. She walked toward it, her right hand outstretched. When she touched the wallpaper, she followed it along the wall then back two steps, then forward.

Thomas wanted to speak up, but he suspected it wasn't the right time. *Would she find the door?* He could tell she was remembering what Ham had said about the wife that didn't like the doors to show. Thomas hadn't liked that wife. He hadn't liked any of them. He did like Adeline. She seemed right for his house. *Well, her house now. If she stays and doesn't put it up for sale, scared away by the wind or what the wind sometimes causes to happen. Or me.*

He watched as Adeline found the slight ripple in the wallpaper that concealed the door. She traced one finger up and down and then pushed: once, twice. The door creaked and opened, tearing some of the wallpaper.

"Oh, no." Adeline looked over her shoulder, then shrugged. "Well. It's my house after all."

Thomas thought her voice held a touch of satisfaction.

Pushing the door wide, she felt just inside the doorway for a light switch, found it and illuminated the steep stairs immediately in front of her. Undeterred by the climb they presented, she smiled and started up the stairs. "Now this is more like it."

Wondering what she meant, Thomas went to the door, still a voyeur in his own home. Any minute he knew she would reach the room where some of the paintings were kept. He made himself count to ten, then twenty. *That should do it.* He made himself visible. He was ready to meet Adeline.

Reminding himself not to float, Thomas climbed the stairs. He knew the room to which they led. He knew what was stored in the room. He hoped Adeline would find it as interesting as she did the house. She certainly seemed fearless, but what she was about to discover might finally frighten her.

Reaching the little room near the top of the house, Thomas entered, pretending he didn't expect to find anybody there. He saw Adeline kneeling in a corner, pulling the framed paintings toward her, studying each one as if she were trying to understand the images.

"Ah. Hullo," said Thomas.

Adeline turned her head quickly. She pushed the paintings back against the wall and stood up. "Hello." She brushed at her jeans. "You startled me. I didn't think anyone else was here." She paused. "I haven't met all the staff yet. Just Mrs. Folly and Ham. Short for Hamlet."

"So it is. Yes. Well." Thomas shrugged. "I'm not a member of the staff. I'm more of a regular resident." He took a step forward. "I'm sorry I startled you." He held out his right hand. "I'm Thomas."

Adeline walked forward and shook Thomas's proffered hand. "I'm Adeline. I just bought this house."

"Indeed."

"Yes."

The silence lengthened.

"Did you say you were a regular resident?" Adeline asked.

"Ah. Yes. I've been staying—renting—a few rooms. In my defense, I haven't received a notice to vacate. Yet." Thomas rubbed his hands together for a moment. "I've been staying here and cataloguing the rooms. Difficult to do, as you can see.

"This room for example." He waved his right arm to indicate the small space. "I've been looking for the door to this room for some time." He chose distraction over truth. "And the paintings, too."

Adeline glanced over her shoulder. "I was just looking at them. I've only been here since last night, but I noticed there weren't any paintings on the walls, just bare spaces. And yet, these aren't at all what I expected."

"Oh?" Thomas feigned ignorance. He went to the wall where the paintings leaned. He knew how many there were, and how many there were yet to be found, plus one more that he had hidden away. He pointed at the first painting. It was of the house. It depicted a sky gray with coming rain and the house appeared dreary, tired even.

Thomas turned to Adeline. "It's not very cheerful, I admit. What sort of paintings were you expecting to find?"

Adeline joined him. "In a house this old there are usually portraits. You know, of the very first owners then the next and so on; people who represent the history of the house." She pulled a painting from behind the first. "But all of these are of the house. And, it's very strange, but each painting is the same but different."

Thomas peered at the painting that had been behind the one Adeline held in her hands. He remembered the painting, but he pretended surprise. "It must be that different artists painted the house. It's rather famous for its unique architectural style, its location, and of course, its weather."

"Hmm, the weather." Another silence. "I heard that it was haunted."

They regarded each other for a minute. Thomas finally spoke. "I heard that too."

Adeline smiled and returned her attention to the paintings. She pulled out one and set it beside the first. "Same angle." She leaned close. "But there's something odd. Something spooky. And there isn't a signature." She stepped in front of Thomas, and pulled a few more of the paintings forward, her gaze intent. "Definitely spooky. Almost ghostly. In this one, the house looks like it's about to disappear."

"An illusion caused by the weather, perhaps?" Thomas waited for her reaction. She was unafraid of the mystery and that pleased him very much.

"Perhaps." Adeline carefully set the paintings back and faced Thomas. "I'm sorry. I can't stand an unsolved mystery. I tend to get obsessive and now it's made me forget my manners.

"You said you were here to catalogue the rooms. Where do you stay? Are you writing a book? Is there anything you could tell me about the history of the house?"

"Ah." Thomas fidgeted. "Well, I reside on the far side of the house. I suppose you could say I'm a bit of a recluse."

"Oh? Why?"

"Unexpected circumstances."

"Such as?"

Thomas tilted his head to one side and smiled his lopsided smile at Adeline. "You are inquisitive, aren't you?"

She nodded. "I am. I'm also hungry. I've been wandering all over the house this morning. Will you join me?"

"In your wandering?"

"For lunch."

Thomas hesitated. He hadn't thought this far ahead. *Still, what have I to lose now? Adeline is as interesting as she is lovely.* "I'd like that very much. Thank you." He waved his right hand toward the door. "Lead and I'll follow."

Adeline headed toward the door. As she started down the stairs, she spoke over her right shoulder. "I must let Mrs. Folly know I've found a hidden room. She seems a bit afraid of the house."

"Do you think so? Because she does know about the hidden doors. She and Ham just don't remember where all of them are located or what's behind them."

"Oh. You've asked them? Have you interviewed them for your book?"

"I must correct your assumption; my fault entirely, I'm sure. I'm not writing a book. This house is more of a . . . hobby. I've been staying on to learn more about its history. More for my own interest."

"That's something we share then. An interest in the house, I mean. And the paintings."

They reached the bottom of the stairs and Adeline walked forward into the room. Thomas pulled the door closed. He paused as he noticed Adeline regarding him with curiosity. For a moment, he thought he might be losing his cohesion, but she didn't look alarmed.

"What is it?" he asked.

"You said you'd been looking for this door and that room for some time. Why?"

"Well, being a bit of a student of history, this house especially, I knew there were paintings missing. And I knew there were doors that had been disguised. I'm not certain of the reason and I suppose I'm not as avid as you about mysteries. More just interested. Nothing better to do with my time."

Thomas sauntered over to Adeline and they left the room and started in the direction of the main staircase.

"What do you do with your time, Thomas? How long have you been here?"

"Oh, a long time. In fact, I've lost track. I'm not particularly organized. One of the luxuries of early retirement."

"What did you retire from?"

Life, thought Thomas. Aloud he said, "Not a great deal. My money was inherited. I went to school. I was a bit of a gad-about for a time. But all I really wanted to do was live simply, get married, perhaps have children. I must sound awfully boring."

"No. Not boring, just familiar; I've wanted the same thing."

At the center staircase, they each took a separate curving stairway to the main floor. At the bottom, they teamed up again and went down the hallway to the kitchen. As they walked along, Adeline pointed at empty spaces on the walls. "See there? The paintings we found of the house weren't big enough to cover all these spaces."

Thomas smiled. "You're much more than inquisitive. You're more like a detective."

Adeline laughed. "I'm obsessing again. The portraits were probably sold or loaned to an art gallery."

"That's a possibility. But I have a feeling you're placating your curiosity."

Thomas stopped at the door to the kitchen and waved Adeline ahead of him. She went to the refrigerator and took out the soup that Mrs. Folly had made the night before.

"Don't worry," Adeline said as she took the large bowl to the stove. "I'm a wonder when it comes to re-heating things. Mrs. Folly made this yesterday."

Thomas reached for a pot. "You don't cook?"

"Not really. I got married very young and my husband was very rich."

"Husband?"

"Ex-husband." Adeline took the pot from Thomas, set it on a burner, and poured in the soup. "So, now I'll finally get a chance to learn how to cook."

"I don't suppose you left him so you could take cooking classes?"

"No. I sued him for divorce, so I could be free of him . . . and his mistress. Such a civilized sort of word, isn't it? Mistress. As if it meant Mistress of the House or the Manor and not—" Adeline stopped and stared for a minute—"the bed."

Thomas reached for a large spoon and handed it to Adeline. "I'm sorry."

She stirred the soup. "Please don't be. I wasn't happily married." She pointed to the loaf of bread, wrapped and sitting on a cutting board. "Would you mind slicing that?"

Thomas looked at the bread and then at the bread knife next to it. "I'm not any good at slicing bread. It always comes out too thin, or lopsided."

"You're as bad as me." Adeline smiled up at him. "Can you stir soup?"

"That I think I can manage."

Laughing, Adeline left the spoon in the pot and went to slice the bread.

Thomas put his right hand on the spoon and gripped it firmly. He pushed it slowly around the pot. He knew he could remain visible for as long as he liked, if he didn't get distracted. And spending time with Adeline was proving to be more than he had hoped for. *What had I hoped for?* He glanced down at the soup and noticed that his hand on the spoon was slightly transparent. Quickly, he concentrated and just as quickly his hand became solid again. He set the spoon aside. "Ah, I think the soup is ready."

"Great. I've sliced the bread." Adeline held up a plate. "There are bowls in one of these cupboards." She went to the table and set the plate down. "I haven't had time to get to know what goes where yet."

Thomas smiled. "I think a little detective work is called for." He walked along the line of cupboards toward the sink. "If I were a soup bowl, where would I be?"

Knowing perfectly well where to look, Thomas still took his time. Finally he opened a cupboard, looked inside, and turned to Adeline. "Apparently I'd be right here." Thomas reached inside the cupboard and took out two bowls.

"I'm impressed. You should use that approach to help me find more paintings."

Thomas took the bowls to the pot of soup. "Why are you so intent on finding a few old portraits?"

"I told you," Adeline joined Thomas and served the soup. "I get obsessive."

"What else do you obsess about?"

"Everything."

They sat down at the table and Thomas regarded his soup. He hadn't eaten or even felt hungry for a long time but since he was visible at the moment, he should be able to eat, drink, even wash up the dishes after they finished lunch. Dipping his spoon into the hot soup, he took a cautious sip. "It's very good."

"Yes. Mrs. Folly was very nice to make it." Adeline paused. "You know, she's a bit of a talker and yet, she didn't mention you."

"Oh?"

Thomas became aware of Adeline studying him with a steady gaze. She leaned forward. "I think you're hiding something from me, Thomas."

"Hiding something?" Thomas sat back. "Whatever do you mean?"

Adeline pointed her spoon at him. "It was you that painted the paintings of the house, right? That's why you're a recluse; you're a painter, I mean, an artist. And I bet you know exactly where the portraits are hidden."

"Hah." Thomas looked away so Adeline wouldn't see the relief on his face. His identity was safe as was the truth of his existence. *She doesn't suspect I'm a ghost, she suspects I'm an artist.* He almost laughed. *Now, how should I respond without complicating our rather tentative relationship with more lies?*

"I'm sorry to disappoint you, Adeline, but I'm not an artist. I simply know a little of the history of the house. But I'd be happy to help you find the portraits if you like."

She smiled. "I'd like that very much." Turning her attention to her soup, she paused and looked at Thomas again. "Why do you suppose the doors are covered with wallpaper?"

"Poor taste?"

"I think it's more than that."

"Perhaps another mystery to be solved?"

"Yes."

"I see." They finished their lunch; the silence now companionable. Thomas helped with the washing up then spoke. "This has been delightful, but I had best get going for now."

"But, Thomas, you said you'd help me find the paintings."

There was a plaintive tone in Adeline's voice that made Thomas pause. "I just have to check on a few things. My part of the house requires a bit of routine maintenance: watering the plants, making sure the rooms are aired; simple but important. Let's meet in the library at about, oh, four o'clock?"

He saw disappointment on Adeline's face but he continued. "The paintings—wherever they are—will still be waiting for us to discover them."

Her face brightened. "You're right. That will be fun."

As Adeline looked at him, Thomas noticed that he was only a little taller, but he still liked that she had to look up. He liked that she looked at him and when she did, she looked him in the eyes, and called him Thomas instead of Tom. As he looked down into her eyes, he realized he could easily love Adeline. "Ah, the, ah library isn't far from the Great Room. Think what fun you'll have trying to find the adjoining door."

"How do you know there will be an adjoining door?"

"Well, I have been here a while, as I said."

"Yes. As you said. I'll see you at four then?"

27

"I promise." Thomas smiled and went to the kitchen door. He turned and waved his right hand in what he hoped was a carefree manner. Then he left the room and walked down the hallway. When he felt certain Adeline couldn't hear him anymore, he made himself invisible. He wanted to spend more time with her, but without being seen, to gather his thoughts and feelings.

He stood against a wall and waited for Adeline. Before he saw her walking along the dark hallway, Thomas could smell her perfume. It was a soft, floral scent. *Like a garden in spring after rain,* he imagined. A memory poked at his mind. The house had a sunroom facing the sea. *Perhaps that's what I'm recalling.* He frowned. *Still, I think there is a small garden somewhere.*

Returning his thoughts to Adeline, he watched her approach. Her steps were quick, purposeful. She called his name and he jumped, thinking she could see him, but then realized she was only hoping to see him, perhaps catch up with him.

Her steps slowed. She stopped and looked around. Finally she turned to her right and walked along the shorter hallway. Thomas knew it led to a sitting room. He followed Adeline. This time she didn't pause at the doorway but instead walked into the center of room and turned around in a slow circle, seeming to appreciate the delicate furnishings. Then Thomas realized she was studying the wallpaper. *She's looking for the door.*

After a minute, Adeline went to the bare wall opposite the room's main doorway. She ran her right hand along the flowery wallpaper: up, across, down. She stopped halfway down and pushed. The wallpaper broke apart, revealing part of the hidden door.

Thomas smiled and watched as Adeline pushed hard and the door gave way, tearing the old wallpaper and giving passage to the room beyond. It was a small library.

"Very clever," Adeline said aloud. She entered the little room.

Quietly, Thomas followed her. A clock on the wall chimed and he remembered that a favorite television program was about to begin.

He didn't remember who had been responsible for putting televisions in various rooms of his house, but he did remember he had been more than annoyed that they had the temerity to put one in a library. True, the shelves were mostly bare. The older, valuable first editions had been taken away by the wives. Stolen, in Thomas's opinion. The children's books had been the next to go 'missing.' Now there were only a few books on each shelf, mostly history and geography and a few uninteresting novels.

One shelf had been adjusted to hold a small television. Two chairs had been placed close to each other but not too close to the television's screen. When it had first been installed Thomas had left the room each time it had been turned on, but eventually his curiosity prevailed and he had studied the operation of the machine.

One afternoon he had watched two programs in the company of a person he guessed to be the cook, based on the large white apron she wore over her dress. When she turned off the television and left the room, Thomas had stayed, waited until it was dark, the house quiet, and then turned the television on again. He had hoped to see more of the programs the cook had watched but soon figured out that they changed according to the time of day.

He settled on a movie and found he enjoyed it very much. It had been like seeing a play produced just for him. It was a bit lonely because he had sometimes gone to the theater with friends and once they had gone to a movie together. He had never imagined that such a thing would eventually be available for private viewing or that he would turn to it for company.

He noticed Adeline wasn't paying attention to the television. She was looking at the books and reading the titles. Her back was to Thomas.

Time for action, Thomas told himself. *After all, she does enjoy a mystery.* Quickly, before Adeline lost interest in the books, Thomas went to the television and turned it on. Then he went to one of the chairs and sat down.

Adeline spun about, obviously surprised, but she didn't seem afraid. "There must have been a power surge," she said. "Probably caused by the wind."

She went to the television and examined it. Someone on the program said something amusing and she laughed. "A library with hardly any books and a TV, I shouldn't be surprised. This house is wonderfully strange."

Adeline went to the chair next to where Thomas was sitting. She sat down and leaned back. The two of them watched the program together, Adeline unaware of sharing the time with Thomas.

When the clock chimed four, Thomas stood up and walked through the wall into the Great Room. He had decided he would open the connecting door from there, proving to Adeline that he meant what he had said. He would help her find the paintings. Well, most of them.

Chapter Four

Adeline stood up and turned off the television. She looked at the blank screen, but she wasn't thinking about the program she had watched. She was thinking about Thomas. She had been so taken with his company that she had forgotten to ask his last name. But then, she hadn't told him hers. It was as if, when they introduced themselves, they already knew each other.

His eyes were kind, his voice warm, and his slightly lopsided smile was friendly and sincere. Adeline liked that he didn't wear a tie with his white shirt. It had a wing-tip collar and the open neckline suited him. His loose-fitting gray trousers and black shoes were casual, meant to be worn around the house. He slouched slightly and it made him seem to droop, but his stance only made him more appealing. It made him appear resigned and she empathized with that feeling. All this she had noticed in an instant and only now remembered the details because she had talked so much.

It wasn't like her to talk and talk. No one had ever listened before. And she had rarely talked about herself because no one had been interested in her or her fascination with mysteries and all things mysterious. But Thomas had listened. He had been interested and this was new to Adeline.

Dear Thomas. He'd been very patient to listen as I chattered on about missing paintings and he was so kind to offer his help. When he said he had to leave, I panicked. Why did I panic? "Because I wanted him to stay." She shook her head. "Still the romantic, which is just a soft word for fool. I can't believe I'm still hoping to find somebody who will really, truly love me."

Her husband had lured her away from her family home with promises of a beautiful, romantic life. Once they were married, he returned his attention to his business and neglected Adeline. He took her love and attention for granted, expecting, insisting, that she always be agreeable, compliant, and never argue with him.

For six years she had tip-toed through their marriage, trying to solve the mystery of what she was doing wrong. When she discovered him in their bed with another woman, Adeline had felt relief more than anger. The mystery was solved. She hadn't done anything wrong except to believe the lies of the man she had married. He didn't love her; if he loved anyone at all it was only himself.

She left that night and went home to her mother and father, her aunts and uncles. They arranged for the family lawyer to make certain she was well paid for her years of silence, subservience, faithfulness, and trust. Her divorce was settled quickly. But life at home no longer agreed with Adeline. Even in the stifling atmosphere of her marriage, she had grown up. She was twenty-nine and yearning for independence.

Adeline knew she had to find a home of her own. It would have to be a place far away from society, from what was expected of her; a place where she could be herself. She had thought about such a place for a long time, she even had a picture in her mind. It would be a house: large and old and beautiful. Elegant but simple, with a view of the sea. It was possible such a place existed, if you had the money and the desire. Adeline had both.

Despite her parents' concerns, she consulted the family lawyer. He contacted a respectable realtor who showed her pictures of several suitable houses. But Adeline didn't want suitable. She put her finger on a page with pictures of the house. "I like this one."

The realtor had shook his head and told her that the house was rumored to be haunted. "My apologies. This house is most unsuitable for a young lady such as you. Why, it's only listed because of its historical value."

Adeline was intrigued. "Historical value? What does that mean?"

"Simply put, it means the house is very old and, in its current condition, almost worthless. The estate is trying to use the size and age of the property as selling points, when in fact, they want to get rid of it because of the high taxes. The land that is included in the sale is worth far more than the house. True it is listed as a mansion, but it has been rented out over many years and no doubt fallen into as much disrepair as ill repute." Annoyance had colored the realtor's voice as he told her that the house would be a foolish investment. It would need updating and extensive renovations. He looked at Adeline with expectation. "I think you should continue looking."

'Should' was a word Adeline had grown to dislike. She especially disliked being told what she should do. She stood up, lifted her chin, and straightened her shoulders. "Please make the arrangements for me to buy it at once. I'm not worried about any updating or renovating. Just arrange for a room to be ready and the refrigerator filled with assorted foods. I can look after everything else by myself."

Now she looked around the room. For a library, it was not only poorly stocked, but small. It was an inside room and the only light was provided by tall lamps on low tables. The large pattern of the heavy, velvet wallpaper was overwhelming. *Where was the hidden door this time?*

"Maybe it's behind a bookcase, concealing a secret passage like in the movies." Adeline pursed her lips. She was letting the headiness of being on her own take hold of her already vivid imagination.

She started searching the bookcases. None of them moved at her push and pull attempts. She stopped as she heard a small sound: a thump and then the turn of a door's handle. The wallpaper on the wall beside the TV was moving. Against that wall, instead of a bookcase, there was a table with a lamp.

That must be the door. And that must be Thomas on the other side. Adeline felt a sudden leap of happiness. Quickly she unplugged the lamp and moved it and the table, setting them down in front of a different bookcase. She turned to face the wall. The paper must have been loosely applied because it fluttered a little, then abruptly broke away from the rest of the pattern. A door swung open.

"Hullo." Thomas stood in the doorway, his black hair spattered with dust from the wallpaper. "Are you ready to hunt for paintings?"

Adeline beamed at him. "Are you sure you don't mind?"

"I don't mind at all. In fact, I'm feeling very keen to find the paintings. I even have an idea where they might be." Thomas stepped back and Adeline walked past him through a narrow corridor. The door at the end was open; it led into the Great Room.

"I hope I didn't spoil your fun," said Thomas.

Adeline looked at him. "Spoil my fun? How?"

"By opening the door."

"I might never have found that one. How did you know about it?"

Thomas swung his left arm forward. He had been holding it behind his back and now he presented Adeline with a book. "I had a bit of an advantage. It's a record of the history of the house."

"That's wonderful." Adeline took the leather bound book. She flipped it open. "This is odd. It seems to have been written by many different people."

"Yes. It dates back to when the house was built. It appears to be a rather unique log of upgrades, improvements, and renovations. Oh, and the weather."

Adeline looked up at Thomas. "You mean the wind. Mrs. Folly says the wind is the weather."

They smiled at each other. Thomas spoke first. "Yes, the wind." He cleared his throat. "Shall we begin?"

"Yes. Where to first?"

"Over there." Thomas pointed.

"But that's just a fireplace. I was looking at it this morning."

"Ah. But it's not just a fireplace." They crossed the room to the huge fireplace and then stepped inside, just as Adeline had done that morning. Then Thomas went to the right hand corner, stretched up his right arm, and pulled on a circular piece of iron that looked like a doorknocker. With much rumbling and billows of dust, the back of the fireplace moved to the left about a foot.

"That's fantastic!" Adeline hurried over to Thomas. She peered into the darkness beyond the back of the fireplace. "How did you know about this?"

"It's mentioned in the book. The original family had it constructed to hide not only their jewels and monies, but themselves if necessary."

"Let's go inside! Do you have a flashlight?"

Thomas stepped into the darkness, turned right, and returned with a lantern in his right hand. He lifted it up to his face. "An emergency lantern, operated by batteries. It probably replaced an oil lantern and that replaced a candle."

"Is that what it says in the book?"

"No. But it does make sense. General upkeep, as it were. Now, let's find those paintings." He shone the lantern's light around the small room. A small, sturdy looking wood table stood in one corner. There were no chairs.

Adeline went to the table. She ran one finger across its surface. "It hasn't been kept up recently; it's very dusty." She crouched and looked at the floor beneath the table. There the dust had been disturbed, revealing four lines within the confines of the table legs. She looked over her shoulder at Thomas. "I think there's a trap door in the floor."

"That's very good detective work."

"Not really. I watch a lot of movies."

Thomas set the lantern on the floor and knelt beside Adeline. He leaned forward and traced the lines slowly, carefully. "There's a groove in one corner." He stood up. "I think we should move the table. Beneath that trap door must be the stairs to the original basement. In the book it's referred to as 'the room beneath the room.'"

Adeline stood up. She didn't bother to dust off her jeans. Instead, she took one end of the table and waited for Thomas to take the other. They lifted it together and moved it over a few feet.

"This is so exciting," Adeline said.

"It is, isn't it?" Thomas knelt down again beside the now exposed trap door. He pulled up hard. The door didn't move. "I think it's stuck."

"We'll do it together." Adeline knelt beside Thomas and put her right hand next to his. "On three."

"On three what?"

"We pull."

"Right."

Adeline counted and they pulled up. The door didn't move. They looked at each other.

"Maybe it slides?" Adeline suggested.

"I suppose it's possible. To the right?"

Adeline nodded. "On three."

Together they pulled the door; it slid slowly to the right and disappeared under the floor.

"That is either very clever or very spooky," said Adeline.

"I'm going with 'clever.'" Thomas picked up the lantern and walked down several steps. He shone the lantern's light ahead of him, then back and forth. "It appears to be a room carved right into the rock."

Adeline stepped down two steps and looked over Thomas's left shoulder. "Definitely a place to put something you don't want found. Ever." She held tight to a guard rail on her left and they descended. The smell of old earth, rock, and dust filled her nose. She coughed.

"Are you all right?"

"Yes, thank you."

"Be careful of the last step." Thomas reached the room and turned to help Adeline.

The last step was a little too high. Adeline stepped down from it awkwardly. "I'm sorry. I'm a bit clumsy."

"Not at all. It's the stairs. They're a very poor design."

"I'm impressed that they have stairs and not just a ladder."

"Obviously a very enterprising family."

"Or maybe they just had a lot of enemies."

Thomas tilted his head to one side. "You do like to look on the dark side of things, don't you?"

"Years of practice." Adeline looked around the small space that had been chiselled and carved from the rock. "Thomas? Would you raise the lantern, please?"

He lifted the lantern and shone it around the little room. Shadows parted. The light glinted on something set against the wall to their right. They walked toward it, the sound of their footsteps bounced in the still air. Adeline looked behind her, but no one was there. She turned her attention to Thomas. He had lowered the lantern and was now leaning over an oversized tarpaulin. It was encircled with a leather strap and a silver buckle to keep it closed.

That must be what glittered in the dark, thought Adeline.

Finishing his inspection, Thomas tugged on the leather strap. Time had dried the leather and aged the silver. The strap broke apart and slipped free of the buckle's tongue.

Adeline held her breath for a moment, then walked forward and lifted one corner of the tarpaulin. The rough material hurt and she released it quickly. It fell to the floor and Adeline gasped.

Thomas smiled. "I think we've found your paintings, Adeline."

"So it would seem." She looked at the portrait facing her and, stepping forward, picked it up carefully, holding it on either side with the palms of her hands. "She's beautiful. I wonder who she is. I mean, was. Does it mention her in the book?"

"What? Oh, no. That's just notes about construction, as I said." Thomas reached down and grasped the corner of a canvas. A thin piece of linen protected the next painting from the first. He pulled away the linen and picked up the painting. It was a portrait of a man with two dogs lying at his feet. "Dour looking fellow."

Adeline was peering at the bottom left corner of the painting she held. "That's strange. It doesn't say the year." She looked up at Thomas. "But artists always put the year. And their names."

"There are no years or names on the paintings of the house."

"True." Adeline studied the portrait. "It's another mystery."

"Oh, good." Thomas set down the painting he held, leaning it against the rock wall. "How many are there do you think? The portraits, not the mysteries."

"I've no idea. Do you think it's okay for us to look at them?"

Thomas chuckled. "Now you're concerned about right and wrong?"

Adeline set her painting against the wall. "It's not that. It's just, now that I look at them, well—they're real people. Or they were. I feel like I'm invading their privacy."

Thomas smiled a little. "I don't think they would mind."

Encouraged, Adeline started unpacking the paintings; Thomas helped her. When they were finished there were twenty-two portraits of various women and men. Thomas and Adeline walked back and forth in front of the impromptu gallery they had created.

All the backgrounds were muted with hazy colors that reminded Adeline of the paintings of the house. "There's your 'spooky.'" She pointed to one portrait's background as she told Thomas what she thought. "It's as if they're portraits of . . . ghosts."

"Ah. Well, that would be quite the discovery."

"Are you making fun of me?"

"Not at all. I was just wondering how one would get a ghost to sit for a portrait."

Adeline stepped back to look at the portraits as a group. "That's odd."

"What?"

"Something's wrong. There aren't any family portraits; no children. The backgrounds and clothes, hairstyles, too. They usually depict the year somehow." She returned to the first portrait and ran a fingertip along the frame. "Why were you hidden away? And for how long?"

Finally Adeline turned to Thomas. "We'd better put them back."

"Whatever for? Don't you want to hang them up?"

"Yes, but not today. These were hidden here for a reason and I don't want to upset Mrs. Folly. She seems afraid of the house and if I want her to stay—which I do, at least for now—then I don't want to upset her. After all, I've only just arrived and I'm already poking about secret rooms, ripping wallpaper off walls, and probably damaging the historical value of the house." Adeline started putting the paintings back against the wall.

Thomas folded his arms against his chest. "Historical value? That doesn't sound like you. As for Mrs. Folly, she is an employee of the family who own, or rather, owned, this house. She was hired by their solicitor, a Mr. Pemberton, I believe. She receives her instructions as to the care of the house from said solicitor."

"And now, of course, from you."

"Of course. It's just that all the arrangements were handled by my lawyer and my realtor. They didn't mention many details. They certainly didn't mention you or your lease."

"My what?"

"Your lease. For the rooms you've been renting. Mrs. Folly and Mr., um, Pemberton?"

Thomas nodded.

"They didn't mention you either. You did sign a lease, didn't you?"

Thomas was caught off his guard. "Well, I . . . I suppose there's something in writing somewhere. I'll have to look. I am sorry for the inconvenience."

Adeline reached for another portrait. "I'm not concerned, Thomas. But I think I'd better check with my lawyer for more details about the purchase of the house. I did buy it and the land, and, as far as I know, all the contents whether or not they're hidden away. We can put these up tomorrow. They really are beautiful."

"I see. Yes. Well, might I suggest that you say you found the portraits with the paintings? Don't mention secret passages or mysterious books. Mrs. Folly will provide her own answers. She'll most likely blame the wind." Thomas paused. "Or the ghost."

Adeline considered Thomas. He looked so earnest, and he was so much fun to be with. "All right. That's as good an idea as any I can think of. Just enough information to placate and Mrs. Folly is just the type to fill in the blanks to suit herself."

"I agree." Thomas put the tarpaulin over the paintings. He left the broken strap and buckle on the floor and took a step back.

"Thomas**?**"

He turned to Adeline. "Yes?"

"You said Mrs. Folly would blame the ghost. Do you believe the house is haunted?"

"In a way. But not by a ghost."

"Don't tell me; the wind."

"Very possibly." Thomas took Adeline's right arm with his left hand. "Now, let's go and see if we can't solve another mystery."

"Which one? Who painted the portraits or why they were hidden away?"

"Or, what we are going to have for dinner?"

"Thomas?" Adeline and Thomas were walking toward the main staircase after dinner.

"Yes?" He looked at her.

"I don't mind you being here at the house, even if you don't have a lease."

He stopped walking. "You're very kind."

"Am I? I think I'm just selfish. You know so much about the house. Maybe we'll even find out more about the ghost. Together, I mean. If you like."

"I would. Like that, I mean." Thomas started up the right hand side of the staircase. He stumbled and stood still.

"Are you all right?" Adeline called to him from the left side of the curved staircase.

"Fine. Fine." Thomas put his left hand on the banister and started up the stairs again. It had been a long time since he'd climbed them.

When he reached the landing, he walked toward Adeline, stopping just in front of her.

"That was a lovely dinner," Adeline said. "You cooked the steaks perfectly."

"Thank you. Of course, your salad was delicious."

"Thank you."

They stood for a minute in silence, looking at each other. Adeline pointed with her left hand. "My room's at the end of that hallway."

"Ah. Well, my room is that way." He pointed down the right hand hallway. "More of a suite, really."

"More room for the flowers."

"Pardon?"

"For the plants you look after."

"Yes. There's a sunroom for the flowers."

A crash of thunder made them both look up.

"When there's sun, that is." Thomas smiled.

They looked at each other again and Thomas resisted the urge to kiss Adeline. He wanted to wait a little longer. "You're not afraid of storms, are you?"

"No. Storms don't frighten me. In fact, I like a good storm. As long as I'm not out in it."

"You do seem to be fearless."

"It's easy to be fearless if you know someone will rescue you." Adeline looked up at Thomas and smiled.

"I used to specialize in rescuing," he said. "Usually small dogs and wet kittens. But I would make an exception in your case."

They gazed at each other for a minute, then Thomas cleared his throat. "I, uh, guess I'll be going now."

Adeline nodded and took a step toward the hallway that led to her room. She turned. "Are you a morning person?"

Once again unprepared, Thomas hesitated. "A what?"

"Which part of the day do you like best?"

"I hadn't really given it much thought."

"Oh." It was Adeline's turn to hesitate. "Would you like to join me for breakfast? About nine?"

"Yes. Yes, I'd like that very much."

"Then I'll see you at nine." Adeline turned and walked down the hallway. She paused at her bedroom door and looked back. "Goodnight, Thomas."

He waved one hand. "Goodnight, Adeline."

Thomas watched as Adeline opened her door and went inside her room. He waited until he heard the door close, then he disappeared. A moment later, he was in his room. Funny how he had taken such ease of transportation for granted, but just tonight his feet had felt heavy and he became oddly aware of them and stumbled. He had remained visible almost all day and now it was past ten at night.

What would have happened if I'd kissed her? Thomas drifted about the large room and out onto the stone balcony. The storm didn't bother him, but his conundrum did. *What would happen if I tried to make love to Adeline?* Aside from the obvious complications of a ghost having a love affair with a person still alive, there were a hundred little details of being alive that no longer troubled Thomas. If he wanted to be with Adeline he had better familiarize himself with all of them. But first, he had to fix the little problem of a lease. *That should be easy enough.*

Thomas visualized the study that was beside the little library. Then he was there.

It had once been part of the Great Room even in the time when Thomas had been alive. The Great Room was enormous then and used for parties and dancing. One of the wives had divided it into smaller rooms, hoping to keep the house warmer.

Thomas considered what he should write. Mrs. Folly had often decried the rearrangement of the original floor plans. Now, with a missive from Mr. Pemberton and with Adeline's enthusiasm for the house, Mrs. Folly would soon get what she wanted: the house as it was meant to be.

Sitting down at an antique desk, Thomas picked up a pen, pulled a piece of linen paper toward him and began a letter to Mrs. Folly.

Chapter Five

Adeline stepped into her bedroom, aware that Thomas was still watching her. She closed the door slowly and waited, but he didn't knock. Disappointed that he hadn't pursued her, she didn't lock the door. *Had she misread their connection or was the mystery of the paintings proving to be more of a distraction than Thomas had admitted?*

She looked at the book Thomas had given her and went to sit on the bed. Flipping through the pages, she stopped at a page that mentioned the wind. The person who had written the entry had decided the only way to combat the wind was to make the larger rooms smaller, then wallpaper over the doors to prevent the wind from—she squinted at the handwriting—"following me," she read aloud.

The wind again. She set the book down and went to start a shower. A half hour later she was tucked in bed, trying to pay attention to the words on the pages of the book. Finally, she closed the book and listened as the storm outside strengthened and the rain pummelled the window. The storm hadn't frightened her when she was with Thomas, but now that she was alone she felt uneasy. She set the book on the bedside table and left the light on. Then she pulled the duvet up against her chest, clutching it each time the storm thundered. She stared at the door, wishing Thomas would knock or peek inside to see if she was all right.

Adeline tried to listen for a knock but the storm was too loud. *The wind is loud, too. The wind.* She closed her eyes and imagined she was safe and warm in Thomas's embrace. *Safe and warm.* She fell asleep.

She woke suddenly to silence and darkness. Sitting up, she reached for the light on the table. It wasn't there. She peered around the room, letting her eyes adjust to the moonlight. *Moonlight?*

Adeline threw back the duvet and climbed out of bed. She went to the window and pulled back the drapes. A full moon lit the lake's surface. She spun about as she heard noise coming from downstairs. It sounded like many people talking. *What's going on?*

She went to the bed, picked up her housecoat and pulled it on. Hearing music, she didn't take time to find her slippers. Instead she slowly opened her bedroom door just wide enough to look down the hallway. The voices and music became louder.

Adeline hesitated then stepped into the hallway. She walked to the center railing of the double staircase and looked down. Laughter echoed up the stairs. A woman in a beautiful ball gown hurried from under the stairs and across the foyer. She paused for an instant and dropped her fan on the floor, then she smiled and went into the Great Room.

Adeline thought the woman looked familiar; like one of the women in the portraits she and Thomas had found.

Her thoughts were interrupted as a young man strode quickly from under the stairs. He noticed the fan at once, as if he were expecting some sign that he should continue his pursuit.

Adeline studied his clothes as he knelt to pick up the fan. He wore a black, tailed jacket with a high collar, a white shirt with a cascade of lace down the front of his shirt and lace cuffs draping over his hands. His trousers fit tightly against his legs and were tucked into tall boots. His dark brown hair was pulled back in a ponytail and tied with a long ribbon. He tapped the fan thoughtfully against his chin and then went to the Great Room's doorway, apparently looking for the lady. Then he entered the room.

It's like a scene from a fairytale. She had been reading about the house, but her thoughts had been on the people who had lived there. *There has to be an explanation.*

Quietly, she descended the right hand staircase. At the bottom, she looked behind her but the hallway under the stairs, although brightly lit, was empty. Then she noticed the lights on the walls: they were lanterns. She looked up at the chandelier. It was lit with candles and a rope swung away from it and was secured to a wall.

Seeking an explanation, she went to the doorway of the Great Room, hanging back just enough so as to remain unnoticed. She looked inside.

Women and men, dressed much the same as the couple she had first seen, danced in the center of the room. Near the walls, several groups of men talked loudly, raised their drinks and laughed, only occasionally glancing at the dancers. Women stood in smaller groups and whispered to one another.

To the right of the doorway, more women and men sat at round tables set with white table cloths, champagne glasses, and candelabras. Left of the doorway was a long table burdened with large platters of food and stacks of plates. Two men stood at either end of the table, armed with large bottles of champagne. They wore white wigs and matching uniforms.

The room appeared to be much bigger, as if the smaller rooms behind it were no longer there. The wallpaper too was absent and the clean, white lines of the walls were interrupted only by sconces that held lanterns.

From somewhere near the back of the room Adeline heard violins and guessed a band or perhaps an orchestra was providing the music.

When the dancing couples occasionally parted, she could see a huge fire burning in the fireplace.

It must be a costume party. But who are they? And how did they arrange to change the room so quickly? The house, too. Adeline looked at the dancing couples, hoping to see Thomas. *He would be able to explain.* When she didn't see him, she scanned the small groups of standing men and followed their glances to the women sitting at the tables waiting to dance. But Thomas wasn't there.

A cork popped. Adeline jumped and took a step back. A log in the fireplace broke apart and the sparks caught her attention. As the flames leapt higher, she looked up. It was then that she noticed the painting above the fireplace. It was a portrait of Thomas. Startled, she backed away another step then hurried from the doorway, up the staircase, and along the hallway to her bedroom. Once inside, she locked the door.

"What's happening?" The room was silent. A crack of thunder seemed to answer Adeline's question. From the window, a mist floated into the room and spread across the floor. The room seemed to tilt to one side. She grabbed onto the doorframe. The light from the moon disappeared.

In the sudden darkness, Adeline stayed absolutely still. Then the light on the bedside table came on; it was the electric light. The mist was gone and outside it was raining. Lightning brightened the room for an instant. *Wherever I've been, I'm back. Or was it a dream? But if I was dreaming, why are my feet cold?*

Needing a distraction, Adeline looked for her slippers. One was near the bed. She went to it and then knelt down and felt under the bed for its mate. Her fingers touched something hard and gnarled. She moved her fingers back and forth along the surface of the object then grasped it and pulled.

The object was heavier than she expected and she had to use both hands to haul it out from under the bed. She sat down abruptly and stared. It was a large picture frame. Dust coated its elaborately scrolled edges as well as the painting it safeguarded. Pulling the frame closer to her, Adeline leaned forward and blew across the center of the picture. *Was it another painting of the house or a portrait? And why was it hidden here, beneath her bed?*

The dust lifted only enough to tease, but Adeline persisted. Finally she lifted the hem of her nightgown and gently brushed at the layers of dust. It was a portrait. But not just any portrait: the man looking at her from the canvas was Thomas.

The oil paint was cracked with age but Thomas's smile was the same. And his eyes, too, smiled at her with a glint of mischief that she had liked the minute they had met. She hadn't noticed what he was wearing in the portrait downstairs, but in the one before her he was dressed in a high collared shirt with a heavy frill down the front, the black jacket he wore also had a high collar and the trousers were tight and fit snugly into high, black boots. His right leg was lifted, supported on the seat of a chair and Thomas was leaning his right arm upon that leg.

To Adeline, he seemed to be trying to look nonchalant and failing miserably. *Still, his slight discomfort couldn't be the reason to hide the painting.* She checked the bottom of the painting; it was unsigned.

She studied the portrait. *It must be one of Thomas's ancestors.* She gently ran one finger along the mouth. *But what about the smile? Could a person inherit a smile?* She pushed the portrait back under the bed, exhausted by mysteries, her mind overwhelmed by everything she had seen and felt since she first entered the house. *I'll ask Thomas tomorrow.*

I'll tell him about the painting and I'll tell him about my dream, too. Except I don't think it was a dream. And I think very much that somehow, that's a portrait of Thomas. Maybe something faked for the party? She set her slipper down and climbed into bed. A strong feeling that she wasn't alone made her look around her room. It was empty; her only companion was the storm outside.

Adeline pulled the duvet close about her shoulders. "It's this house. This beautiful, strange house. Or is it the wind?" She rolled over onto her left side. "Don't think about it now." She closed her eyes, feeling tired all over. *Ask Thomas tomorrow. He'll explain. Tomorrow.*

———————

From one of the chairs in front of the fireplace, Thomas watched Adeline. He had intended to return to his side of the house, but the ferocity of the storm changed his mind. The house often did strange things when storms were particularly strong. After he had written his letter, he went to Adeline's room and, when the house began to change, he stayed near her, shadowing her when she went downstairs to investigate the party. He had seen it before many times. He hoped desperately that she would be drawn to the mystery it presented, instead of being frightened and running away.

Invisible, Thomas stood close to Adeline, watching her intently for her reaction to the party. *Yes, she was curious, but sensibly cautious, too.* When she saw his portrait and raced for her room, he disappeared and was already there waiting for her, still invisible, careful to sit down and stay out of her way. After she discovered his portrait under the bed, he was curiously pleased. It wasn't the best portrait of him, but it was the only one.

Now what? He watched Adeline turn onto her right side and stretch one arm across the empty space next to her. She seemed restless.

I'll stay until she's sound asleep, he decided. *And tomorrow I'll pretend that everything she tells me—if she tells me anything at all—is entirely believable. Just another mystery to be solved. Yes. That's it. Or was it?* Lies were always more troublesome than truth.

Thomas made himself comfortable in the chair. He thought about his portrait. *I was a fool. Not even an old fool, just a romantic fool.* He turned old memories over in his mind. He remembered flirting unsuccessfully with several women. The party, unlike Thomas, was a great success. But after several glasses of champagne he had asked a friend to look after the guests for him and said his 'goodnights.'

I went upstairs. I remember feeling a bit sick to my stomach. And then . . .

Then? Thomas rested his right elbow on one arm of the chair and leaned forward. He frowned. It was frustrating not to remember, particularly since the details of his demise seemed to be intertwined with the house. He had thought about his murder many times over the years but it had remained a mystery.

A mystery. He looked at Adeline; she lay quiet now, her breathing slow and steady. *What if Adeline can help me remember? Better still, she could solve the mystery.*

Thomas sat back in the chair and crossed his legs at the ankles, forgetting he had intended to leave. He hadn't realized how much it had bothered him: dying so young. Murdered. If the loneliness of being a ghost had been tolerable, it was only because he had been lonely when he was alive. And he had never been good at mysteries. He had given up and just quietly looked after the plants, watched the television, and occasionally wondered about the party downstairs. And the wind.

Outside the house, the storm weakened and the wind blew away, up the mountain and out to sea. The house was still.

The sound of water running woke up Thomas. He rubbed his eyes. "I fell asleep!" He clapped one hand over his mouth. The water stopped and Adeline's voice called from the bathroom.

"Hello?"

Thomas didn't answer. He heard Adeline call his name and hurriedly chose a destination. He ended up in the kitchen pantry. "Fine. That's just fine." He opened the door and looked around the kitchen. "I'll make breakfast."

A half hour later, Thomas looked up as Adeline entered the kitchen. "Good morning."

"Good morning." She joined him at the counter. "What are you making?"

"It will either be an omelette or just scrambled eggs."

"Sounds lovely. I'll slice bread for toast." Adeline moved around the kitchen, already starting to feel at home.

"Did you sleep well?" Thomas asked.

"Yes. No. I—" Adeline paused, bread knife in her right hand. "I had a strange dream. And then this morning, I thought I heard someone in my room."

"I see. Well, it takes a bit of time to get accustomed to an old house. What was the dream about?"

Adeline told him as they continued making breakfast together. Thomas listened; he didn't laugh and he didn't interrupt. As they ate their scrambled eggs, Adeline told him about the painting she'd found under her bed.

"Ah. Another mystery."

"Is it? The man in the painting looks exactly like you."

"Does he?"

Adeline narrowed her eyes. "Yes." Her voice was firm. "You could be twins."

"Really?"

"Yes. Really." She leaned forward. "What was his name?"

"Who?"

"You know very well 'who.' The man in the painting that was under my bed." Adeline pointed her fork at Thomas. "My instincts tell me that you know and that you're hiding something from me." She set her fork down. "Please don't make it a lie."

Thomas sighed. He ran one hand through his hair. "Well, if you must know, it is my portrait. I'm posing as an ancestor of mine."

"Who?"

"I don't recall his first name. But he was the first Éclair to be part of the aristocracy."

"Éclair? Like the dessert?"

"Quite. In fact, he was a lord, of sorts. It was rumoured he won the title in a game of cards. Anyway, it doesn't matter. What matters more is—"

There was a knock on the back door.

Thomas stood up quickly. "Ah. I just remembered that I forgot something." He hurried to the kitchen doorway. "I'll be right back. Please don't mention me. I'm terribly private."

"All right."

As Thomas exited the kitchen, Ham entered the back door, soaked from rain he stood just inside. "Morning, miss. I'm just heading to town and, what with the weather and all, I wondered if you might be needing anything. I'm afraid I won't be available for a few days. Stormy days like these take up a lot of my time at home."

"Thank you for thinking of me, Ham." Adeline rose and stood in front of the second place setting. "I'm fine. And the weather doesn't bother me. I'll just keep myself busy with the house. You know, rearranging furniture, dusting, redecorating a bit."

"All right then, miss. I understand how you ladies like to rearrange." He turned to leave and stopped. "Might I be so bold as to make a small suggestion?"

"Certainly."

"Don't change things too much." Ham glanced around the kitchen.

"I won't."

Ham touched his cap, turned to leave and stopped again. "You might want to keep the door locked, miss. There's no one about to fear, but the wind can get powerfully strong. Blow the door open or even off its hinges."

"I see. I thought it was locked."

Ham held up a key that looked like the one Adeline had used to unlock the front door. "As the handyman, I have a spare. Mrs. Folly has one, too. Would you like them back?"

"No. That's all right, Ham. You should have a spare key in case of an emergency. Mrs. Folly, too. But thank you for knocking first."

"I didn't want to frighten you, miss." He glanced around the kitchen once more. "You had a quiet night then?"

"Yes. Very quiet."

"That's fine. Fine. I'll just be off." He left, closing the door tightly behind him.

Adeline waited a minute then called to Thomas. "You can come back now."

He walked into the kitchen. "Sorry about that. I don't socialize much. Recluse and all."

"Are you shy? Because you haven't been shy with me."

"Shy? Well, I suppose I am in a way. Let me explain."

"Please do." Adeline started clearing the table.

"You might want to sit down. In fact, yes, sit down, please. If only so you can jump up in shock or surprise. Preferably surprise."

Adeline put down the plate she held and sat down in her chair. "If you're going to tell me you're married—"

"What? No. I'm not married. I already told you I wasn't. I just don't want you to be frightened—" Thomas stuffed his hands into the pockets of his trousers— "I want you to understand, that's all."

"You have a terminal illness."

"No, no, no. Listen—"

"You're a criminal, a fugitive?"

"Don't be ridiculous. I'm nothing of the sort. Stop guessing and let me tell you. Will you please just listen?"

Adeline nodded.

"I'm dead."

"You mean, you feel dead inside."

"No. No, I mean I'm dead."

"Dead?"

"Yes. Dead, deceased. Your instincts were correct. That *is* me in the painting. It was for my birthday party. I don't remember being murdered. I passed out and when I woke up the next day there was my body on the bed. And I wasn't in it. I was a ghost."

"You think you're a ghost."

"Yes. No. I don't think I'm a ghost; I am a ghost. I wanted us to be better acquainted before I told you. I was waiting for the right time. Because I was . . . afraid."

"Afraid? You just said you're a ghost. What could you possibly be afraid of?"

Thomas shrugged. "That you wouldn't like me anymore." He tilted his head to one side as he looked at Adeline. "How about this? You watch me right now and don't look away for an instant. Promise?"

"All right. I promise."

Thomas disappeared. He didn't disappear slowly or in a mist, simply one moment he was there and the next he wasn't.

Adeline gasped, glad she was sitting. She clasped her hands together to steady herself. After a minute she spoke to the empty kitchen. "Thomas? Are you still here?"

"I am." He appeared again, just where he had been standing.

Adeline shook her head slowly. "I must be dreaming again. You can't be a ghost."

"Why ever not? I just disappeared, didn't I?"

"Yes, but . . . ghosts make rooms cold and, and—" Adeline pointed at a small bouquet of flowers on the kitchen windowsill— "they make flowers wilt."

"That's all you've got to base your argument upon? I wasn't given a book of rules. I'm just going along as best I can." He sat down, shoulders drooping. "I don't even remember all the details of my life, let alone my death."

"When did you die?"

Thomas smacked one hand on the table. "I told you, I was murdered."

Adeline stood up. She picked up the plate again and took it to the sink. "It's no use being angry at me, Thomas."

He followed her. "I'm not angry at you. I'm angry that I was murdered. I'm sorry. Please, Adeline. Listen to me. Look at me. Please?"

Adeline turned to Thomas. She looked at him. "Well?"

He flinched at her tone. She sounded angry. "Adeline, you are the first person I've let see me since I was murdered. And that was, I don't know, a very long time ago. I'm truly sorry that I didn't tell you the truth when we met."

He looked out the kitchen window. "I like you very much. And . . . we've been having such fun together." Finally, he looked at her. "Haven't we?"

Adeline smiled a little. "Yes." It was her turn to look out the window. "I was hoping it might become something more than fun."

"I'm still hoping."

"You are?" She looked up at Thomas. His hair had fallen over his eyebrows. Impulsively, she brushed at it with the fingertips of her right hand. "How can I do this? How is this possible? Who murdered you? And why? And why are you here?"

She walked away from the sink, then stopped and spoke over one shoulder. "What about those people I thought were a dream? Are they here, too? Ghosts, like you?"

Thomas shrugged and went to stand beside Adeline. "I don't think so. They seem to be connected to the house. In what way, I don't know."

"Oh." Adeline started toward the kitchen doorway. She tried to sort her thoughts, but Thomas interrupted them.

"Are you still angry with me?" he asked.

"No. And I wasn't angry. I was hurt."

"I see. Well, where are you off to then?"

"To get the portraits." Adeline stopped in the long dark of the hallway and turned to Thomas. "Will you still help me?"

"Of course." He smiled. "Will you help me?"

"Of course. If I can. What would you like me to do?"

"Find out who murdered me. Perhaps why."

Adeline started walking again. "I'll do what I can."

"And I will appreciate it very much."

They walked in silence until they reached the Great Room. Again Adeline turned to face Thomas. "Maybe you're not a ghost."

He started to protest, but Adeline held up her right hand for silence. "Maybe you're caught in another reality or another time. After all, if those people who were having a party aren't ghosts, then what are they? Where are they? And how long have they been here?"

"I've no idea."

54

"I think we may find a clue in the portraits."

"Ah-hah! I knew you'd love another mystery."

Entering the Great Room, they walked toward the fireplace. "It's not just the mystery," Adeline almost whispered.

"Oh." Thomas's voice was equally quiet. He stepped into the fireplace and opened the door. "Then what is it? What makes you think the portraits hold a clue to my murder?"

"The clue might be more about the mysterious people. And the people—"

"Might be from another time?"

"I don't know. I confess, I watched a lot of television during my marriage. And from the time I was a little girl I was told I have a vivid imagination."

"I think you just see beyond the ordinary. A different point of view, as it were."

Adeline smiled. "Thank you, Thomas."

They made their way down the stairs. Thomas was first and held out his right hand to Adeline at the bottom step. She took it and, as she stepped down, she looked up at him. "It feels different."

"My hand?"

"No. The air." Adeline took the lantern and moved past Thomas, past the portraits. She lifted the lantern above her head. "I feel outside air. There must be another entrance." She almost bumped into Thomas as she took a step back.

"It would explain why the paintings are in such good condition," he said. "Try shining the light over there." He pointed at the wall beside the paintings.

Adeline did so. "You're not hiding more from me, are you, Thomas?"

"Not that I'm aware. If I am, it's only because I don't remember clearly."

Adeline narrowed her eyes, peering at the shadows. A slight waft of cold air lifted a strand of her hair. "There it is again. It's as if the cave has been carved to make shadows look solid." She took a step forward, her right arm outstretched to touch whatever might be in front of her. She felt along the rough rock, then stumbled when nothing was there.

Thomas caught her about her waist.

"I've got you," he said. "Are you all right?"

"Yes. Yes." Adeline brushed her hair away from her face and shone the lantern directly at the place where she had stumbled. "Look. There's a fissure in the wall."

"It hardly looks big enough for anyone to fit."

"If we go sideways we can fit."

Skeptical, Thomas stepped ahead of Adeline. "Give me the lantern. I'll go first."

"But you don't have to go at all, do you? Can't you just disappear and reappear at wherever this ends?"

"If I knew where it ended I could. But I don't. More than that, I won't because I won't abandon you. We'll do it together or not at all."

"All right. But if I get stuck . . ."

"I'll unstuck you."

"That's not a word."

"No. But it's still true." Thomas lifted the lantern and, turning his right shoulder toward the fissure, he squeezed into the opening. "It opens up a little after the first few steps," he called back to Adeline.

"Good." She squeezed into the fissure, glad that Thomas was just ahead of her; the lantern's light a small beacon in the heavy darkness of the rock. "It's almost a tunnel."

"Almost."

"I can feel more air. Can you see how much further?"

"Yes. In fact, I think I remember where this leads." Thomas stopped and gently took Adeline's right hand. "Here, the floor is slippery now and a bit wet. There's some moss, too."

"Moss? Like in a garden?"

"Precisely. And—" Thomas moved ahead with more confidence, then stopped—"here is the garden. My garden."

Chapter Six

Following Thomas, Adeline became aware of the tunnel opening up. Thin branches poked at her legs. Thomas was pushing them away, holding them aside. A few more steps and she could stand beside him. He lowered the lantern. The air was clean now and the cloudy sky familiar. Rain tickled her face.

They were standing in a thicket. Across from them was a stone archway with hydrangeas on either side. They were just beginning to bloom in the late spring rain. Brown grass was becoming green and needed trimming. Decorative stones were set on either side of a short path that disappeared off to her right behind a large tree.

"It's beautiful, Thomas."

"It will be. Hamlet looks after it when he can. I've watched him and it seems to me that he's not really comfortable here." Thomas started down the path, still holding Adeline's right hand. "The last wife was going to tear it down." He stopped and looked around the small garden. "That was the only time I intentionally tried to frighten someone."

"What did you do?"

"Oh." Thomas shrugged and started walking again. "Nothing terrible, really. I kept shutting and locking the garden door, and then the doors inside the house. With her in the room."

"I see. And it worked."

"Yes. She left and I got to keep my garden. I've always liked it very much. In fact, I think I was going to come here the night I was murdered."

"Let's not keep saying murdered. Let's say . . . disappeared."

They stopped in front of the archway. "If it makes you feel better." Thomas led Adeline under the archway to a large wood door. Releasing her hand, he pulled on the iron ring in the center of the door. "It looks pretty, but it always sticks."

The door opened a little. Adeline stepped forward and helped Thomas pull. Together they opened the door. Not far beyond was the steep hill that led to the barn and beyond that, the moor.

Adeline looked to her left. "The kitchen should be that way."

"It is. Come on." Thomas held out his left hand again and Adeline accepted his warm grasp.

"I was supposed to look over the estate," she said. "And do some sort of inventory. I don't recall any mention of a garden. But then, I wasn't paying close attention. I wanted so much to see the inside of the house first."

"I'm glad you did."

They hurried across the muddy lawn to the kitchen door. "Do you have a key?" asked Thomas.

"Just the one for the front door."

"That will work."

Adeline reached into the back right hand pocket of her jeans and withdrew the large key that had allowed entrance into the house and all its mysteries. She opened the kitchen door, stopping long enough to take off her wet shoes. As she leaned against the wall, she noticed Thomas wasn't wet at all.

"Why aren't you soaked from the rain?"

"When I'm outside the house, I become a little less, solid, as it were." He held up one hand. "Don't ask me why."

"All right. I won't ask now. But I am going to ask you lots of questions later. After I've dried off and changed my clothes."

Adeline stood up straight, looking up at Thomas. "If this is a dream, if I'm lost in some sort of madness, don't wake me, don't cure me. I'm feeling so happy."

He touched her right cheek gently with the fingertips of his right hand. "You're not dreaming, Adeline. Or mad. And I'm happy, too." He bent toward her and kissed her lips lightly. "Sorry. Sorry. I should have asked or something. I'm quite out of practice."

"So am I." Adeline stepped close to him and kissed him. His lips were warm against hers. Impulsively, she hugged him and then went quickly to the kitchen door. She turned back to face him. "I won't be long. Will you wait?"

"Yes. I'll even make a pot of tea."

"I'd rather have a beer."

He smiled and went to the refrigerator. "Two beers then. Maybe I can find some pretzels." He started opening cupboard doors.

Adeline turned and hurried down the hallway. Her bedroom seemed strangely ordinary after the events of the morning. She changed into jeans and a sweater then returned to the kitchen.

Thomas was waiting for her. On the kitchen table were two bottles of beer, two tall glasses, and a bowl of pretzels. "You look lovely," he said. "And thirsty." He poured a beer and held it out to her.

"Thank you." Adeline took the glass of beer and drank. "That's better."

"You have a moustache."

"I have a what? Oh." Suddenly self-conscious, Adeline grabbed a napkin from the table and wiped her mouth, deliberately removing the lipstick she had applied. "Better?"

"Much." Raising his glass, Thomas drank and then stood up. "Where shall we begin?"

"The dining room."

"The dining room? Why?"

"Because I haven't seen it yet and because Mrs. Folly seemed particularly afraid of it."

"I don't blame her. It's an awful room. At least, it is now."

"Why?"

"Disuse, neglect. And there's a large picture of one of the wives. She had a very high opinion of herself."

"The one who wanted to tear down your garden?"

"That's the one."

"Now I have to see the dining room."

Thomas emptied his glass. "I thought we were going to get the portraits and discover a clue."

"Oh, I've already discovered one clue." Adeline set her glass down on the table.

"You have? Where? When?"

"In the garden." She smiled. "Come on. Let's look at the dining room."

"But, but—"

Adeline took Thomas's left hand. "Come on."

"All right." His voice was deep with reluctance, but his fingers wrapped easily about hers. "Let's get it over with and then you have to tell me the clue."

They headed out of the kitchen and down the hallway. "I will." Adeline looked at the doors on her right. "Tell me which one, will you, Thomas?"

"Which one what?"

"Don't be silly. Which door is the door to the dining room."

"Oh." He stopped and pointed at the door they were approaching. "That one."

The two of them walked up to the door. "I feel like I should knock," Adeline confessed, her voice almost a whisper.

"Yes. It does give off an unpleasant . . . uh, vibration, doesn't it?" Thomas reached for the doorknob and turned it quickly. "You have to do it quickly, rather like pulling a tooth."

He pushed the door open; it creaked. Reaching for the light switch, he flipped it up. The dark room turned gray as a large, ugly chandelier weakly spread light across shadows. The table and chairs were draped with sheets, covered in dust, but what drew Adeline's attention was the picture directly across from the door. It was a full length portrait of a very angry woman.

"No wonder you didn't want her in your house," Adeline remarked.

They moved together around the long table and toward the painting. The woman in the painting was tall and thin, her dark hair, though short, was pulled back from her face with barrettes. Her dark eyes were piercing, with heavy brows that seemed to agree with the slight downward turn of her mouth. Her clothes were tailored and either faded or already gray.

"She looks like she's going to step out of the painting at any moment," said Adeline.

"If she does, run."

"Mrs. Folly said the room was unfriendly. She didn't say it wasn't ready at all."

"Perhaps she hadn't the time or, more likely, the inclination to clean it." Thomas glanced around the room. "Do you find it cold in here?"

"It just needs airing," said Adeline, still engrossed with the painting. "Okay. Well, I think I've seen enough for now." She looked up at Thomas, aware that they were still holding hands. "Have you?"

He nodded and they retraced their path back to the door. Their places were now reversed and Adeline reached for the light switch. She paused. "It is cold." She released her grip on Thomas's hand and faced the painting. "I don't think that's the original painting." She narrowed her eyes. "I'll ask Ham to take it down and set it in the Great Room."

"Whatever for? Why not get rid of the bloody thing? And why don't you think it's the original?"

"I want to get a better look at it. It could be another clue." She smiled up at him. "Let's get out of here."

"By all means." Thomas waved one arm toward the door. Adeline moved slowly, pausing in the doorway and looking back at the room. "Was this room once part of the Great Room?"

"I don't remember. The book I gave you—the diary of the renovations?"

"Yes?"

"It ought to mention something about this room and any others that were created after the Great Room was diminished in size." Thomas glanced over his shoulder. "Let's go."

"All right, all right." She stepped into the hallway, Thomas right behind her.

The door swung shut behind them. They exchanged looks of surprise laced with anxiety.

"Probably not level. Old house and all," said Thomas.

"Of course." Adeline smoothed her hair and headed up the hallway. Together the two of them returned to the secret room below.

The portraits were heavy and it took several trips to bring them up to the Great Room. Together they lined the portraits against one wall. In the drifting daylight, the details in the paintings were astonishing.

Adeline brushed dust and dirt from her hands. "These were definitely painted by the same artist," she announced. "And look here," she pointed at the backgrounds of several portraits. "As I suspected, they were painted in your garden."

"What?" Thomas looked closely at the background in each painting. It was not, as it had first seemed, just a wash of color. It was instead most definitely a wall of green and stone with a few hydrangeas off to one side. He slapped one hand against his forehead. "Of course!"

"What is it?"

"I'd forgotten until just now." He turned to Adeline, excitement making him grab her shoulders. "I was in the garden the night I died. I went there first and there was someone there I didn't know. But she seemed to think she knew me. And . . . and we went upstairs to my room." Thomas paused.

"And?" Adeline waited, wanting to hear and yet feeling somewhat jealous.

"It's not what you're thinking. I told her I didn't feel well and she said I ought to lie down. By myself. Which I did. I fell asleep. And when I woke up—" he shoved his hands into his pockets—"well, obviously I didn't exactly wake up."

Compassion overwhelmed Adeline. She put her right arm about Thomas's waist and hugged him. "Come on."

"Um. Where are we going now? I thought we were going to hang the paintings."

"We will. But right now we need to eat and think."

"I don't really need to eat, you know."

"I do. And I've seen you eat, so we know you can. Whatever rules apply to other ghosts obviously don't apply to you. Let's take advantage of that."

They returned to the kitchen and had lunch, talking only of how good the food was and when would the weather change. After they had cleaned up, they returned to the Great Room and confronted their mystery.

"Do you recognize the woman you met in the garden in any of these portraits?" asked Adeline.

Thomas shook his head at first, walking back and forth in front of their gallery. After several minutes, he returned to stand in front of the painting of a woman alone. She was very beautiful, her hair swept up in an elaborate set of curls, her dress fit for a fancy ball. "I think that's her."

Joining him, Adeline peered closer at the painting. "That's the woman I saw when I first saw the dancers."

"Are you certain?"

"Yes! Absolutely!"

"How very curious. I wonder if she's my murderer?"

Adeline stepped close to the figure in the center of the painting. The portraits were mostly of equal size and all their frames had an antiquated patina. But this woman's portrait was slightly larger and the frame thin, as if the original had been removed and replaced. "She's certainly beautiful enough to be a murderer."

Thomas frowned a bit. "Whatever do you mean?"

"Well, on television, it's almost always the beautiful woman who's the murderer."

"This isn't bloody television," Thomas's voice was almost angry. "It's my life. Or was."

"I'm sorry, Thomas. Still, from what you've remembered so far, and the difference between the size of this painting and the others, she was obviously someone of importance. And importance often means power."

"Then perhaps she had me killed by someone else."

"Perhaps. From what you've told me, it sounds like you were poisoned. Maybe she was keeping an eye on you to make sure the poison worked. You did say you didn't feel well. And that you fell asleep."

"And never woke up. Not properly that is." Thomas turned away from all the portraits. He went to one of the large windows and looked at the rain as it slithered down the glass. "Like a snake."

Adeline turned to him. "What did you say?"

"Sorry. Sorry."

She went to stand beside him. "Are you okay?"

"Yes. I'm fine. Just feeling a bit sorry for myself. Look." He faced her and his voice softened. "Let's start hanging up the portraits. It might help me remember something more."

"Are you sure?"

"Yes."

Adeline looked at the long line of paintings. "Okay. But we're going to need a lot of nails."

They found Ham's spare toolbox near the backdoor and, armed with hammer and a box of assorted nails, the two began hanging the portraits. Adeline strived to put the paintings where the discoloration on the wallpaper dictated.

"It's probably not the right one," she said, as they struggled with a particularly heavy frame, "but it will do."

They stood back and looked at their project. Thomas adjusted the angle a bit. Satisfied, they moved on to the next until only the portrait of the beautiful woman remained. They looked at it and then each other.

"Do you suppose we could put her up in the dining room?" Adeline asked.

"She would definitely be an improvement. At least until we know more about her."

"True. Let's do it for now, until, as you said, we know more. Then I'll air the dining room, Ham can replace that awful chandelier, and we can have our dinners there. Her portrait might inspire us."

"You mean, it might inspire you. I'm just an interested bystander, as it were."

Adeline smiled. "Oh, no, Thomas. You're much more than that."

"Whatever do you mean? You're the one who solves mysteries. And Hamlet won't be back for a few days," Thomas reminded her.

Forgetting what she had wanted to say, Adeline asked, "Were you eavesdropping?"

He looked offended. "You do realize that, because I'm a ghost, you can hardly accuse me of such a thing. Especially in my own home."

"You're right. I'm sorry."

"Come on." He nudged her with one elbow. "Let's at least get the portrait to the dining room. We can eat in the kitchen for now."

Returning to the dining room, they leaned the portrait against the wall. Adeline looked at the painting they were going to replace. "Does she look disapproving to you?"

He looked at the severe gaze of the dark eyes. "I think we're imagining it, but just in case I'm wrong—" He strode to one of the tall windows cloaked with a heavy drape and yanked the drape aside.

The dim light of late day drifted through the rain and into the room. "Tah-dah. What do you think? Any improvement?"

Adeline did the same to the other window and thought the room began to feel differently, as if it had been too long neglected, forgotten, and now was ready to be renewed.

"Definitely an improvement," she acknowledged. She sighed. "I also think I'm tired and hungry and have had more than enough mystery to suit me. For now."

Thomas chuckled. "Let's go."

"We'll leave the door open. To start airing the room. And I'll take this drape cloth and throw it away." Adeline grabbed the drape cloth from the table and pulled.

An enormous amount of dust billowed from the cloth and made her cough as she freed the mahogany table from its confinement. Then she gasped.

Thomas, unaffected by the dust, had been standing in the doorway. He went to Adeline. "What's wrong?"

He looked at Adeline's astonished face then to the tabletop. There was another painting.

Chapter Seven

"There's only one explanation," Adeline decided. She and Thomas sat at the kitchen table. They had studied the new painting carefully and agreed it wasn't him at the side of the beautiful woman.

"And what do you suppose the explanation to be now?" Thomas was feeling irritable which irritated him because he hadn't felt irritable in a very long time. He had remembered nothing new about his life or death as they hung up the paintings, but when Adeline discovered the new painting in the dining room a curious calm helped him recall something peculiar about the night he died. They discussed it over dinner in the kitchen and Adeline was still relentlessly coming up with possible scenarios.

"You said you didn't know the man who poured the glass of champagne that made you feel sick."

"I said I didn't invite him to my birthday party." Thomas sat back in his chair and ran one hand through his long dark hair. "I also said he could have come along with someone I did invite."

"Yes. But from your description of him, Thomas, he's the young man who followed the beautiful woman into the Great Room. And there isn't a portrait of him in our gallery; just the new painting of a man who looks almost exactly like you standing with his arms about the waist of our mysterious beautiful woman."

"What if he was the painter or artist as it were?"

"Exactly."

"Exactly what?"

"He was the artist. He painted the two of you, I mean, your lookalike. He suspected you and she were lovers and, jealous, put poison in your drink. That would explain why it tasted bad and made you feel sick." It was Adeline's turn to sit back. "And then killed you."

"I'm beginning to prefer the doctor's supposition; that I had a heart attack."

"The poison probably simulated that. Was there an autopsy?"

"What a horrible thought. I hope not."

"Well if there wasn't, who would suspect murder? I mean, other than people who already thought the house was haunted by you?"

"Of course," Thomas mused half to himself, "I was only thirty-nine."

"You said forty-three during dinner."

"All right, all right. But I looked thirty-nine. Anyway, the point is—" he stopped and looked at the stove, then back at Adeline—"I've quite forgotten the point now."

"The point is you were murdered by the artist. He thought you were the man in the painting having an affair with the woman he was in love with."

"With whom he was in love."

"What?" Exasperated, Adeline stood up. "You asked me to help you, Thomas. I'm only trying to do what you asked."

"I'm sorry." Thomas stood up and went to Adeline. He put his arms on her waist and looked into her eyes. "You've come up with a truly brilliant possibility."

"Explanation."

"I stand corrected." He stood still and waited until the annoyance left Adeline's face. Then he stepped closer and kissed her. "What do we do next?" Seeing her surprise he dropped his arms. "I mean, to confirm your theory." He held up his right hand. "Explanation."

Adeline, still overwhelmed by the warmth of the long kiss, blinked several times as she tried to think. *What do we do next?*

"I don't know," she confessed. "We still don't know who the artist is, was. He cleverly didn't sign the paintings of the house or the portraits. And we don't know who the woman is, was. And it's far too late to report your murder to the police."

Thomas smiled and tilted his head to one side. "You're very beautiful."

"What?"

"I'm not going to say it again. Not tonight. Look. It's late. Go to bed and we can discuss it all over again in the morning."

"I don't want to go to bed. Not alone."

Thomas sat down again. "What did you say?"

"You heard me." Adeline turned and walked slowly to the kitchen door. "Are you coming with me or are you just going to disappear and then reappear in my bedroom?"

Thomas jumped up from his chair and hurried to join her. "With you, of course."

She held out her left hand and he clasped it tightly with his right. "I think you should know I'm out of practice."

Adeline nodded and started down the hallway. "So am I."

"But you were married."

"Not happily."

"Still—"

Adeline stopped walking. They were in front of the dining room. The door was closed. "Thomas?" her voice was a nervous whisper.

"Yes?"

"The door's closed."

He looked at the door. "Ah. Now that is a mystery I can solve." He drew her away and they continued down the hallway. "Very few doors in the house are level now."

"Because of the wind?" Adeline let him lead her away but couldn't help glancing back.

"No. Because the house is old."

"You know, sometimes I think you don't take this whole 'there's a mystery to be solved' seriously."

"Quite the contrary. I take it very seriously. I am, after all, part of the mystery."

They reached the stairs and started to climb the left staircase together. "We should have put a chair under the door handle," said Adeline. "I've seen that in movies."

"Adeline?"

"Yes, Thomas?"

They reached the top of the stairs and he stepped next to her. "Shall I tell you a secret?"

"Of course!"

He bent his head a little until he could whisper in her right ear. "This isn't a movie. That door isn't level. And I'm beginning to think you don't want me to spend the night with you."

Before she could answer, he kissed her, there, at the top of the staircase, just like in a movie.

After a minute, Adeline said softly. "You couldn't be more wrong." She turned and started down the short hallway to her bedroom.

Thomas followed her.

"That was amazing," said Adeline.

"Really? Here, try this one." They were sitting curled up against one another on Adeline's bed. Hungry after their lovemaking, Thomas had disappeared to the kitchen and returned with a plate of assorted cookies.

"How did you get the plate and cookies to come with you?" Adeline managed to ask, her mouth still full of a chocolate cookie.

"I told you, I don't know. I can't explain that any more than I can explain how I could make love to you an hour ago. And you said you wouldn't keep asking me questions."

Adeline smiled, feeling gloriously happy. "You're right. I am trying not to keep asking, but you're my own, personal mystery, Thomas Éclair. The tall, dark, handsome stranger with the mysterious past. Irresistible."

Thomas held back the cookie he was about to offer her. "Is that why you wanted me to spend the night with you? Because I'm a mystery?"

"No. Because I like you very much. And you're irresistible."

He threw the cookie over his shoulder and tackled her. She laughed as they hugged and kissed. "Tell me again what you told me in the kitchen," said Adeline.

"Kiss me first."

She kissed him. It was much later that Thomas leaned on one elbow and caressed Adeline's hair. "You're beautiful."

"No one's ever told me that before. I think you think that because you've been alone for such a long time. You've only memories and portraits to compare me to."

"That's not what I think at all. When I first saw you and followed you around the house, I thought, 'she's beautiful.'"

"I haven't seen the entire house yet. You might change your mind." Adeline sat up. "I want to see your side, and your room."

"It needs tidying and you need sleep."

"Don't you?"

"Not really. But I'll stay with you and hold you and when you wake up, I'll still be here."

Satisfied, Adeline lay back and turned on her left side. Thomas lay down against her back and put his right arm around her waist. "Now go to sleep."

She closed her eyes, thinking she'd never be able to sleep.

Several hours later she woke up. "Thomas?"

"I'm right here."

Adeline blinked in the dull sunlight. Thomas stood by the window, drapes open so he could look out at the lake. "The view is much better from the sunroom."

Pulling the sheet with her, Adeline joined him. "Will you take me there today? To the sunroom?"

"Yes. But right now you should shower and get dressed."

"I don't like that word."

"Which one?"

"Should."

"Then, I suggest that you shower and get dressed. Otherwise—" he put his arms around her—"we'll have to spend the day in bed."

"Tempting." Adeline kissed him. She looked out at the bleak morning light. The rain was almost a sun shower. "I'll shower." She turned away then back. "Don't disappear on me."

"I won't."

She went to the bathroom and ran the shower. A short time later, returning to the bedroom, she noticed that Thomas was at the window again, this time dressed. And the bed was made. He turned as she entered the room and smiled at her. Something in his smile made her feel happy, as if she'd never experienced happiness before.

I suppose I haven't really.

"Don't watch me, Thomas. I'm going to get dressed."

"But I just spent the night with you and we—"

"This is different. Now just look at the lake. And don't turn around until I tell you to. I'm going to be all awkward legs and arms. There's nothing attractive about a woman wiggling into a bra and jeans."

"What if you need help with a zipper?"

"I'll let you know."

Several minutes later, she was dressed and, hair wet but combed, she went to Thomas. "I know it's silly, but I suddenly felt clumsy and shy, not at all beautiful like you made me feel last night."

"Then I'll have to keep trying until it's a constant state of mind for you."

"Will you? You won't disappear on me?"

"I won't disappear on you. And I'm not going anywhere except to the kitchen for a very late breakfast."

Adeline reached for his right hand and clasped it with hers. "Take me with you, Thomas."

"What? Now? I don't know if it's safe."

"What's the worst that could happen?"

Thomas frowned. "You might die."

"Well. Then you'd be stuck with me, I guess."

"You guess! You can't guess. This is not the time to start guessing. We haven't even solved the mystery of the portraits, or the dancers, or my murder."

Adeline didn't release her grip. "Guessing is part of solving mysteries. I'm guessing I'll be fine. Now let's go. I'm hungry."

Thomas sighed but instead of drooping, he straightened his shoulders. He counted to three. And they were in the kitchen.

"Wow!" Letting go of his hand, Adeline hugged him. "That was fantastic! I don't know how to describe it. It . . . it was like being tickled from the inside."

Returning her hug, Thomas still felt anxious. "Hold on. I think we have to do a test."

"A test?"

"Yes." He pointed at the shiny kettle on the stove. "Breathe on that."

"Why?

"I want to make certain you're still alive."

Adeline went to the kettle, lifted it, and exhaled onto its shiny surface. Her breath left a small smudge.

"There." She rubbed the smudge with a tea towel. "Let's make brunch."

"Oh, the view of the lake is much better from the sunroom. I can even see the sea." Adeline turned to Thomas. "I still think we could have transported here or whatever it's called."

"I wanted you to see the house."

"Hmmm. It is lovely. Will you mind much if I change it a bit?" Before he could answer, she hurried to tell him about her plans to restore the house back to its original design. She'd ask Ham to do some of the renovations and maybe he would know someone else who could help. They would do one room at a time. In this way, she and Thomas could avoid strangers and contractors who would feel intrusive instead of helpful.

Thomas listened, appreciating Adeline's desire to preserve his privacy. He did not want it known that he was alive, more or less, and residing at his home. He especially liked how Adeline called the house 'our house' and not 'my.' The plural made him feel cared about and, watching her as she moved about the sunroom, gesturing excitedly with her hands, he thought that perhaps at last he had found the woman he was meant to love. It certainly had felt like it when he had made love to her. *How did I manage that? I just wanted to so very much. It was easy and natural. What strange and curious circumstances are happening?*

"What do you think about that?"

Thomas started. "Sorry. What?"

"I'm sorry. I'm talking too much." Adeline went to him and gave him a kiss and then leaned back against his chest. Thomas wrapped his arms about her waist and they looked out at the lake.

"You're not talking too much. It's wonderful that you're so excited." Thomas held her closer. "But promise me something."

"Of course."

"Don't you disappear on me."

"I won't. I promise."

"When will you start the renovations?"

"As soon as Ham is available. Don't worry. I'll tell him I want to keep my privacy and that's why I want it done with just one or two other people at a time. Oh, and I have to telephone Mrs. Folly. We need more groceries. Except, I'll say I need more." She turned to face him. "It feels strange to pretend I'm here alone when I'm with you. But I don't mind."

"Speaking of pretending"— Thomas fidgeted a little— "before I told you the truth about me, I forged a letter from Mr. Pemberton to Mrs. Folly."

"Why?"

"Well. When you were asking me about a lease, I—"

"Oh, Thomas. I'm so sorry. How awful for you. What did you say in the letter?"

"Just that this side of the house was let, ah, rented, some time ago. It's sort of a lease, really, giving me permission to retain this room and its bedroom."

"Where's the letter?"

"In the study."

"Let's go to the study then. We probably don't need it now. I mean, I know you're here and Mrs. Folly believes you're here. In fact, I think Ham does as well."

Thomas looked surprised. "Anyone else?"

"The realtor warned me the house had a reputation for being haunted."

"How rude. Except for that one wife, I've been very quiet."

"I'm sure you have, but both Ham and Mrs. Folly seem to acknowledge that you're here somewhere. I'll just pretend that I've not heard or seen you." Adeline smiled up at Thomas. "And more. Now let's disappear to the study."

"All right."

A moment later they were there. Adeline took the letter from the desk and said she'd tuck it away just in case. Then she moved about the room, fingers lightly grazing the walls. "The wallpaper's loose. Someone was very hasty."

"The wind frightens people. It's more than cold sometimes. Sometimes it feels alive."

Adeline pursed her lips for a minute. When she spoke, her voice was thoughtful as if she were putting together a puzzle. "The wind." She stopped herself. "The wind! It was windy the night I saw the dancers. And there was a storm. What was the weather like the night you were, you know?"

"You can say 'murdered.'" Thomas tried to pull the fragments of his memories together. "I'm not certain but I think there was a storm coming in from the sea. It was probably windy. Why?"

"I think the wind and the mysterious dancers might be connected."

"Life with you is never going to be dull, is it?"

"What a nice thing to say. Come on. Let's go to the kitchen. I'm hungry again."

"Shall we walk?"

"For fun." They held hands and walked to the kitchen. As they prepared their meal, Adeline continued to speculate on the interaction of the wind and the dancers. When had Thomas first seen the dancers? Could they see him? Could they see her? Did he think it would be windy tonight and did it also need to be stormy, too?

Thomas felt exhausted by the time they sat down. He didn't mind; he luxuriated in feeling again. Especially the feelings he had for Adeline.

They had almost finished cleaning up when the phone rang.

Adeline froze and looked at Thomas. "Who do you think it could be?"

"Answer it and ask."

She went to the phone on the wall. "Hello? Oh, hello, Ham. There'll be a storm tonight but clear tomorrow? Thank you for letting me know. Yes, I'm fine. But I do need you to come up to the house in the morning. Please bring any extra tools you might need to start some simple renovations."

She continued to explain what she wanted as Thomas listened. A ladder for tearing down wallpaper, whatever tools required for knocking down walls. Yes, she wanted him to start immediately and then let her know how much help he needed. She preferred to keep it to a minimum of people. Cost didn't matter, just privacy.

"Thank you, Ham. Oh. Yes, please. How thoughtful of you to ask. I do need to restock and whatever other groceries Mrs. Folly thinks would be helpful. I've been extremely hungry. It must be the weather. Thank you, Ham. I'll see you in the morning."

She hung up the phone. "We start tomorrow."

"Wonderful!" Thomas hugged her, lifting her slightly off her feet. He set her down and kissed her. "What about tonight?"

———◆———

Thunder woke the lovers. At first they tightened their embrace, but a second boom made the room seem to shake.

Adeline sat up. She reached for the bedside light. It wasn't there. "Oh, no. Thomas?"

He sat up beside her. "I'm right here. It's just another thunderstorm. Ham warned you about it, remember?"

"It's not just any storm," Adeline felt about the bed for her robe. "It's the kind that makes the house change. The kind that brings the dancers."

Finding her robe, she pulled it from the bed and stood up. "Listen. Do you hear music?"

Thomas, still sitting on the bed, listened. "I hear the wind." He glanced around the room. "Adeline? I can barely see you. Where's the light?"

"It's not there. I told you. Somehow the wind changes the house and brings the dancers." She pulled on her robe, tying it tightly at the waist. "We have to investigate."

Reluctantly, Thomas got up and dressed.

"Hurry." Adeline was at the bedroom door and opened it a bit. Light laughter and music drifted into the room. She glanced back as the room was suddenly brightened with moonlight. "Why did you get dressed?"

"If we're going to a party, I'm not going naked." He joined her at the door and the two of them opened it wider. They peered out into the hallway.

"You're right," Thomas agreed. "I hear music."

At the end of the hallway, the tree outside scratched against the window as the storm increased. "And wind."

"Let's go." Adeline opened the door wide and stepped into the hallway.

Thomas grabbed her left hand. "Wait a minute. Don't you think you should get dressed?"

"We may not have time before the wind changes and the dancers disappear. Anyway, I don't think they'll be able to see me. Not if I'm holding your hand."

"And how did you come to that conclusion?"

"As long as you're holding my hand, we know we can disappear together, right?"

"Right. And don't ask me why or how."

"I won't. But it seems logical to conclude that when we're holding hands, I can be invisible too."

"I hadn't thought of that." Thomas stepped into the hallway. "All right. But don't let go of my hand."

"I won't."

Together they hurried down the hallway. When they reached the top of the double staircase, they stopped.

"Look at the chandelier," Adeline whispered. "Candles, instead of light bulbs."

Thomas looked up, then suddenly pulled Adeline closer to him. "Look down over the railing."

They looked down. The doors to the Great Room were open and the music was loud and festive. Occasionally a dancing couple swept past the open doors.

Thomas took the lead now and they moved quietly down the left staircase. At the bottom, he became invisible, but Adeline could feel his right hand holding hers. She tightened her fingers about his. "Thomas? I can't see you. Can you see me?"

"Well of course I can see you. But we're going to have to test your logic somehow. Let's stand near the door. If someone notices you or me, I'll immediately whisk us back to your room."

The two crept near the left side of the Great Room's doorway. Inside, the scene was almost identical to the first time Adeline had stood near there and watched, except for one thing: the portrait of Thomas wasn't above the fireplace. She pointed and whispered her observation to him. He nodded. After a minute, he took a step forward. Still holding Adeline's left hand with his right, Thomas beckoned casually to one of the servants standing at one end of the long table of food. He wasn't noticed. "You there," he called. No response.

"They can't see or hear us, Adeline. What do we do now?"

"I'm not sure."

"What do you mean, you're not sure? Now is not the time to lose your confidence."

Adeline thought quickly. "On the count of three, let go of my hand."

"I will not. Someone might see you."

"Exactly. If they do, you grab my hand and whisk us away, okay?"

Thomas drooped. *Investigating a mystery*, he decided, *was extremely nerve-wracking.*

Adeline was counting. On three, he let go of her hand. A pair of dancers passed near them and the woman gasped. She said something to her partner and he looked at Adeline.

Frightened, Adeline grabbed Thomas's right hand. "Get us out of here."

Abruptly, they were back in Adeline's bedroom. She hugged Thomas, not realizing she was shaking. The room started to fill with mist. Then it began to tilt. She held him tighter.

"Don't let go of me, Thomas."

"I won't."

There was a long silence, then the sound of the thunderstorm. Adeline heard rain. She kept her head pressed against Thomas's chest.

"Are we safe now?" Her voice trembled.

"Yes."

Adeline leaned against him. "I'm so sorry. That was a foolish thing to do." She looked up at him. "Maybe even dangerous."

Thomas kissed her gently. "We had to try. Anyway, you're fearless, remember? And I rescue wet kittens. We'll be fine."

"How?"

"I've no idea. That's your department. I'm just, what do they call me in movies? The sidekick?"

Adeline smiled and hugged him again. "Oh, no. You're not the sidekick. You're the hero. My knight in shining armor."

"Am I really?" He pulled back from her a bit. "I suppose I was rather brave. Still, they can't harm me. And I certainly won't let them harm you."

Adeline stepped back, turned and went to the bed. Thomas followed her. As they lay down together, she spoke, her voice calm and steady now. "Well, we proved something, at least."

Thomas was untying her robe and kissing her neck. "What? That you were right? Again?"

"Yes. No. That we've definitely got another mystery."

Chapter Eight

When Ham knocked on the front door the next morning, Adeline paused before the mirror in the foyer. She smoothed her hair. She felt like she had been cast as the leading lady in a movie. A mystery, of course. She knew Thomas stood near her, invisible. And, when he said she looked beautiful, she knew only she could hear him.

Smiling, she went to the front door and pulled it open.

"Morning, miss," said Ham, touching his cap.

"Good morning, Ham." Adeline took a step back, then blocked the door a little as she saw the older man standing behind Ham. "I see you've brought a friend."

"Yes, miss. You did say to let you know how much help I'd be needing and Samuel here is the best restorer in the country. He'll be much better able to assess who else we might need. That is, if we can't do the renovation ourselves."

"I see." Adeline opened the door wide and allowed the two men to enter. Hamlet introduced her properly to Samuel. His hair was as white as his teeth were yellow. He wasn't much taller than Adeline and his face was lined with age, but his blue eyes were shining with happiness. He grinned as he shook her hand thoroughly.

"Very pleased I am to meet you, miss. Might I add it's an honor to be here at the house? Such a beauty it was in its time. When Hamlet mentioned you wanted to restore it instead of making it modern, I offered my assistance quick as a fox."

"How very kind." Noticing the truck parked in the drive, Adeline asked when Mrs. Folly would be arriving.

"She's here now, miss," Ham answered. "Already in the kitchen. We made sure to help her with the bags of groceries first."

Feeling a little overwhelmed, Adeline smiled. "Thank you. Please do come in and we can walk around the rooms." She paused. "I should warn you, I'm determined that the house be as it once was when Thomas Éclair was alive. Perhaps even before then."

The two men exchanged glances. "Well, then. I suggest we start with the Great Room," Samuel said. "From there we can have a look at one or two other rooms that you would like attended to first."

Thomas coughed a little and, knowing he had Adeline's attention, said, "I like Samuel. But have a care how often you mention my name. It might scare them off. You never know how people will react."

"Of course." Adeline smiled, knowing the men thought she was speaking to them. The three went into the Great Room and Adeline began describing the changes she envisioned.

Samuel and Ham produced measuring tapes from their tool belts and nodded, not interrupting. When they returned to the foyer, Adeline pointed at the two suits of armor at the bottom of the stairs. She wanted them removed at once. Without hesitation, Samuel lifted one suit by the waist while Ham took the other. They carried them out to the truck, returning with a ladder and toolboxes.

"We'll start the measurements now, if that suits you, miss," said Ham.

"Almost. I'd like to show you the dining room first. I want to start using it but it needs new curtains and a new chandelier. I'd appreciate measurements of the windows. In fact, you might have to install new windows. As long as they look antique."

"Certainly." Ham nodded and the men followed Adeline down the hallway.

"Ah! I see you've found the portraits." Samuel paused to admire one. "I'm glad you like them. Might I ask where you found them?"

"In a small room above the Music Room. That reminds me." She stopped and turned to Ham. "I'd like the Music Room restored. And I'll need a piano."

"What sort of piano, miss?"

"A grand one, please." She continued to the dining room door. She had braced it open with a chair and explained that it would stay shut but not open. Ham and Samuel at once began discussing how to hang the door properly.

Adeline stood back. She felt Thomas beside her and wanted to hug him. But her part demanded that she speak of him only in the past tense. She put on a smile and joined the men in the dining room. They were looking at the large portrait on the wall. Adeline explained she wanted it removed and the 'picture of the lady' put in its place. If they were startled, they didn't show it. Setting up the ladder, Ham climbed up while Samuel kept it steady.

"As you thought, Samuel, it hangs on a single wire. But that nail looks terrible large." He lifted one corner of the frame. "Weak, though. We'll be leaving behind a big hole."

Samuel looked at Adeline. "We'll not be able to avoid a bit of damage, miss, but we will fill and plaster. Might you be liking paint instead of wallpaper?"

"Oh, yes! I dislike the wallpaper, not only here but in all the rooms. I know it will take more time, but I'd much prefer paint."

"That's grand with me, miss," said Samuel and grinned. "Paint's a fine choice. My grandson has a good eye for the task. He wants to be an architect one day; go to school in the city. He calls it art.

"But he's a fine assistant," Samuel hurried to allay any doubts Adeline might have. "Strong and able, too. That is, if you wouldn't mind having another person on the premises."

Adeline nodded, interested but still determined to play the part of 'Lady of the Manor.' "That will probably be fine, Samuel, but I want you to look at the Music Room first."

"Quite right, miss. No need to rush." Samuel looked up at Hamlet. "Come down and we'll lift the frame from the bottom."

Ham complied and Adeline stood well back. She didn't want to be in the way, but she wanted to watch.

Setting the ladder safely aside, the two men gripped the ugly frame on the bottom corners. With effort, they lifted it up and pulled. It almost toppled forward but they wrested it to the floor and leaned it against a wall. As they did so, a small piece of paint fell from the portrait.

Adeline hurried forward. She knelt and picked up the piece, then looked at the portrait.

"I'm most terribly sorry, miss." Ham apologized. "I didn't think the painting was so old it would fall apart."

"Don't worry, Ham." Adeline ran her fingers over the small hole in the painting. Impulsively, she gave a ragged edge a pull, creating a long tear. "It's a pentimento! This portrait was painted over something else. Hold the frame upright for me, please."

As the men did so, Adeline wished Thomas could help her. But she stuck to her part and the newer paint cooperated. It seemed to be acrylic instead of oil, peeling off like bits of rubber.

After several minutes, only a few lines were stuck along the inside of the frame. The original painting was revealed. It was Thomas's garden.

"Oh, it's lovely!" Adeline pretended never to have seen it before. "We'll have it reframed, of course. Something delicate to suit the flowers.

"Ham, is there a garden somewhere near the house?"

"Yes, miss. Just beyond the kitchen on the leeward side. Small, but as you said, lovely. I do my best to keep it tidy."

"I'm sure you do and thank you." Adeline wiped at her hands. She looked at the slight damage to the wall. "If you would, just put the other portrait up for now. Then, I'll take you to the Music Room."

"Very good, miss." Ham looked pleased; Samuel, too.

Once it was in place, they regarded the beautiful woman in the painting.

"I think she was once above the fireplace in the Great Room," Thomas remarked. "But we can switch paintings later."

"Of course." Realizing she had spoken aloud, Adeline rushed to add, "This portrait was probably meant for the Great Room. Above the fireplace. But let's leave it here for now. I do want to have the painting of the garden reframed." She paused. "Um, would you mind taking down those dreadful curtains? A good, strong yank or two should work."

"Aye. And the original window frames with them," said Samuel. "How if we take them down carefully and then away to the truck? It may well be there's original wood under the sloppy paint work."

"That's very sensible of you, Samuel. Thank you. Would you like to see the Music Room now?"

"Lead on, miss. There's plenty of morning left in the day and we can work till sundown."

It was half past ten when Adeline finished her abbreviated tour of the house. She explained that she only had plans for the rooms she had shown them and had not yet decided what would best suit the other rooms.

The two men agreed it would be best to leave the other rooms as they were for now and start with the rooms she intended to use first. Samuel asked if he might telephone his grandson and have him join them as they were going to start knocking through the wall that connected it to the Great Room. Adeline agreed and left the dining room.

She went to the kitchen and stopped in the doorway. Mrs. Folly was standing at the long wood island in the center of the room. Several loaves of bread and packages of sandwich meats were on either side of a large cutting board. On the counter behind her, beside the stove, were baking bowls and apple peels. From the oven came the delicious aroma of apple pie.

"Good morning." Adeline strode into the room, still playing her part.

Mrs. Folly looked up. "It seems it will be good after all." Her eyes narrowed a little. "You've not been disturbed by the wind?"

Adeline went to peek through the glass front of the oven. "Not at all. I rather like the wind. And I love the house."

"Do you now? Ham said you were going to restore it. I was glad to hear of that. If you'd been like those others I've heard tell, then I wouldn't have stayed."

"So you'll stay?"

"I will. I'm making a bit of lunch for the men. No doubt Samuel will have his grandson up by noon. I've done a good shopping for you. Your solicitor set up an account at the grocers in town. Under the name of Parker."

"Thank you very much, Mrs. Folly."

"I do what I can." She faced the island. "I'll have the sandwiches ready soon enough."

Adeline went to stand beside her. "Mrs. Folly? Do you know anything about the large portrait that was in the dining room?"

Mrs. Folly paused; a knife in her right hand dripped a little mustard on a slice of bread.

"Only that the wife that had it painted was right full of herself. And that she hated the house."

"Do you know who painted it? It wasn't signed."

"Most likely someone from the city. Someone the woman knew." Mrs. Folly spread the mustard on the slice of bread. "Why do you say 'was?'"

Adeline told her what had transpired earlier in the dining room.

Mrs. Folly continued making the sandwich. "And what was the painting beneath?"

"It's a painting of a garden."

"Ah, yes. She was just spiteful enough to have it painted over. That was his garden."

Adeline kept her voice steady. "Who's garden?"

"The last owner of the house: Thomas Éclair." Mrs. Folly's voice, so calm and factual, suddenly dropped to a whisper. "The one who was murdered." She straightened her apron. "He's most likely a ghost now. It's said he doesn't care for visitors."

"Oh. Well, I'm not a visitor. And it's a beautiful painting. Ham said the garden's on the leeward side of the house."

"That's right. To protect it from the wind. I've not stepped inside, but Ham tends to it occasionally." Mrs. Folly picked up a serrated knife and sliced the thick sandwich. "I hope your plans don't include changing the garden. I don't think he'd like that."

"Who wouldn't like that? Ham?"

"The ghost, of course."

"I thought you wouldn't stay after dark because of the ghost."

Mrs. Folly scoffed. "A ghost can't scare me for long. What's the use of an old woman's scream? I doubt he was the type of man to enjoy being cruel, otherwise that spiteful woman might have stayed. No. He's here somewhere. Perhaps in this very room right now. Restless because of his untimely end; unable to pass what with being so near to where the waters blend." She shook her head. "Poor soul"

"I was hardly poor," Thomas said.

Adeline resisted speaking to him. She spoke to Mrs. Folly instead. "Where do the waters blend?"

"Where the lake catches the sea," Mrs. Folly explained. "That's a powerful magic there," she continued, unaware of Thomas. "And this house, it's been full of mystery and magic since the first stone was laid centuries past. A ghost is the least of my worries. Or yours. As for the garden, well, it's rumored that the ghost appears there sometimes. No doubt mourning the loss of his life and him so young and murdered, too.

"No. It's not the ghost I fear, but the wind and the waves and the storms. And the magic. Everyone knows magic is more powerful at night. So I'll do what I can during the day, as I said when we met, but not at night."

"I understand. Perhaps you'll be glad to know, I've no plans for the garden. If it's half as lovely as it appears in the painting, I'll be happy to leave it in Ham's care. When I see it for myself, I'll let Ham suggest what he thinks would be best for the garden." Adeline swallowed a giggle as Thomas nudged her in the back. "And the ghost."

"I hope you're not laughing at what I'm telling you."

"Not at all. Please believe me, Mrs. Folly, I've nothing but love for this house. In fact, I like a mystery and a house with a past."

Again Mrs. Folly paused in her work. She turned toward Adeline and studied her. They stood facing each other for a long minute. "You've seen him then."

The statement caught Adeline off guard. "Seen who? The ghost? No. No, I haven't seen anyone. It's just that I know so little of the history of the house. I was told it was haunted, but that didn't stop me from buying the house. As for the ghost—"

Adeline changed the subject. "When will lunch be ready?"

"By the time the beer's delivered."

"Beer?"

"Yes. I ordered six cases. Be certain not to let the men have more than one beer at lunch. They can have two at the end of the day's work. Men are like donkeys; you've got to hold a carrot in front of them."

"Thank you, Mrs. Folly. I'll remember that. Oh, and thank you for doing the shopping."

"You're welcome, Miss Parker. Will you need any help with the cleaning today?"

"I'll make certain the men clean up after themselves." Adeline turned to leave. "The pie smells delicious."

There was no answer. Adeline did not really expect one. Mrs. Folly had said what she wanted to say and the conversation was over.

Mrs. Folly answered the knock on the kitchen door. "They're in the Great Room. I'll take you there. Mind you wipe your boots."

The young man obeyed, then quickly took the tray Mrs. Folly held out to him. The two walked down the hallway, Mrs. Folly leading. When they entered the Great Room, she led the young man to the folding table and chairs that Ham and Samuel had set up.

Adeline was talking to Samuel about installing a balcony. She hadn't mentioned the book in her possession and let him think it was her idea.

"Begging your pardon, miss." The young man set the tray down on the table and Adeline looked up. He was extremely tall, perhaps six foot four, with broad shoulders. Wearing a plaid work shirt and jeans with a tool belt already about his waist, the unnamed fellow pointed to the far corner of the Great Room. "I couldn't help but overhear. There used to be a balcony there. I would place money that, taking down those poorly made walls, it's there still."

"That's wonderful." Adeline stood up. "You must be Samuel's grandson?"

Samuel pushed his chair back and stood up, looking proud. "That he is, miss. This is Robert."

"It's nice to meet you, Robert." Adeline extended her hand to the younger man. He wiped his right hand against his shirt and shook her proffered hand carefully.

Adeline noticed that, even as Robert shook her hand, his eyes strayed to where he said there was a balcony. She asked him how he knew that.

"I can tell by the lines on the wall. And too, there's a book in town about this house. At the library, miss."

"Does it say anything about the paintings and portraits?"

"I don't think so, miss. I'm sorry but I was studying it for the design." He hesitated then seemed to come to a decision and said, "You see, I hope to be an architect one day. For me, the architecture is the art. The design and layout, what the house was first intended to be when it was first built, is what I was giving my attention."

"I think that's a wonderful point of view and a good goal. I'll have to get a library card."

"No need, miss. I've the only copy of the book and it's still in my possession. I can have it here for you tomorrow if you like."

"I'd like that very much, Robert. Thank you." Adeline moved away from the table a few steps. "Will you have some lunch?"

Thanking her, Robert sat down and Adeline left the men to their single beers and large plate of sandwiches. She wanted very much to talk to Thomas.

Chapter Nine

"Well?" Adeline whispered to Thomas again. "What do you think?"

"I think I'd still like to know what we're doing in the hall closet."

"I told you. I don't want anyone to hear me talking to you."

"Couldn't we discuss this in the sunroom?"

"Oh." Adeline stopped herself from becoming more insistent. She had been preoccupied all morning and now she was not thinking sensibly. "I'm sorry. I wasn't thinking. We should talk in the sunroom. Would you whisk us there now? Please?"

Thomas smiled and they were in the sunroom. "There. Now we can converse."

Adeline heard the slightest tinge of jealousy in Thomas's voice. His voice was already pleasing to her, its timbre just deep enough to make her listen for more, its warmth almost touchable. Now he was jealous and they had to discuss the new information Robert had unwittingly disclosed. She went to look out the windows of the sunroom and Thomas joined her. After a minute, she turned to him.

Adeline faced the potential problem right away. "There's no need to be jealous of Robert. He's just a boy."

Thomas scoffed. "Whatever makes you think I'm jealous of Robert? Other than he's tall, blonde and blue-eyed. Young, handsome, and, oh, yes, alive."

"You're being silly. I need you to help me make an important decision about the restoration and you're jealous." She slipped her right hand about his left. "Do you want to know a secret?"

He looked away. "All right. If you must."

"I think I'm falling in love with you, Thomas Éclair. Not because you're living a mystery. And that's the word: living. In some strange, maybe magical way, you're alive. You know you are." She looked up at him, staring until he faced her.

"If our nights together aren't proof enough of that, I don't know what is except this." She kissed him, putting her arms about his neck and stepping close against him.

Returning the kiss and embrace, Thomas finally relaxed. He lifted his head and looked steadily into Adeline's eyes. "I think I've already fallen in love with you. And it makes me feel alive. And that, more than anything, is very probably why I can make love to you. And feel love. And jealousy."

He took one step back from Adeline, his hands on her waist. "But it's not a lover's jealousy, it's, it's just so damn frustrating to stand by and watch you have all the fun. I know it's childish but we were having such fun together. Just the two of us. Weren't we?"

"Oh, Thomas." Adeline stepped into his arms again, hugging him. "Of course we were having fun together. It was stupid of me not to realize that you felt left out. It's not childish at all.

"There were several times just this morning that I wanted to turn and ask your opinion. But I couldn't. It was frustrating because I knew you were there. And I could hear you.

"Just continue to give me your opinion and I'll pretend it's mine. We can make this work. It's only for a few months, maybe less. I'll do anything I can to make it easier for both of us. But you did agree to the restoration of the house. Don't you want that anymore? Don't you want to understand what's happening here?

"We have to understand why those people show up and have a party. And the wind, it's definitely strange but you already knew that. The paintings and portraits. Your murder. A case of mistaken identity? Now the balcony that I suspect has a room behind it. But I wasn't certain and I didn't want the workmen to start tearing down walls before we had discussed what would be best. For us. Just tell me what you want."

Thomas kissed her lightly. "I just want you. But you're entirely right. Again. And I do want the house restored. But just the one side. I want this side left alone. Agreed?"

"Agreed."

Thomas thought for a minute. "By the way, there is a room behind the balcony. It used to be the library. It was fairly large and very beautiful. I think you'd like it. You should let the boy open it up."

"I will." Adeline paused. "Are you starting to remember your life, Thomas?"

"Only the small parts that don't matter."

"I think they do matter. Maybe more than we realize. Anyway, they matter to me. And when the men are gone this evening," she continued, "the library will be ours." She smiled. "We can plan and arrange it anyway you like. The way you remember it once was."

"I remember walls full of books."

"Done. I'll start making a list of titles."

"And would you do something very silly for me?"

"You know I will."

"Put my portrait up somewhere. Perhaps in the library. Maybe it will help us with all the mysteries we have to solve. It seems I want to be remembered after all. Even in that small way."

"I'll get it from my bedroom after the men leave. We can put it up together. That would be nice, wouldn't it?"

"Yes. But even nicer would be if you start spending the nights in my bedroom. Yours was mine when I was a boy and it's been renovated. Tastefully, but not to my taste."

"I see." Adeline smiled. "You're asking for a very intimate thing, Thomas. Don't you think you should show me your room first?"

"I do." He held her right hand and led her from the sunroom. The brightness of the sunlight dimmed as they walked down a short, wide hallway. Thomas stopped at a large single door with a brass handle. Turning it, he opened the door and, releasing Adeline's hand, he stood back. "After you."

Adeline walked into the room. It felt sprawling compared to hers. There was a huge wood burning fireplace with a comfortable looking arm chair in front of it. Beside the arm chair was a little table with a brandy decanter and a glass. A book lay on the seat of the arm chair.

"What are you reading?"

"Shakespeare's Romeo and Juliet."

Adeline kept her smile to herself and started walking about the room, much as she had when she first investigated the house. The walls were bare of wallpaper or paintings. There was a large window open to catch the day's first spring air, a chest of drawers, a writing table and chair. And a bed draped in beautiful colors of blue and green.

"Oh, my god."

"What?" Thomas looked around his room. "What is it?"

"It's enormous." Adeline hurried to the king size bed and jumped. She landed on the soft mattress, laughing. "Oh, it's marvelous. And bed curtains, too. And a view of the mountain. This is a wonderful room."

Adeline bounced a bit on the bed before getting off. She smoothed the silky covers she had crushed. "I'm definitely accepting your invitation, Thomas. I'll pack an overnight bag tonight."

"Why not just move all your belongings?"

"Because Mrs. Folly would get suspicious, or worse. Even though she's accused me of seeing you, I don't want her to know exactly how much of you I've seen." Adeline went to Thomas. "She's a bit of a gossip and we don't want people to talk now do we?"

Thomas laughed and the lovers hugged.

"You know, I was a bit jealous, too," Adeline confided.

"Of what?"

"The beautiful woman in the portrait."

"Ah, but her companion wasn't me. Although it does appear I was murdered for resembling him. Someone, perhaps the mysterious artist, thought I was her lover as you said."

"Hmm." Adeline glanced out the window at the changing light. "We'd better get back. I'll give Robert his new instructions about the balcony and the room beyond."

"And I won't be jealous."

"Oh yes you will." Adeline kissed him quickly. "I've never had anything like what you've given me, Thomas. And a little jealousy can be flattering."

"How do you suppose that?"

"Because you think I'm beautiful and I thought you were jealous of Robert for maybe thinking the same thing."

"I'm certain he does."

"I doubt that very much. Anyway it doesn't matter what Robert thinks. Only that he does a good job of restoration or reconstruction or whatever it's called. Come on. Whisk us back."

"To where?"

"The hall closet of course."

Thomas laughed again. "I love it when you don't think clearly."

Before Adeline could ask what he meant, they were standing at the door to the dining room across from the hall closet.

"But—" Adeline began.

"Hush. It's Mrs. Folly."

Mrs. Folly was coming down the long hallway with a tray of beer. "Evening, miss. I put aside a bit of dinner for you seeing as how you missed lunch. You might want to inspect what the men have done before they leave and give them their orders for tomorrow.

"I'll be leaving now. I'll be back tomorrow morning. I'll bring samples of fabric for the new drapes." She glanced into the dining room. "Yes. It's long past time this room be used again." She continued down the hallway. "I'll see you in the morning, Miss Parker."

Accustomed already to Mrs. Folly's mannerisms, Adeline quickly called a thank you and good night. Then she turned to Thomas. "Let's go see what's been done so far."

"Now that is clear thinking."

Adeline went to the Great Room, Thomas just one step behind her but invisible again.

Robert had a broom and was sweeping the floor diligently. Samuel and Ham were supervising, beers in hand. They stood up as soon as she entered the room and set their beers on the table, keen to hear her approval of their first day of work.

Adeline managed to prevent a gasp of astonishment as she surveyed the knocked out walls of the dining room; several of the walls had been stripped of wallpaper and washed. The buckets still sat on the floor and Ham hurried to assure her they would be emptied and put away.

He was quick to point out a ladder that now leaned against the wall with the balcony. Lines had been drawn to show where Robert had been carefully measuring the next step for tomorrow, if Adeline approved. Robert was certain he had found the balcony and that, instead of it branching off the upstairs hallway, Ham said Robert still believed it likely there was a large room behind the balcony because he had made a small hole with his hammer to test the surface of the drywall.

The dining room was shown to her by Samuel. With pride he explained that Robert had found wood beneath the painted window frames and already begun stripping the wallpaper as she had requested. They could start knocking down the frames that had held the flimsy drywall and wallpaper as soon as she agreed.

"When can the framework come down?" Adeline asked.

"First thing in the morning, miss," Samuel answered.

"Will you need more help?"

"I believe we can manage just fine, miss. Robert's strong, as I said. True that I'm old, but still able. And Ham's the best handyman in the county."

She turned and beamed at each of them in turn. "It's a wonderful start. Do sit and have your beers. Robert?"

He had put aside his broom when she arrived and stood by as she did her inspection. Now he stepped forward. "Yes, miss?"

"I'm very glad that you found the balcony. I'd like you to go ahead with whatever's necessary to completely restore it and the room behind as well."

"Yes, miss." His grin was much like his grandfather's but with whiter teeth. "And will you still be wanting that book, miss?"

"Yes, please. Do go and have a beer or two. But no more than that because I want you all to drive home safely and return early to get back to work. Mrs. Folly will provide your lunches. I can make a work schedule for you, Ham. I know you also work at your property and perhaps a few others."

"Not a problem, miss. This time of year, I'm free and available whenever you need me. Especially for whatever this job requires. Time and effort well spent, isn't it Samuel?"

"It is indeed. And it will be gratifying to see this house as it once was and was always meant to be."

Adeline agreed and then asked Ham if he knew of anyone in town that could reframe the painting they had discovered that morning. He gave it a minute of thought, asked Samuel's opinion, and they both agreed that Old Boy would do a very nice job for her and likely also have an antique styled chandelier she might like for the dining room.

"But with newer wiring, miss. I can install it myself."

"That's sounds wonderful, Ham." Adeline looked around her at the almost magical beginnings of the past coming back not to haunt but to life. "It's all wonderful." She turned to face the men. "I'm very pleased. Ham?"

He stepped forward and Adeline discussed the costs and details of payment both for the men and the vendors that Ham would deal with on her behalf. Then she thanked them all and wished them a good evening.

"I'll see you at nine," said Adeline.

"We can make it eight, miss," Robert said eagerly.

Thomas grumbled about getting out of bed too early, but only Adeline could hear him.

She immediately said she'd prefer nine to five. Six as the days lengthened. It was agreed and she made an elegant exit.

Thomas kissed her on her left cheek. "You were marvelous."

Her smile reflected a happiness she had never thought possible. Not because of the compliment, but because of Thomas. He thought he was in love with her. And now, whatever the consequences, she knew she was in love with him.

———◆———

"This door is locked too," said Adeline. It was late and she and Thomas were investigating the hallway on the second floor that led to the library. It had six doors before the end where the library had once been.

"I wasn't given a key to anything but the front door. But I'm not comfortable asking Ham to open anything before we check it for ourselves."

Thomas looked over her right shoulder at the book she held; the one noting the renovations over the years. "What does it say in the book?"

"Only that she, no name, had locked all the doors against the wind. Apparently this part of the house wasn't used."

"That's not true. I used it. Well, when I was a boy. I just don't remember the details. It seems to me there's something behind all these doors. Something unusual. I seem to recall being scolded for 'hanging about' as my father said. I do have a very strong feeling that it's not wise for me to whisk us beyond a door that might not have enough room even for me."

"Okay. Let's try the next one."

All the doors were locked, and, as they stood in front of last door, Adeline suggested they take the chance of whisking there because they knew the library was behind the door.

Thomas thought about this, arms folded across his chest, head slightly tilted to the right as he scrutinized first the door then Adeline's face. "No. I'll go by myself."

"But you've remembered so much, Thomas. And we know there's a room. It must be the original library."

"There's no use in arguing with me about this, Adeline. True, I remember a library, but what was done to it after I was murdered, I don't know. There could be boxes of books or broken pieces of lumber from the start of a renovation. It could be a storage room full of buckets and mops or whatever one puts in storage. At any rate, I won't risk your safety. I'll go first, come back, and then we can go together. If I think it's safe."

Adeline studied the determined line of his mouth. Reluctantly, she agreed and watched as Thomas disappeared. It felt like he had been gone a terribly long time. She was about to call to him when the door opened. Thomas stood there. "It's still the library."

"Can I come in now?"

"You may."

"Must you always correct my grammar?"

"I must."

Smiling, Adeline stepped into the room. She felt along the wall for the light switch.

"It doesn't work," said Thomas. "Wait for me." He disappeared again.

Adeline waited in the dark with only the light from the hallway to show her shapes of what she decided must be chairs draped in cloths. She stood still and peered into the shadows of the room. It felt large, as Thomas had remembered, and yet it seemed to have the wrong shape to it. *Why do I think that?* There was nothing about this room in the book of notes. It seemed to have been forgotten or dismissed when earlier renovations were taking place.

"Oh!" Adeline almost screamed. She put one hand against her chest. "Don't do that!"

"Sorry. I thought you were expecting me."

"Yes, but— Well it's like sneaking up on me, visible or not."

"I've brought a flashlight." He held up a large utility flashlight. "Am I forgiven?"

"I was never angry, just startled." Taking the flashlight, Adeline turned it on and they began walking about the room. The outside wall had one window but it was stuck shut and shuttered from the outside. The wall opposite the door seemed different, perhaps a quick blocking off of where the balcony was. She told Thomas about how she thought the shape of the room was wrong. He agreed and knocked repeatedly along the interior wall to the left of the door. It too, like the wall behind the balcony, was newer than the stone exterior wall where Thomas remembered shelves of books.

"Someone quite ruined it, didn't they?" His voice was sad.

"Don't worry. We'll fix it. All of it." Adeline shone the flashlight at the interior wall. "I bet that connects to the other room with the locked door."

"It does," Thomas said. He looked at Adeline, surprised at the memory and his certainty of its reliability. "It doesn't just connect, it was never there. Neither were the doors. It's like a game of dominoes. Have the men knock this wall down and the next and the next." Thomas was pacing back and forth in front of the wall like a caged animal.

"It wasn't just a library. It was a gallery and . . . it overlooked the Great Room!"

"You remember! And a gallery makes perfect sense except—" Adeline went to hold Thomas's right hand—"Why cut it up into small rooms? Because they feared the wind? Or, maybe they had lots of guests or children? Still, it's terrible."

She squeezed his right hand trying to reassure him. "We'll make it right again. Just imagine it, Thomas: a beautiful gallery above the Great Room. A library at one end, perhaps tables and chairs for party guests to sit and watch the dancers."

Adeline stopped herself and thought about what she had just said. "You know, when I first saw the dancers, I never thought to look up."

"Neither did I. We'll just have to wait for another storm. Come on. There's no place for my portrait here at the moment. And I'd like a drink."

"Beer?"

"Brandy."

"All right. But what do we do about the door?"

They left the room and discussed whether or not to leave the door open, or leave it unlocked. Finally they agreed that it would be best if Adeline continued her pretense at being unaware of what the men would discover as they continued working.

"Let what's his name find it all then. We found it first."

Adeline nudged Thomas in the ribs with one elbow. "His name is Robert. And we found it first. Remember that. Now where's the brandy?"

"In my room."

"Don't you mean, 'our' room?"

"You're right. I do."

"Then whisk us to our room, please, Thomas."

———————◆———————

"This is lovely," said Adeline. She snuggled closer to Thomas. They were lying in bed and Adeline was enjoying the soft mattress with sheets and a proper bedspread instead of a down comforter.

"I can't believe you're eating cookies with beer."

"I don't like brandy. And I do like the cookies." Recklessly she dipped one in the mug of beer Thomas had brought her from the kitchen. "See? Delicious."

He squeezed her shoulders gently with his right arm and took a sip of his brandy. "That's better. I didn't realize how out of sorts seeing the old library would make me feel. Displaced, as it were.

"I suppose because it's been such a long time since I paid attention to anything much in my life. Seeing the library, all in disarray, made me realize that it's been a very long time since I even had a life."

"I didn't realize that either. I was so happy you were remembering and far too caught up in all the fun." Adeline set her beer and the plate of cookies on the bedside table. Naked, she leaned against Thomas's bare chest and kissed him.

Returning her kiss, he set aside his glass, but Adeline sat up suddenly.

"What is it?"

"Your life. This isn't the bedroom where you were murdered, is it?"

"No. In fact, I was just now recalling that I had chosen to go to a guest room because, as I've told you, I didn't feel well and the guest room was closer."

Adeline relaxed, then sat back up again before Thomas could kiss her. "It could be another clue."

"Is it? I have to confess, at this moment, I don't really care."

Adeline pursed her lips. "But then, we're already pretty sure you were poisoned so which room you went to wouldn't matter. Then we're back to square one."

"Are we?" Thomas stroked her right arm lightly.

Adeline lay back down against him. "How did you get the wood for the fire?"

"I've no idea. You know that."

"We're really going to have to test all your abilities one of these days."

"I'm thinking of a test for right now."

Adeline let him kiss her. "You pass," she whispered.

Chapter Ten

Morning sunlight woke Adeline. She stretched and reached for Thomas but he wasn't lying next to her. Sitting up, she called to him. When he didn't answer, she got up and pulled on her housecoat. Tying it at the waist, she was about to go to the door when he suddenly appeared in front of her.

"Thomas! You said you wouldn't do that. And you promised you'd never disappear on me."

"I'm sorry. You were asleep." Thomas held up his portrait; he had retrieved it from Adeline's bedroom. "I thought I'd surprise you."

"I don't like surprises." She noticed his disappointment. "I mean, usually I don't." She helped him take the painting to the outside wall and they leaned it there beside the window. Before they could discuss where to hang his portrait, Adeline gasped and looked about the room. "What time is it? Where's a clock?"

"I think the clock in your bedroom said just past eight."

"I'd better hurry and get ready. The men will be here soon." She kissed him quickly and disappeared into the bathroom.

Thomas heard water running. A moment later Adeline appeared in the bathroom doorway. "Thomas?"

"Yes?"

"You don't have a shower. Just a bathtub."

"I know. This side of house is almost untouched by renovations and all that sort of thing. I like it much better without wallpaper and carpeting. I have a view. And the sunroom. And—"

"Thomas?" Adeline interrupted him. "I have to have a quick shower. Would you please whisk me back to my bedroom?"

He sighed. "All right. But remember, you agreed not to renovate this side of the house."

"And I won't. You and I will supervise the restoration together on the other side of the house. Now please take me to my shower."

Thomas went to her and clasped her right hand with his left. They disappeared.

"Thomas?"

"Yes?"

"This isn't exactly what I meant." They were standing in Adeline's bathroom, in the shower. The water was running from the shower head.

"Too hot?"

———◆———

Adeline smoothed her wet hair at the mirror in the foyer.

"You look beautiful," Thomas said.

"I look wet. A Lady of the Manor should look polished."

"You look polished. And sleek. Fashionable." He drew her to him and kissed her.

Loud knocks on the door interrupted them. They pulled apart. Thomas made himself invisible as Adeline went to answer the door.

Less than an hour later, instructions given and the day's work begun, Adeline was in the kitchen waiting because Mrs. Folly insisted on making her a 'good' breakfast.

"With real coffee. None of that instant nonsense. And you can't supervise those men without something solid in your stomach. Sit down. It won't take more than a minute."

It took almost a half an hour, but Adeline had to admit Mrs. Folly made a delicious omelet and, though she didn't care for coffee, she added milk and sipped a little.

Mrs. Folly announced she'd take coffee to the men. "It'll keep them going until lunch."

Content to have Mrs. Folly take charge of such minor details, Adeline waited until she left the kitchen, then whispered to Thomas. "I've saved you a bite."

"I don't really need it." He appeared at the table opposite her. "Although it smelled delicious." He looked at the half a slice of toast and the small slice of omelet on her plate. "And you were obviously hungry."

With a smile, Adeline pushed her plate toward him. "I was. It seems fantastic love-making gives me an appetite."

Thomas had already bitten into the toast. His mouth full, he waited to speak then suddenly disappeared, plate in hand. Mrs. Folly was returning.

"I see you've already cleaned up after yourself."

"Uh. Yes. Yes, I have. Thank you for the breakfast, Mrs. Folly. I'm sure I'll be better organized tomorrow."

"No need to worry. It's part of my job to see after your health. That's cooking and shopping and cleaning. And here." She went to the back door, picked up a large canvas bag and brought it to the table. "These are the samples I mentioned. I think the rose print will brighten the dining room nicely." She paused and looked around the kitchen.

"Is something wrong?" asked Adeline.

Mrs. Folly straightened her apron. "Not at all. Just had a strange tingle at the back of my neck." She went to the refrigerator and started taking out food for lunch. Speaking over her shoulder, she asked if Adeline knew that the dining room had once had double doors leading from the Great Room.

Admitting that she didn't, Adeline asked how Mrs. Folly knew. "It's common knowledge. Don't think that half the town hasn't had a look at that book young Robert brought you. And now they're waiting to hear what you'll be doing to the house.

"They'll not be hearing anything from me, of course."

"Of course."

"None of anybody's business but yours."

"No. It isn't."

"Still, you might want to take a look at the book in the dining room. And the rose print sample of fabric."

"I'll do that right now."

Adeline took the bag of fabrics and left the kitchen. Going to the dining room, she sat down at the table and picked up the book that Robert had brought to her as he had promised. She flipped the pages. There were dozens of old black and white photographs of the interior of the house. She found one of the dining room and sat back a little in her chair.

"It was nice once, wasn't it?" Thomas remarked. Still invisible, he stood quietly behind Adeline, looking over her right shoulder at the picture of the dining room. It had double doors at one end. Wood framed windows. And floor length curtains with a rose print.

Adeline shut the book. "I'll go and tell Ham to measure the windows and order the curtains."

Standing up, she turned, imagining she could see Thomas and most definitely sensing his presence on some new, intimate level. "If you agree." She wanted to add 'darling' but didn't, deciding the endearment should wait for a private moment.

"I agree," Thomas said. "I recall my father sitting at the head of the table. My mother sat on his right and me on his left."

"That's a nice memory."

Ham appeared at the open framework. "We're ready to start taking down this framework, miss." He knocked on the cheap wood.

"Samuel says we can have it done by lunch. If you're ready to vacate the room, that is."

"I am, yes. I didn't mean to slow your work. But there is something I wanted to discuss with you." Adeline went to show Ham the page in the book and the sample of fabric.

Thomas stood nearby, listening to their conversation. He was unspeakably happy and at the same time a little afraid. Everything he had wanted in life was happening now and he had no idea how long it would last. He only knew he was going to hold on to it, to Adeline and her love, for as long as he possibly could.

"Thank you, Ham. I'll see you at lunch." Adeline left the dining room and headed down the hallway and up the stairs. Thomas walked beside her. "Don't you want to supervise the men?" he asked.

She heard laughter in his voice. "I'll look in on them after lunch," she whispered.

"Where are we going then, if not to wait about and watch?"

"I have to dry my hair. And make the bed look like I slept in it. And open the windows."

They reached the top of the stairs and started down the familiar hallway that led to Adeline's room.

"You dry your hair," said Thomas. "I'll muck about with the bed and open the windows."

"All right. But don't let Mrs. Folly see you."

"She's busy in the kitchen. Anyway, anybody could have forgotten about holding a plate. You covered for me very nicely."

Adeline opened the door to her room and stopped. It seemed uncomfortably small now that she had spent the night in Thomas's room. In Thomas's bed. With Thomas.

Resisting the impulse to ask him to appear so she could kiss him, she went to the bathroom and plugged in her hair dryer.

Thomas went to the bed, pulled back the comforter and lay down, rolling back and forth a bit. "You know she won't check up on you," he called to Adeline, trying to be heard above the noise of the hair dryer. "Mrs. Folly follows instructions."

Leaving the bed, he went to open the windows.

"What did you say?" Adeline looked out the bathroom doorway. She had turned off the blow dryer and her hair was tossed and wild.

"I said would you like me to make the bed and tidy your room for you?" It was Mrs. Folly. She stood at the bedroom door.

"Oh." Adeline fumbled to set the dryer down. She grabbed her hairbrush from the bathroom countertop and started brushing her hair, deciding to wear it in a ponytail instead of a bun. "That's not necessary, Mrs. Folly. I'll do it myself."

"Very well. I'll just open the windows. It's going to be a fine day and fair weather for a week or more. The house needs airing."

"Yes. Yes it does." Adeline realized she sounded nervous. "How many windows do you think we should open?"

"Six. I've already started. And I'll close them before I leave."

"Thank you." Adeline returned to the bathroom mirror and fixed her hair. Finished, she looked at her reflection. Then she put one hand to her mouth, stifling a gasp. She could see the faintest reflection next to hers. It was Thomas.

I'm going to have to make another list, thought Adeline. *One that covers all the amazing things Thomas can do.*

She left the bathroom. Mrs. Folly was gone. The windows were open. But Adeline's heart still beat too fast. The sooner the restoration was over, the sooner she and Thomas could live together without pretense. She didn't understand how it was possible that they could be together now, only that it was happening and she was going to hold on to it for as long as she could.

The morning went quickly and, as Robert worked carefully to reveal the balcony, he discovered the start of the railing. Adeline stood at the bottom of the ladder and feigned excitement. She said she definitely wanted him to restore it. "In the book there's a picture that shows it once went all along that wall."

"Yes, miss. I saw that. But I'll have to go slowly so as not to cause damage to the rooms behind."

"I don't want them. I want an open gallery."

"And a library," Thomas added. "Tell him about the bookshelves and the library."

Adeline did so and Robert nodded with a grin. "That sounds fine, miss. It's almost always a good idea to use the original features when you're doing a restoration."

"It was my idea," Thomas said to Adeline. She refused to answer, thanking Robert instead and letting him get back to his work.

At the end of the day, she once again inspected what the men had accomplished. It was astonishing. Not only had the framework that had blocked off the dining room been removed, but Robert had uncovered the balcony, knocked through the fake wall behind it, and begun knocking through the library's interior wall. He had also started working his way forward to where the railing began.

Adeline had stood next to Robert as they discussed a picture in the library book. Thomas had one arm about her waist as he, too, examined the original photograph. "It's going to be beautiful," he told her.

She repeated his words to Robert. "It will be, miss. All it takes is a bit of patience."

"Don't forget about the Music Room," Thomas reminded her.

Again Adeline repeated his words to Robert. "That will take more time, miss. But we've not forgotten. I couldn't find a picture of it in the book. But I'll follow along the lines of the room when I remove the wallpaper. There could be another room that's also been hidden, like this one here and the ones next to it."

He looked over the balcony at the railing and said it definitely ran the length of the Great Room. He couldn't give Adeline an estimate on how long the restoration would take for the project or for the Music Room.

"Don't worry, miss. I know you're anxious to see it done. But, if I'm to do it myself, which I'd prefer, it will take a bit more time. If I had to guess, we'll have it ready by summer."

"But that's fantastic, Robert. It's much sooner than I'd hoped."

"Mind you that's without finding more rooms."

"I understand. Just go along as best you can. A steady pace with a clear goal is better than rushing to meet a deadline." She was getting tired of repeating everything Thomas said and realized she was hungry. Excusing herself, she went to the kitchen.

Mrs. Folly was taking off her apron and getting ready to leave. She told Adeline that she'd left stew on the stovetop for her dinner and she'd baked biscuits. "I put them in that basket there," she pointed to a spot next to the stove. "Under a towel to keep them warm."

Thanking her, Adeline remembered to ask if there were keys to the locked rooms on the second floor.

"None of which I know. There's your key; copied twice. One for me, one for Ham. It's the only key you'll be needing, seeing as the other half of the house is his. And you won't be restoring that side." She looked at Adeline, eyes steady. "Or will you?"

"No. No I won't be restoring the other side of the house." Adeline felt a strange kinship with Mrs. Folly because, in her way, she had acknowledged Thomas's presence. Impulsively, Adeline mentioned that she had ordered the rose print for the curtains in the dining room.

Mrs. Folly stopped as she opened the back door. Then she turned and did something extraordinary: she smiled. "I'll see you tomorrow morning," Mrs. Folly said and left.

"I think she's happy," Adeline said to Thomas.

"I've never seen her smile. Anyway, I'm happy. Are you?"

"Oh, yes, Thomas. I'm very happy."

Two weeks went by. As Mrs. Folly predicted, the sunshine stayed. The men worked hard but with enthusiasm. At the end of each day, Adeline would do her inspection, no longer hiding her happiness as Robert uncovered and restored the gallery and its railing. Samuel and Ham, when not working with Robert, restored the dining room.

At night, when everyone had left, Thomas and Adeline would stroll about the rooms, holding hands and discussing paint colors and furnishings. They often sat in the dining room now to share dinner, but the kitchen was still their preferred place. In a way, it was where they had really met for the first time because it was where Thomas had revealed he was a ghost.

He most certainly wasn't like any ghost Adeline had ever seen in movies or read about in books. Each night they'd return to his room and, after making love, they'd lie next to each other: Thomas with his brandy and Adeline with a small plate of cookies. Only occasionally would she have a beer, saying it was fattening.

"That's something you don't have to worry about," Adeline told him one night. "Getting fat. Growing old. I don't want to grow old, Thomas. Not alone."

"I told you, you won't be alone. I'll be with you."

"And there's another thing I'm still worried about."

"What? That I'll be with you?"

"No. No. I'm worried that we haven't made any progress on solving the mysteries."

"We will."

"How can you be so certain?"

"Mrs. Folly isn't the only one who can predict the weather. There's a storm out to sea. It will here in a day or two." He set his brandy aside and leaned over and kissed Adeline. "And then the dancers will return."

Putting her plate on the bedside table, Adeline turned her attention to Thomas. "And what do you suppose will happen? Have you remembered anything more about your life?"

"No. But I only just now remembered something terribly important."

"What? Another mystery?"

"Yes. Why have I only made love to you once tonight?"

Adeline wrapped her arms about his neck, pulling him close. "Well we can solve that mystery right now."

In the morning, the routine at the house was interrupted by the ringing of the telephone as Adeline descended the stairs. She crossed the foyer and picked up the receiver. It was Mrs. Folly. It had rained all night and she wouldn't be up until it stopped. There was a storm coming.

A few minutes later the telephone rang again. It was Ham. He could make the trip by horse, but he and Samuel thought it better to wait out the storm. They had supplies in the truck and it would most likely get stuck in the mud and clay.

"Better to wait then, Ham," Adeline agreed, keeping her disappointment from her voice. They had all warned her how suddenly the weather could and would change. "I'll see you and Samuel in a day or two? Three days. That's fine, Ham. Please let Robert know. He knows. Of course. Thank you, Ham."

She turned to Thomas as he became visible. "We have the house to ourselves."

"I told you a storm was coming."

"So you did. Come on. Let's go and make breakfast."

Thomas felt comfortable as he and Adeline ate. He felt he had exactly what he had wanted just in a different way. Perhaps not all, not a wife, but he had a lover and friend. No children, but Adeline's love was more than enough. After clearing the table, he turned to her. "Do you like children?"

"They're okay, I guess. I never gave it much thought. After all, I wasn't happily married. Why?"

"I just wondered." Thomas continued with his tidying. "We've a few days alone now. I thought we could talk about our future, as it were."

"That sounds nice. Our future." Adeline joined him at the sink. "Well, I don't want children. Maybe a dog or a cat. But children? No."

"What if I weren't here? I don't want to deprive you."

"But you must be here; you promised you wouldn't disappear on me. Please keep your promise, Thomas. Stay and I'll stay and we'll be together." She hurried to say more before he could object. "You said you thought you were falling in love with me. Haven't you decided yet? If you love me, I mean."

"Well of course I love you, damn it."

She smiled. "It's settled then. We'll stay together, just the two of us. No children."

"I don't want a dog either. Perhaps a cat."

"Fine."

"You're certain?"

"Yes."

"Well then let's have a look around and see where we can hang my portrait. Perhaps I'll remember the name of the artist."

Leaving the kitchen, they wandered about the house with a hammer and nail, finally going upstairs to the library. Adeline said she thought Thomas's portrait would look very nice next to the window or near the balcony that overlooked the Great Room.

He went to get the portrait, disappearing and reappearing quickly this time. "Here?" He balanced the frame carefully next to the window. "Or here?" He held it next to the balcony.

Adeline considered her choices carefully then chose a third location. "How about over there?" She pointed to the interior wall of the room that was slowly being transformed into a gallery. She and Thomas had already picked out a few sets of tables for two with chairs. The furniture would be delivered after the restoration of the walls and the railing was complete. The interior wall had been cleaned and taped, ready now for painting.

Thomas took the portrait to the wall. "It does look rather good. With room for more on either side if we choose."

"I hadn't thought of that. What portraits would you want beside yours?" Adeline eyed the wall and then hammered in a nail. Thomas helped her hang his portrait and they both stood back.

"Yours, of course. And perhaps the painting of my garden."

"That sounds lovely. Except . . ."

"What?"

"I don't want my portrait painted. At least, not until we solve the mystery behind the other paintings. It's . . . spooky."

"I see. Well, what about the painting of my garden?"

They walked to the railing and looked down at the Great Room. "I like that idea. And we could put up one of the paintings of the house beside your portrait. Why don't we decide after the wall is painted?"

"All right then. Let's go." Thomas held out his left hand and Adeline clasped it with her right.

"Where are we going?"

"To the room above the Music Room."

And they were there. Thomas released his grip and went to the wall where the paintings of the house still leaned, half forgotten in the rush of events that had recently taken place. He started pulling each one forward, tilting his head and finally choosing one near the back. It was the house in summer. Dark green grass seemed to hug the house before it met the gray of the cliffs and then sloped down to the deep blue of the lake.

The artist had painted the roofs of the house in a soft reddish pink, the walls varying shades of beige. Its background was the blue and green of the mountain with soft white clouds in a blue sky.

"That's beautiful," said Adeline. They drew it out together and set it in front of the other paintings. "I didn't see this one before you came into the room." She looked at Thomas. "It will definitely look fantastic in the gallery. But let's leave it here until the room is finished. Even with the delay because of the storm, it won't be long now."

A rumble of thunder made them both jump. "And it won't be long before the storm arrives. Let's get back to the kitchen." Thomas grabbed Adeline's right hand.

Suddenly, everything was dark and the walls felt close, the room cramped.

"Thomas?"

"Sorry." She heard him fumbling with a doorknob. Opening the door, Adeline stepped into the kitchen. "How did we end up in the pantry?"

"I wasn't concentrating. And I was rushing. I was in that room once, when I was boy. A storm began and the door stuck. It took quite some time before I managed to open the door and get down the stairs to the Music Room."

"How terrible for you. Why were you in the room?"

"I wanted to see the paintings. I thought perhaps they were magical. Hidden away and all. Magic is exciting stuff for a boy."

"That's it." Excited, Adeline hurried to explain. "Magic. That's what we haven't taken into consideration. We've been trying to come up with a rational explanation for what happens to the house when there's a storm. And it's anything but rational."

"I suppose you think the dancers are magical, too?"

"They could be. Or perhaps they're caught in some sort of spell." She saw the skepticism on Thomas's face. "Oh, come on. You must have read fairy tales at some time. Stories of spells cast on castles and princesses? Maybe by a dragon or a witch?"

Frowning, Thomas went to the kitchen window and looked out. He considered Adeline's suggestions as he tried to recall a bedtime story his nanny told him. A vague memory returned: one night she had been telling him something about the lake and the house. She said both were magic. "The magic bein' here long before the house."

When he had asked why, she said she'd tell him what she'd been told; a sort of a story "that begins with a knight and his lady."

He turned to Adeline, feeling excited, too. "Robert's book. The one from the library. Does it have the history of the house?"

"It has a couple of pages that I've only had time to glance at so far."

"Where's the book?"

"In the dining room."

"Let's go." As he reached for her hand he noticed Adeline's hesitation. "Don't worry. It doesn't have a pantry. Or a closet. And I'm not in a hurry. Much."

They disappeared together.

Later that night, as the storm and the wind met outside the steady stone walls of the house, Thomas and Adeline lay side by side on their bed. He held the library book on his lap as they read the brief history of the house.

"Read it aloud to me? Please? It's so beautiful."

"Aren't you a bit old for a bedtime story?"

"It isn't nice to mention a woman's age; it's indiscreet. Anyway, it isn't bedtime. Besides I love to hear your voice and it's such a sad story. It's easier to accept if you read it out loud."

"You just said it was beautiful."

"It is. In a sad way."

"All right." Thomas began to read aloud.

Adeline closed her eyes and imagined the knight and his lady standing near the edge of the cliffs. Cold wind blew across the lake below creating waves that battered the cliff's side. The knight swept his right arm at the green landscape below them, telling his lady about the caves beneath the cliff and how they would make a good stronghold and foundation for the castle he would build for her.

"This place is touched with magic," the lady warned. "I feel it in the wind."

Despite his love for her, the knight did not listen. The land was a gift from the knight's king. He could not refuse. He promised his lady that he and his men would build her a fine castle, worthy of her beauty and her love.

"In one year, I promise we shall have a home to share. The cliff and the lake will be no more than a pretty view for you to gaze upon."

"May it be as you say. But build me a grand fireplace to keep the house warm and strong walls of stone to protect us from enemies, storms and . . . the wind."

"It will be safe. And if ever you are afraid, there will be a secret place to hide."

Behind them, the wind made the surface of the lake roil and then crashed the angry waves against the cliffs.

"A secret place to hide." Adeline repeated. "That must be the cave where we found the portraits. But why were they hidden? There's still so much we don't know."

"Shall I finish the story?"

"Yes, please."

Shortly after construction began, lightning struck the castle. The unfinished walls could not withstand the storm and the wind. They shuddered and crumbled; only the fireplace remained. Fleeing on horseback, the knight and his lady tried to make it to the village, but in the rush of rain and wind, the lady's horse stumbled and the lady was thrown. She landed against a rock. Her neck was broken and she died.

Devastated, the knight cursed the castle and the wind and its storms. He returned to service for his king and was killed in battle.

Thomas closed the book. "There. It's almost exactly the same as what I recall my nanny telling me. The author of the book says that, according to her research, this is the first time the story has been written down. It's been told for generations as part bedtime story, part myth. Probably embellished to suit the storyteller."

"The lady said the land was touched with magic," Adeline murmured. "The house could be touched with magic, too." She sat up. "Suppose you were touched with magic? That would explain not only your existence but your unique, unghostly abilities."

"Unghostly? That's not a word."

"All right. Less than ghostly." Adeline got out of bed. "We'd better get dressed."

"Whatever for?"

"To go downstairs and watch the dancers. Maybe they're touched with magic, too."

"You're not afraid?"

"This time we'll both stay invisible. And we'll look for the balcony and the gallery."

Thomas sighed. He got out of bed and dressed, then waited for Adeline.

She emerged from the bathroom several minutes later wearing jeans and a t-shirt. "Let's walk this time."

"I promise I won't put us in a closet."

"It's not that. I want to see the house." She took his right hand in her left and together they headed for the Great Room. They strolled down the short, wide hallway from Thomas's room. He steered Adeline to the right and, as they continued along the slightly frayed runner, she looked at the walls, lit intermittently with small electric lights that looked like lanterns.

"Why don't you have any paintings or portraits on the walls?"

Thomas shrugged. "The paintings of the house were put in that little room when I was very young. And no, I don't know why."

"What about the portraits?"

"They were taken down. One day they were there and the next day, gone."

"Who took them down? And why? And when?"

"I promise you, I don't remember. I only remember seeing them when I was very little. And before that dreadful party, I told a friend about the portraits. John. John somebody. Anyway, it was his idea for me to have a portrait painted of myself. Very convincing fellow."

"Do you remember the name of the artist?"

"No."

Frustrated, Adeline tightened her fingers about Thomas's hand. They walked in silence for a few minutes then stopped as the long hallway intersected with another. "Why, we're here already. This is the hallway that leads to my room. And there's the main staircase."

"Let's go to the library," Thomas suggested.

"Good idea."

Suddenly the lights dimmed, flickered, and went out. For a moment, the house felt like it was floating on water. Then everything went dark.

"Thomas?"

"Yes. Wait for a minute."

Holding hands, they waited in the darkness. Abruptly, the hallway was alight with torches along the walls. The runner was gone and the cold floor was white stone and bare. They moved forward cautiously.

Thomas whispered to Adeline. "Don't worry. I'm invisible and so are you. But this time, don't let go of my hand."

"I won't."

They went to the library. The door was open. To their left, seated at small tables, were a few couples. The ladies wore floor length, voluminous gowns with low bodices and the men wore high collars, ruffled shirts, and high boots. The library and the balcony were vacant.

Thomas and Adeline went to the balcony and looked down at the people in the Great Room. They were dancing their dances, eating and drinking, laughing and talking.

Watching the party guests, Adeline thought about all the years Thomas had watched them. It must have made him feel very lonely. She looked up at him. "Do you see the man who gave you the drink of champagne?"

Thomas looked over the party guests. He looked at the couples in the gallery again and then down at the room below. "I don't think so. It was a very long time ago."

"Try again."

Thomas looked at the men standing in tight groups near the outside wall. A tapestry fluttered as one of the servants opened a window.

"There he is!" Thomas pointed. "That's the man who poisoned me."

Chapter Eleven

Adeline looked at the man that Thomas pointed out. He was tall and thin. His hair lay against his skull like threads of gray and white, and his long face and nose almost disappeared against his pale complexion. He was dressed much like the other men in the room, but over the frills of his shirt and the high collar of his jacket he wore a long coat, almost like a cape.

"Look!" Adeline pointed as the beautiful woman walked toward the tall man. She spoke to him for a minute. He nodded and went to stand in front of the fireplace, his back to the room.

The beautiful woman clapped her hands and the orchestra stopped playing. "My dear friends, I hope you are enjoying this evening."

There was applause.

"I have arranged entertainment for us all on this most special of occasions." She nodded to the conductor. There was a brief drum roll and the man in front of the fireplace spun about, the cape floating around him. Colored smoke billowed from within the folds of fabric.

The man began to speak in a foreign language.

"What's he saying?" Adeline asked Thomas.

"I don't know. It's not French. Or Italian. Or even Spanish."

"You speak all those languages?"

"No. I just know a few words."

Adeline returned her attention to the man. He was waving one arm dramatically; a tall hat appeared from his cloak. He swept the hat high and flowers flew up to the ceiling, then floated to the floor. For the next several minutes the man amused the crowd with simple card tricks, instructing different people to shuffle the deck, pick a card, and hold it up while he looked away. Then he described the card. Finally, he stopped and, after speaking a few more words, he bowed, lifted his long coat, then spun about. The fire burned higher as a mist swirled in front of it.

When the mist dissipated, the man was gone. The crowd applauded. They applauded louder when he reappeared at the doors, sans hat and coat. A smile distorted his mouth. He gripped a bottle of champagne in one hand and a rose in the other. Going to the beautiful woman, he gave her the rose and, without touching it, made the cork pop free of the bottle. Champagne sprayed the floor in a small half circle. Laughter and more applause followed this last trick.

The man spoke slowly in English. "It has been a pleasure to know you all. My assistant has hung your portraits in various rooms and hallways about the house at the request of your hostess, the beautiful Lady Moorhouse."

A servant with a tray hurried forward and the man gave him the now half-empty bottle. Then he escorted Lady Moorhouse to the center of the room. The orchestra began a waltz.

"He's hardly attractive," said Thomas. "I wonder what she sees in him?"

"I'm sure she's just being polite. She's the hostess. And now we know her name!"

"Title."

"It's a start. She must own the house at this time. She hired him to paint portraits of her guests. He said his assistant hung the portraits.

Maybe he's the one who killed your lookalike. You know, to remove the competition." Adeline leaned over the balcony a little, noticing the couples that had been seated in the gallery were doing the same thing along the railing. They didn't see her.

"But you said it was the unknown artist who murdered me. That man is some sort of magician. Still, I'm certain he gave me the poisoned champagne. Anyway, I'll bet money that it was his assistant who painted the portraits and that man took the credit."

"Why do you think that?"

"Look at his hands."

Adeline looked at the tall man's hands. They were bent and the fingers curled: arthritis. He couldn't have held a paintbrush properly to do the detailed work of the portraits.

She was about to ask Thomas to whisk them back to his room when Lady Moorhouse suddenly pulled back from the man and slapped him hard across his face. She lifted her head imperiously and went to join a young, handsome man that stood near the doors.

The tall man stood alone for a moment, then he went to where a servant held his coat and hat. Taking them, he turned to look over the people in the room, then at the people in the gallery. His dark eyes seemed to measure each person and the expression on his face was not one of embarrassment but disdain.

"You think me not good enough for your company? I think a demonstration of my superiority is in order." The tall man lowered his voice and began to speak in some sort of rhyme, but again, Thomas and Adeline couldn't understand what he said.

Adeline felt an urgent need to hide and, pulling Thomas with her, stepped quickly from the balcony and pressed against the wall of the library.

"Get us out of here now," she whispered.

"To where?"

"Anywhere. Hurry!"

They stood in Thomas's garden, just under the arch that led to the cave beneath the house. The wind hurled rain against them.

"We have to get further away. Take us to our bedroom, Thomas."

They stood in front of the fireplace in their room. Adeline was soaked, but Thomas was dry. He lifted her right hand and kissed it. "I'll get a towel."

"No! Don't leave me." She clung to him and he hugged her.

"You said you weren't afraid this time."

"I wasn't until that horrible man looked everyone over, as if he were sizing them up. And when he started to speak in that strange language, I felt frightened. I mean really, really terrified."

Thomas kissed her softly. "Come on. Let's get you dry. The house will change again any minute."

"How do you know?"

"After all this time? I know."

The house changed. The room looked very much the same after the mist had gone.

Outside, the thunder was further away and the rain lighter.

An hour later, Adeline sat cross-legged on the bed, naked beneath one of Thomas's house coats. She had forgotten to pack hers. She set aside the towel that she had been rubbing against her hair, still damp from the unexpected stop in the garden.

"I bet it was a spell. You know, the words that seemed to rhyme?"

Thomas sat next to her, his back against several pillows, legs crossed at the ankles. The library book lay open on his lap. "Don't be ridiculous. That's all superstitious nonsense."

"Said the man who's a ghost."

Thomas raised his right hand in protest. "A unique ghost, if you don't mind."

Adeline lay down next to him. She hugged him with her right arm, resting her head against his right shoulder. "Very unique. But—"

"No more tonight." He shut the book and set it on the table beside the bed. "I think I've had quite enough of magic and mysteries for now." He gently rolled Adeline onto her back and kissed her.

Near dawn, Thomas got up and went to his bedroom window. He glanced back at Adeline, asleep in their bed, and then peered out at the slowly lightening sky.

He thought about Adeline's speculations of the night before. It had never occurred to him that he could be the victim of anything else but murder, but Adeline now believed he could be the victim of some sort of magic spell. *Nonsense.* And yet, he felt a curious truth about not only his circumstances but that of the dancers. He had never taken time to discover more about them until he met Adeline. He had been entirely pre-occupied with his own dilemma and then, as the years past, he had quite simply lost interest.

Watching the dancers for the first time from the balcony, recognizing the man who had given him the poisoned drink, he wondered when he had first seen them. *And how did the man get from the past to the present? Or did I travel back in time? No, no, no.*

Thomas had asked all his guests to dress very grand for his birthday party. But he hadn't recognized any of his old friends, only that one man. The dancers had to be part of something that had taken place in the past. His presence, his party, had somehow overlapped with theirs the night he died. *Yes, that made some sense.*

If the man was a real magician, capable of making things disappear, as in his act, it follows that he could have made the dancers disappear. Doesn't it?

There was also Mrs. Folly's truth: it had long been said, even when Thomas was a little boy, that far out on the lake, where the waters connected with the sea, there was a magical place. No one ever ventured there. They didn't just fear the weather and the wind, they feared the magic.

Magic! And yet, I have to admit I am a bit magical myself in some mysterious way.

Thomas looked over his shoulder; Adeline turned a little in her sleep. She had felt something just before the man 'cast his spell.' A warning fear that most likely saved them from whatever had happened to the dancers.

If the man had control of some sort of magic, the magic on the lake, perhaps stirred by the storm, could have strengthened it and made almost anything possible.

Thomas ran his right hand through his tousled hair. He looked out the window again. The sky was streaked with pink clouds. The mountain across the lake was turning different shades of green in the early morning light. It wouldn't be long until it was summer. *What then?*

He dropped his head, feeling tired. It was wonderful to feel tired. Returning to bed, he snuggled close to Adeline. Life was wonderful again, at last. It wasn't the sort of life he had expected, but it was much more than he had lost when he had become a ghost.

If I am a ghost. I might be unique, but perhaps it is because of magic. This new theory deserves to be taken seriously. I must stop teasing Adeline. I love her.

He sighed and closed his eyes. Rain started to drum lightly against the window and he listened to it for a long time.

Thomas's thoughts meandered. He wondered how the magic of the house might have been affected by a magician. And, too, what the man had said about having his assistant hang the portraits all about the house.

But what if his assistant had done more than that? What if it was the assistant who had painted the portraits? The magician had hardly used his hands at all during his magic act at the party. What if the magician could no longer paint?

"My god. I'm beginning to think like Adeline." He looked at her, still asleep in their bed. "What would Adeline say? Proof. We need proof. But what kind and where?"

Adeline had said the portraits had been painted in his garden. But he was certain nothing was hidden there. *But what if the magician or his assistant had discovered the cave?*

"The cave!"

Adeline stirred and reached for Thomas. She sat up. "Thomas?"

"I'm here. By the window. I'm sorry I woke you. I was thinking aloud."

"It's all right." She rubbed her eyes. "What time is it?"

"What? Oh. I've no idea. Early still. Go back to sleep." Thomas got dressed.

"Where are you going?"

"To the garden. Uh, cave. The garden's cave. You know what I mean."

"What were you thinking? And why are you going to the garden?"

"I want to check something."

Adeline flung back the covers and got out of bed. "Not without me." She started getting dressed. "Don't watch. And don't you dare disappear and make me come after you. I'll only be a minute."

Torn between a frown and a smile, Thomas's mouth lifted a little on one side. "All right. I'll wait."

"Good."

A half hour later they were in the garden. This time Adeline was protected from the rain by an umbrella. She watched Thomas as he wandered along the path, pausing occasionally to look at the flowers that seemed to brace the large stones of the garden walls.

Finally he returned to Adeline and, taking her right hand, led her under the arch and into the tunnel.

"Why do you want to see the cave again?" she asked, trying to see as the gloomy light behind them dwindled.

"I think there's another cave."

Adeline stopped abruptly. "Another cave? What makes you say that?"

"I'll tell you in a minute. Come on. We're almost there."

Reaching the cave below the Great Room's fireplace, Thomas went to a second battery operated lantern they had left there. He turned it on, then turned to Adeline.

She wished there was a chair she could sit upon as she listened to Thomas's theory. It made perfect sense, especially when you added magic to the mystery, just as a puzzle becomes clear when you add the last piece.

"Well?" Thomas tilted his head to one side. "What do you think?"

"I think your theory provides a very good explanation for the lack of a signature on both the paintings and the portraits."

"But is it right?"

"I'm not sure. We have a magic house, and a magician's magic and an assistant—" Adeline looked steadily at Thomas. "I think we should look for proof, like you said."

"Because of the magic of the house?"

"Or the man. Or the two combined. It's spooky. Let's look for the other cave." She went to the wall left of the stairs. "Do you remember anything about it?"

"No. Only that it's here somewhere."

Slowly, they walked along the perimeter of the cave. Adeline lightly touched the walls with her fingertips. There was only the fissure of the tunnel. Thomas was about to give up when Adeline pointed at where the portraits had been leaning against the wall. "There's a dark mark there. Shine the light, will you, Thomas?"

He did so. A rat hurried away from the wall.

Adeline jumped. "Thomas? Was that what I think it was?"

"If you thought it was a rat, yes. Don't worry. We'll get a cat."

"I thought cats only chased mice."

"We'll get a very large cat."

They sat in the kitchen and discussed their new theory. It matched all the evidence they had uncovered, but they were still missing details. Where the portraits had been, there was a small nook carved into the wall of the cave. A rough piece of driftwood had been placed against the opening. Behind it was their treasure: an artist's oil paints, brushes wrapped in a piece of canvas, several paint-stained cloths, three paint palettes and three empty canvases already nailed to wood frames.

"What do you suppose the empty canvases were for?" Adeline took a bite of her toast.

"I think they were for a 'who' not a 'what.'"

"What?"

Thomas spread more butter on his toast. "I think the assistant intended to paint more portraits. Perhaps he wanted to confess the truth to Lady Moorhouse. It could make him famous or at least popular."

"That would have been dangerous, don't you think?"

"Yes."

They continued their breakfast. "Are you thinking what I'm thinking?" asked Adeline as she stood up and started clearing the dishes.

"I doubt it very much. What are you thinking now in that marvelous mind of yours?"

"I'm thinking that we have to find a way to communicate with Lady Moorhouse." She paused at the sink, hands dripping with bubbles of soap. "That's a strange name, isn't it? Moorhouse. And the house is at the edge, or end, of a moor."

Joining her, dishes in hand, Thomas didn't comment. Instead he asked how she intended to contact Lady Moorhouse. They couldn't have a séance because she wasn't a ghost.

"We don't know that for certain." Adeline rinsed the dishes and handed them one at a time to Thomas. "Anyway, a séance might cause trouble for you. Suppose the medium sensed you? That would be awful."

Adeline let the water out of the sink. She faced Thomas. "We could leave a note."

"A note?"

"Yes. We could write a note to Lady Moorhouse. We could tell her to go to the garden."

"And then?"

"Meet her there, of course. Have a chat."

"A chat? With a dead woman?"

"I'm just thinking creatively. And we don't know she's dead. She might be trapped in, or under, a spell at some other point in time. At any rate, it's worth a try. Besides, you and I do much more than chat."

Thomas smiled. "Yes. Well, let's leave that out of this for the moment." He put away the last of the breakfast dishes and closed a cupboard door. "I think I was accidentally caught in whatever magic or combination of magic occurred. An innocent bystander, as it were."

"I agree. Your party and Lady Moorhouse's party were in the same room during a storm. It's just the years between that are different."

"Centuries, not years."

"I don't think that matters. At any rate, what else can we do? We need more details.

"Have you got any ideas, Thomas?"

"I'm afraid not."

They left the kitchen together, holding hands, safe within the comfort of each other's company. Reaching the dining room, Adeline suggested that it might be a better place to meet Lady Moorhouse because of the weather. She went to look out one of the windows, now framed with new curtains in the rose print. A gust of wind splashed rain against the glass and she stepped back.

"Thomas? Do you think there will be another storm tonight?"

"Unfortunately, yes."

"Maybe it's fortunate. We can write a note now. But where should we leave it? How do we give it to her? We can't let anyone else find it; especially our suspect."

"I can give it to her."

"How?"

"If you fold it up very small, I can slip it into the bodice of her gown. She can't see me, but she's certain to notice the note."

Adeline folded her arms across her chest. "Won't she notice invisible fingers?"

"I'll be extremely careful. The epitome of a gentleman."

"All right. Let's write the note. A very short, small note. To meet us here in the dining room." Adeline thought for a minute. "We'll tell her it's a matter of life and death."

"How long have you been waiting to say such a melodramatic phrase?"

Adeline laughed. "A very long time."

———————⟡———————

That night, the rain increased but not the wind; no storm brought the dancers. Thomas and Adeline stayed up late and spent the next day wandering about the many rooms in the house that Adeline hadn't yet explored.

After dinner they went to the sunroom. Adeline looked at the darkening view for several minutes then announced she was going to get dressed.

"But you're already dressed."

"I'm going to put on something fancy. For the dance."

"What makes you think the dancers will appear tonight?"

"Because the wind is changing; it's getting stronger." She pointed at the view, already being rearranged from sunset to night. "And look at the waves. They're higher and closer together. And on the horizon there's a mass of dark clouds. A storm is definitely coming."

"That's quite the weather report." Thomas joined her. He looked at the lake and sky. "I agree. It's going to storm. And soon. Do you have a frock to suit the occasion?"

"A frock?" Adeline tried not to laugh. "Not exactly. But my mother did insist I pack a few evening gowns. One of them will have to do."

"I still think we should appear together."

"But the dancers can't see you. They can see me when I'm not holding your hand. Oh! What if you held Lady Moorhouse's hand? Do you think then she could see you?"

"Possibly. Let's leave it as a last resort. Finding the note and then meeting you might be all the lady can cope with and we don't know how much time we'll have before she has to rejoin her guests."

"True." Adeline turned away from the view, kissed Thomas on his left cheek and then left the sunroom. She didn't feel afraid as she walked down the short hallway and entered the bedroom; she felt excited. She lifted her large suitcase and put it on the bed.

"Do you need help?" Thomas asked. He became visible at the foot of the bed.

"I'm fine. But you can help me decide which dress." She pulled out a silver and blue evening gown. "My mother thought I might go out to dinner in the city." Reaching for a second gown, she lifted it up to show Thomas. The gown was cream colored and strapless. The waist was fitted and the skirt was full and trimmed with black lace.

"That one."

"Okay."

Adeline undressed and Thomas helped her. His hands caressed her back.

"You're enjoying this," she commented. She reached for the gown and stepped into it, pulling it up quickly before Thomas could distract her more. "Will you do up the zipper, please? And there's a little hook at the top."

Thomas pulled the zipper up and fastened the hook. "There." He kissed her bare right shoulder. "Turn around and let me have a look."

Adeline smoothed the silk fabric and turned in a small circle. There was a soft rustling sound as she moved.

"What was that?" Thomas looked alarmed.

"Taffeta."

"Taffeta? What's taffeta?"

"Expensive. My mother was hoping I'd get lonely and move to the city. She wanted me to start dating 'the right sort of man.'"

"What? No mysteries or magic? That sounds awfully dull."

"I agree."

"You look beautiful, Adeline."

She went to stand in front of the bathroom mirror. It covered the wall above the sink and she could see most of the gown. "It is pretty."

"Not the dress, you."

Adeline smiled and pulled her hair up, twisting it a little to make a soft bun. She pushed three hair combs into place to hold the bun.

"There. That's better." She turned to Thomas. "What do you think?"

"I think you need a necklace." Reaching into a pocket of his trousers, he pulled out a diamond necklace and dangled it from his fingers.

"Where did you get that?"

"From my mother's jewelry box. I hid it under the bed after she died. Did you know that people never look in the most obvious places when they're searching for something?" He draped the necklace about Adeline's neck and fastened it.

She was about to speak when thunder roared and the house began to change. She grabbed Thomas's right hand and held on. When the change stopped, Thomas spoke. "Are you ready?"

"Yes."

He whisked them to the dining room.

In the Great Room, Lady Moorhouse paused to watch her guests. It was still early in the evening and the storm did nothing to dim the happy mood. A servant offered her a glass of champagne from a silver tray. As she reached for it she felt a strange discomfort between her breasts. She set the glass back on the tray and motioned for the servant to leave. Then she went to stand in a corner.

Looking around the room to make certain no one was watching, she glanced down and saw a piece of paper in her cleavage. Curious and confused, she pulled the paper out, unfolded it and read the note.

"This must be a joke," she said.

Another servant paused not far from where Lady Moorhouse stood. "My lady?"

She crumpled the note and lifted her chin. "I wasn't speaking to you. Return to your duties."

The servant bowed and walked away.

Lady Moorhouse studied several of her gentlemen guests, wondering which of her suitors had managed to place the note in such an intimate hiding place. She smiled at no one and went to the doors of the dining room. Two servants opened the doors for her and shut them after she entered the room.

She moved slowly to the table and set the note on its polished surface.

"Very well. I'm here. Where are you?

"Here." Adeline stepped from behind the drapes of one of the windows. "I'm here, Lady Moorhouse."

Chapter Twelve

Adeline took a few steps forward and stopped near the table. She felt uncomfortable under Lady Moorhouse's scrutiny.

"You are not an invited guest," Lady Moorhouse said at last. Her voice was calm, almost conversational.

"No. I'm not. Let me explain—"

"Not yet," Thomas interjected. "You're a lady of wealth and position; you don't have to explain."

"You must be the new mistress of Lord Parnsley."

"What?"

"Do not feign ignorance with me, my dear. You're young and pretty. You could hardly have escaped Lord Parnsley's wandering eye. And I very much doubt you inherited those diamonds."

The insinuation was clear. Adeline was about to retort when Thomas touched her left arm. "Don't respond; she could have you thrown out of the house."

"Was it he that wrote the note?" Lady Moorhouse asked, unaware of Thomas. "Or you?"

"You can answer that," Thomas said. "But tell her only enough to keep her attention."

"I wrote it."

Lady Moorhouse walked gracefully along the length of the table, stopping at the far end. She turned a little to face Adeline. "'A matter of life and death,' you wrote. Yours? Or mine?"

"Yours." Adeline wished she had a fan to snap. "And I'm not anyone's mistress."

"No? Well, then, who are you?"

"I'm a friend of Lord Thomas Éclair."

Lady Moorhouse paled. "The name is not familiar." She walked around the end of the table, moving closer to Adeline. "Whom do you believe to be a threat to my life?"

"I think you know, or at least have your suspicions. The portrait artist; he is not what he seems. He means to cause you harm." The more formal speech calmed Adeline. She was still playing a part but this time she felt more like a chess piece. Lady Moorhouse was the king, in need of protection, and she was the queen.

Lady Moorhouse stopped halfway along the table's length. She frowned. "How do you know this?"

"It doesn't seem to surprise you."

Lady Moorhouse arched her right eyebrow. "You're very observant."

"I am." It was Adeline's turn to move; she walked toward the fireplace and looked up at the portrait hanging above the mantelpiece. It was the one of Lady Moorhouse with Thomas's doppelganger at her side. "Who is this man with you in this portrait?"

"A close, personal friend."

"Yes. He does seem very . . . affectionate. Doesn't your husband object? To have such an intimate portrait in his house could be misconstrued. Even invite gossip."

"The house is mine; a gift from my husband. He travels most of the year, pursuing his love of gambling and investments."

"But this man . . . you haven't mentioned his name, by the way . . . he's special to you. It's in your eyes and his. He's more to you than a lover."

Adeline looked at Lady Moorhouse.

"What about the young man who followed you into the Great Room? And the artist's assistant? They're your lovers, too. Or wish to be. Do they know they have competition?"

"If it is your intention to blackmail me, you will not succeed. My husband is aware of my . . . indiscretions. As I am of his."

Facing Lady Moorhouse, Adeline smiled a little. "How very civil of you both. But that is not my concern. I truly believe the danger lies with the portrait artist."

Lady Moorhouse went to one of the windows. Outside, in the storm, the little courtyard was littered with pools of water. "Ah, yes. Romanivich. He has tried to blackmail me, without success. He wants this house, you see. The land, too. There are rumors of a treasure buried somewhere near. No doubt you are aware of that, as well."

"I am," Adeline lied. Remaining as poised as Lady Moorhouse, she went to stand beside her at the window.

Thomas stepped close to Adeline. He spoke in her left ear. "Remember what I said about people never searching the most obvious places? Why is there a courtyard in the middle of the house? Look. It's small. No garden. Not even a statue. Just a brick floor painted white, and a little tree."

"What sort of tree stands in the courtyard?" asked Adeline, as if she was touring the house.

"I don't know. There's another in the garden and one outside the house. I wanted this one removed and the dining room made larger, but good workers are difficult to find in this part of the country. Especially those who can be trusted."

"Trusted? With what? Your indiscretions?"

"Hardly. No. The rumors are not only about a treasure, but the house as well. It's said it has magic in it. Old stories told too many times and yet there is a stain of truth. See the wind that bends the tree's branches? It gets inside the house; it closes doors and snuffs the light from candles. It takes the warmth from the fireplaces. It is always cold here."

"Any house this large has such minor problems."

"I don't think them minor." Lady Moorhouse looked directly into Adeline's eyes. "I think the house does have a magic.

"I visited Russia some time ago and heard talk about Romanivich."

"What sort of talk?"

"That he has a special gift to see what others cannot. He had modest success as a portrait artist. Under the guise of wanting him to paint my portrait, I invited him to visit. I hoped he might notice something and tell me. I was unaware he already knew about this house. He examined all the rooms, saying he was looking for the right background. When he asked me questions about the house, I mistook it for artistic interest.

"I first noticed he was starting to take an interest in me when he painted my portrait. I then retained him to paint portraits of my friends as well. I thought it would diffuse his feelings, distract him. As you have observed, I have many personal friends. Including Peter, Romanivich's assistant."

"But it didn't work."

"No." Lady Moorhouse placed her right hand against the window. Her fan hung from a narrow ribbon about her wrist. She glanced at her companion. "I've left my guests unattended too long. And I've said too much.

"But you, you asked me here and yet have said very little. As for Romanivich, a jealous man is always dangerous, at least in his mind. Romanivich is old. His work here is finished. He has had time to look about the house and revealed nothing to me. I will dismiss him tomorrow."

"Why not now? Tonight?"

Lady Moorhouse hesitated. "We have an agreement, he and I; a verbal contract, if you will. He wishes me to write a letter of reference praising his talent so he can secure a position in the royal court in Russia. He craves status and desires to be acknowledged as a great artist.

"I only wish he wanted money. It would be simpler than such a lie. You see, it did not escape my notice that his assistant is the artist." Lady Moorhouse smiled, wryly. "How Peter begged me to run away with him. He did not care that his talent would go unacknowledged, only that I love him. Dear boy. Such a child. So passionate and full of romantic daydreams."

"And what did you tell him?"

"That I loved my husband, of course."

"And Peter believed you?"

"Not at first, but I convinced him. Romantics are easily convinced if one uses the right words, the most persuasive phrases." Lady Moorhouse went to stand in front of the fireplace and looked up at the man in the portrait. "You're right about this man. He is my lover. He is my only constant in my world of chaos. I fear he has come to mean much more to me than is safe. I cannot say what will become of us."

She turned away and went to the doors that led to the Great Room. "The storm is growing stronger. You should stay the night. I'll have a room prepared for you."

She lifted her fan and paused. Not looking back, she spoke again, her voice soft. "His name is Sebastian. Sebastian Éclair. He loves to gamble, too. And he's gambling that I will divorce my husband and marry him."

Before Adeline could respond, Lady Moorhouse rapped on one of the doors with the handle of her fan. Immediately, the servants on the other side opened both doors.

Lady Moorhouse swept into the Great Room.

Taking advantage of that moment, Thomas took Adeline's left hand and whisked them to their bedroom. "Are you all right?"

Adeline kicked off her shoes and went to the bed. She flopped back upon its soft mattress. "Yes. But that was exhausting and I don't think it helped us much."

"I think it did. Now we have names and details. And you maneuvered Lady Moorhouse into saying much more than she intended."

Adeline sat up and took the combs from her hair. She pulled her fingers through its length, trying to relax. "At the end of the conversation, I felt sorry for her. She seemed lonely, maybe even a little afraid. A loveless marriage, a dangerous man that she thinks she can just kick out the door. A lover who loves her."

"And she believes in magic. I should have tried harder to warn her about Romanivich." She stood up and went to Thomas, turned her back to him and lifted her hair. "Would you please help me out of this?"

Thomas undid the hook and stopped. "Perhaps we should try again."

"How? When? Tonight Romanivich will cast a spell and make everyone disappear. Or trap them in some portion of time in which they forever repeat the night over and over again. It's horrible."

"We don't know for certain that's what happens."

"But we know something happens." She changed the subject. "I felt you fidget behind me when Lady Moorhouse said the name of the man she loves. Is Sebastian Éclair an ancestor of yours?"

"It's possible. I think he may be the first Éclair to successfully join the upper class. Sort of buying his way in, as it were."

"By gambling with Lord Moorhouse."

"Yes. Perhaps even partnering with him on his investments."

"And is there really a treasure?"

"If there is, I think I know where it might be hidden."

"Under the tree in the courtyard."

"Not only beautiful, but smart."

"I'm tired, Thomas. And hungry."

He finished pulling down the zipper and helped Adeline take off the gown. He watched as she walked naked to the bathroom and returned a minute later wearing one his housecoats.

"I'll whisk to the kitchen and get us something to eat. We can try again tomorrow night. Or whenever the next storm occurs. I think time is, for us, on our side."

"Why do you say that?

"If Lady Moorhouse and her guests are indeed trapped by some sort of spell, they'll still be there until we're ready."

"Isn't it cruel to make them wait?"

"I doubt they're aware of their predicament or the passage of time."

He went to Adeline and kissed her lightly. "I'll be right back."

"What if we find the treasure first?" Adeline bit into another cookie.

"You mean, dig up the tree in the courtyard?"

She nodded.

"What do we do if we find the treasure?" Thomas handed her a napkin.

"We could bribe Romanivich; insist he leaves before he confronts Lady Moorhouse. The spell won't be cast and the dancers will be free."

"I have more than enough jewels to bribe him. They're yours."

"That's very sweet, Thomas. But they were your mother's. No; it doesn't feel right. Besides, whatever we find in the treasure might not even be jewels. Magicians often collect magical items, talismans that add to their power."

"And books."

"Yes!" Adeline took a long drink of her beer then set the glass down quickly. "No! Romanivich would have found it already. Lady Moorhouse said he searched all the rooms. No. He needs more magic."

"Or simply more money. Isn't that often a motivation for murder?"

"Sometimes. He could want revenge." Adeline wiped her mouth with the napkin and got up from the bed. She knelt down, looked underneath and pulled out a large jewelry box.

"Whatever are you doing?"

"Looking for a clue. Your mother may have left a note for you. If the treasure is jewels, then she might have hidden it from your father."

"So he wouldn't use them for gambling."

140

"I was thinking more kindly than that. I think she wanted to protect your inheritance. A house can be sold, gambling money lost. Investments can lose their value, but hidden treasure is a security that lasts."

"You make her sound like a pirate."

"I'm sorry. I didn't mean it like that. She loved you and wanted you to be safe." Adeline ran her right hand over the lid of the jewelry box. "I thought it would be locked, but there isn't a keyhole."

Joining her, Thomas lifted the box onto the bed. "It doesn't have a traditional lock. It's similar to a Chinese puzzle box. My mother showed me once."

He helped Adeline to her feet and they sat on the bed, the jewelry box between them. Deftly, Thomas slid several thin pieces of wood back and forth along the sides of the box. Then he opened it.

Adeline gasped; diamond necklaces and rings shone with a light of their own. "I think we've found the treasure."

"No. These are just the jewels she inherited. Some are probably from suitors before she married my father." He lifted the top tray, revealing more jewelry. The pieces were carefully placed, as if on display. An emerald and diamond necklace caught Adeline's attention. It rested a little higher than the other pieces. Picking it up, she set it on the bed, more interested in what was beneath it. She ran her fingers along the soft material that lined the bottom of the box. One of her fingernails snagged on a bit of metal.

Leaning close, she carefully pulled at what appeared to be a nail. The bottom of the box moved a little. "There's something here." She tugged at the metal. A portion of the bottom lifted to reveal a chain wrapped around something.

Thomas looked. He reached for the chain and unwound it. "It's a locket." Fumbling with the clasp, he opened it. "It doesn't have a picture inside."

"Is there a note?"

"Not exactly. There's an inscription."

"What does it say?"

"The tree that talks will shelter you from the storms of life."

"What do you think it means?"

Thomas studied the locket. "Do you remember I told you that your bedroom was mine when I was a boy?"

"Yes."

"Well, there's a tree outside the window at the end of the hallway. Its branches would scrape the glass when the wind knocked them. I used to imagine the tree was talking to me."

"That's the tree that made the noise that frightened me my first night here."

Thomas smiled. "Yes." He closed the locket carefully. "When I was a boy, I didn't like to nap or go to bed on time. I always felt like I was missing out on something secret that only the grown-ups were allowed to enjoy. I would wait until my mother left my room, then I'd sneak out the window and climb down the tree."

"Where would you go?"

"Nowhere. I'd just sit at the foot of the tree and look out at the lake until the wind brought the rain. Then I'd climb back up the tree to the window, return to my room, and get into my bed." Thomas chuckled. "I wasn't very adventurous."

"I think you were. It sounds like fun."

"It was. I remember the tree had a sort of hole in one side. I'd squeeze inside and think that I had a secret of my own."

"A hole in one side? Maybe that's the tree with the treasure."

"I suppose it's possible."

"We should investigate it right away." Adeline stood up. "Even if the treasure isn't there, we might find another clue."

"It's late. We'll investigate tomorrow. In the morning. After breakfast. Agreed?"

Reluctantly, Adeline agreed. She went to the window. The storm had lessened to a steady rain. She thought about Lady Moorhouse and the people in the Great Room. *How are we going to help them? If we can help them. Each time we learn more about the house and its mysteries, there are more questions than answers.*

Thomas put all the jewelry back into its box except the locket. There was something odd about it and he thought it might be important. After tucking the box back under the bed, he put the locket on the bedside table, then went to stand behind Adeline.

Wrapping his arms about her, he pressed against her back and kissed one side of her neck. "Whatever you're thinking, it can wait for now. I know you'll figure out this entire mystery."

"No, I won't." She turned in his embrace and put her arms about his neck. "We will."

She kissed him. "There is one place we could go tonight."

Thomas sighed. "And where is that?"

"The bed."

Chapter Thirteen

In the morning, the rain fell fast and relentless. Looking out the kitchen window, Adeline knew her umbrella would not keep her dry. She finished washing a breakfast plate and gave it to Thomas.

"Maybe it won't be so bad. After all, it's only water."

"It's too treacherous. The grass will be slippery and the ground muddy. You could fall."

"But you'll be holding on to me."

"I will. But the ground where my talking tree grows is uneven. Worse, when it rains like this, rivulets of water can quickly become rivers. They rush over the side of the cliffs in heavy waterfalls. I won't risk your life."

Adeline couldn't resist a smile at Thomas's protective stubbornness. "All right. We'll wait it out. Besides, we still have to decide what to do next."

"About Lady Moorhouse?"

"About the Music Room."

"Oh. I've had some thoughts about that." He put away the plate and hung the tea towel on the top of a lower cupboard door. "Let's walk."

Curious, Adeline walked beside Thomas to the main stairs, listening as he described what he'd really like. A grand piano in the Great Room would sound better, then the Music Room could be arranged to fit a television.

"I don't play the violin," Thomas said, a little regretfully.

"But you play the piano?"

"A bit. But the Music Room was for lessons and it felt confining. I spent more time standing on the piano bench and looking out the window."

"I play the piano a bit, too. Maybe we can play duets?"

"I'd like that."

Reaching the Music Room, Thomas opened the door and followed Adeline. He pointed at the door that led to the little room, saying a spiral staircase might look nice there and give the room more space. She agreed and suggested a skylight in the roof. She had to describe that. He liked the idea.

"Samuel thinks there's another room behind this wall." Adeline tapped along the wall opposite the window. "We could open it up, maybe put an arch to connect the rooms and make them one, big space. Just for the two of us."

Thomas didn't recall another room, but he agreed that, if there was one to be found, Samuel should do as Adeline suggested. "But if he finds something untoward don't forget to be surprised."

"Are you remembering something?"

Thomas shrugged. "Not so much a memory, more of a vague feeling of apprehension."

Adeline went to the hole that Samuel had made with a hammer. She peered into the darkness, then stood back to let Thomas look.

"Perhaps it's a dumbwaiter," he said.

"Here? Why?"

"I've no idea. It's just that the darkness on the other side feels very near the wall. Perhaps it's the back of a large piece of furniture. Or a closet. I don't remember."

"It's all right. We'll find out tomorrow." Adeline reached for Thomas's right hand and they left the room together. "I'd like to put a larger door here or maybe French doors."

"That will look very pretty."

Adeline started chatting happily about the expected deliveries. She had found a picture of a piano in a magazine and shown it to Ham. He ordered it from an antique store in the city. Something about the curved legs and the elegant design made her think it belonged in the house.

She was expecting the books she had ordered to arrive soon. They were for the new library next to the gallery. A few had to be special ordered because they were out of print. The wall to the small library had been taken down and there was now more space in the Great Room.

"Perhaps that's where we could put the piano," she mused.

"Where?"

"Where the small library was once."

Thomas whisked them to the Great Room. "What about here, near the fireplace?"

"Maybe. But . . ." Adeline went to one of the windows. "If we put the piano here, it would get more light. On a sunny day, that is."

She glanced out the window; the rain was thinner. She could see the road now; its ruts were filled with streams of rushing water. She stepped closer to the glass. "I think someone's coming."

"In this weather?" Thomas went to look out the window. "It appears to be a lorry."

"What's a lorry?"

"A large truck for transporting heavy goods. Still, it's reckless of them to travel today. They must be mad."

"Or very determined."

They watched as the lorry crept along the road. Every turn of the wheel made it look like it might topple over, but it continued its journey. When it reached the gravel of the driveway, its back tires spun for a minute. The sound of the engine changed as the driver shifted gears. Then the lorry moved forward again toward the house and the front door.

"What should we do?" Adeline looked at Thomas.

"Let them in."

Adeline felt self-conscious in her jeans. Looking down, she realized she was wearing one of Thomas's shirts. "I can't be seen like this."

"Of course you can. My shirt isn't going to become invisible." There were several heavy knocks at the front door. Thomas kissed Adeline on her right cheek. "I'll be right beside you." He made himself invisible.

The knocking repeated.

Adeline went to the door and opened it wide, expecting a person in distress.

A short woman looked up at her, hand poised to knock again. "Ah! There you are. And here it is."

"Here's what?"

"Your piano. You are Miss Parker? The one who placed the special order? Rush? Paid in full it is and I'm not one to keep a customer waiting. Though I do admit I hadn't expected the heavens to empty themselves on me and mine."

She turned to the cab of the truck and motioned with her right hand. "Get moving, boys! And be sure you keep it dry."

Two burly looking young men clothed in rain jackets scrambled from the cab and went to the back of the lorry.

"Well, then. Might I come in and see where you'll be wanting the piano placed?"

"Yes. Come in, please. It's just I wasn't expecting you today."

"I tried to call. Collect. But the operator said the line wasn't working. A bit of water and the whole world goes soft." Taking only a few steps inside, the woman pulled down the hood of her mackintosh revealing faded red hair and dark blue eyes. Her face was round like her figure and she smiled at Adeline. "Name's Harold."

"I beg your pardon?"

"Harold. That was me husband. Rest his soul. I kept the name and the business."

"Harold and Sons," said Adeline. "Yes. My handyman recommended you, Mrs. Harold."

"Maude."

"Pardon?"

"Call me, Maude."

"I'm Adeline."

"Pleased." Maude extended one hand and Adeline shook it.

"Is he here, then?" asked Maude.

For an instant, Adeline was caught off guard. *Did she mean, Thomas?*

Maude continued. "Your handyman. The one who called and paid in full. Said his name was a play."

"Oh. Hamlet." Adeline smoothed her hair. "No. He's not here today. I'm sorry. But I can help."

"No need. No need. Full service. I'll even wipe up the floors before we leave. Now. Where do you want the piano?"

"In the Great Room." Adeline pointed at the open doors. "I thought it would look nice near the far window."

Maude wiped her boots on the rug at the door and ambled into the Great Room. A trail of muddy footprints marked the marble floors.

"Be careful not to step in the mud," Adeline whispered to Thomas. "You might leave footprints."

"What's that you said?" Maude turned.

"Oh. I said be careful. The floors are slippery." Adeline went to stand near one of the windows. "Do you think this is a good location for the piano?"

"It would do on a sunny day." Maude looked around the room and pointed at where the small library had been. "That would do better. Comfortable from changes in the weather. You wouldn't always be having to close the windows or the drapes. And not too close to the fireplace. Too much heat is bad for the wood."

"I hadn't thought of that. Well. There will do nicely, then."

Maude went to one of the new pillars that now supported the gallery above. She rapped it with a fist. "Good work. Must be Samuel's. Or his grandson."

"Yes."

A shout for help came from the front door and both women hurried from the Great Room. The piano, well wrapped in tarp, was stuck in the doorway with one man at either end. "Not enough room, mum," said one of the men.

Thomas put his right hand on Adeline's left shoulder. "See that tapestry to the right of the door? Pull it back. The front door was originally double but my father preferred it single."

Maude was looking at Adeline with puzzlement. "Is there another entrance?"

"Just a minute." Adeline went to the tapestry and drew it back, revealing the second half of double doors. "I'd quite forgotten this. If you can help me with the brace, I think we can pull it open."

Maude instructed the men to set the piano down and help with the second door. The one inside easily lifted the oak plank that rested on iron hooks, preventing entry. The one outside put his left shoulder against the door and pushed.

Groaning, the wood yielded and years of accumulated dirt became a mudslide as rain rushed into the foyer of the house.

"That's better," said Maude.

"I always thought so," said Thomas. "But my father thought a single door was more imposing. He wanted to impress visitors, not welcome them."

"I'll have Samuel properly restore it," said Adeline, half to Thomas and half to Maude. "Will it do for today?"

"Yes. Yes." Maude checked the tarp and pointed to the doors of the Great Room. "Take it in there, boys. Between the pillars." She glanced at Adeline. "That will make the piano the feature of the room, not the fireplace."

"I agree," said Adeline quickly. She stepped out of the way as the men lifted the piano again.

"Wipe your boots!" Maude barked. "And follow me."

149

The little procession went into the Great Room, trailed by Adeline and Thomas.

The men undid the many straps that held the tarp in place, but it was Maude that slowly, almost lovingly, drew the tarp back. She gave it to one of the men, then had them lift the piano again until it stood between the pillars.

"Here now. Owen! Go and fetch the bench!" The young man with dark hair hurried away. The other gathered up the straps and tarp, standing by for instructions.

"Take those out to the lorry, Tavish. And bring the mop and pail."

Adeline stood before the piano. It was trimmed with gold and its rich wood gleamed despite the increasing darkness of the room. The curved legs held it aloft as if suspending it in air. "It's perfect."

"It will need to be tuned," Thomas remarked.

Maude was crawling under the piano, checking to make certain it was dry. "It needs to sit a while, then I'll check the tuning for you."

"Thank you," said Adeline. She gazed at the piano. "It's absolutely beautiful."

Owen returned with the piano bench. Maude unwrapped and inspected it, then set it in place. It had curved legs, like the piano, and the seat was upholstered in black and gold brocade.

Adeline ran one hand over the satiny material then sat down. She gently lifted up the lid and looked at the creamy ivory keys. They had a soft hue of age where they touched each other, like in an old photograph. The black keys looked like they had been painted in place: dainty and narrow. Both rows were polished and the piano seemed to be waiting for her touch. Speechless, she sat still.

Maude's voice startled her. "Miss Adeline?"

"What? Yes?"

"I asked where the washroom is. It's a far trip back to town and longer because of the rain. I'm thinking we'll get rooms there and return to the city in the morning."

"There's a washroom down the hallway opposite the dining room." Adeline rose and went to look out one of the windows. The rain had increased to a downpour. She turned to Maude. "But I must insist you stay here tonight. There are plenty of spare rooms and, if you don't mind helping me, I'm sure we can find something to make for dinner."

Maude went to the window. She nodded. "I'll take your kindness and thank you. It's a hard rain out there; likely to drown more than sorrows and not fit for man or beast."

As if to accent her words, a man on a horse appeared at the end of the driveway. Dismounting, he tied his horse to a hitching post and lifted two large bags from behind the saddle. Then he hurried to the house, head and hat down.

Adeline recognized the figure and went to open the front doors. "Ham! Whatever are you doing here in this weather?"

"I saw the lorry from my house, but the phone's not working and I couldn't follow in my truck. The road is bad and getting worse. My mare didn't care for the trip, but I was worried you might need help." He lifted the bags. "I brought a few emergency supplies in case the wind knocks out the power."

"That's very thoughtful of you, Ham."

One of the bags he held was moving. He set it down on the floor and opened it. When nothing emerged, he knelt and pushed the bag a little. A ball of orange fur bolted out and plunked down on the muddy floor, front legs splayed for balance, long tail straight out. It looked up with large green eyes, then, noticing it was the center of attention, began to groom its fur in place.

"I know you said you didn't need company, miss. But this fellow appeared at my back door this morning, crying and hungry. My dogs would have chased him off, but I thought you might give him a home if only until summer."

"I'll be happy to." Adeline picked up the cat, oblivious to the muddy grip he gave her. "He's not a kitten. How old do you think he is?"

"Two years, perhaps three. Most likely he's been living off the land and no doubt a good mouser. I don't mean to frighten you, but sometimes there's a wee mouse to be found, especially with construction noise and all."

Maude came down the hallway. She introduced herself and then her sons. Hands were shaken all around.

"I've just asked Maude to stay the night, Ham. I think it best if you did the same. But where will you put your horse? The lane to the stables won't be safe."

"There's a tool shed near the backdoor. If you don't mind, miss, I can make room for her there. She's big but gentle. And I'll be sure to clean up after her in the morning."

"That's fine, Ham. But will she come up to the house?"

"I think she will now, miss. She didn't balk at the end of the driveway. It was only habit that I left her there.

"I'll fetch her now and bring her round to the backdoor."

Touching one hand to his cap, Ham left and went to get his horse. Owen said there were a few bales of hay in the lorry and that he'd drive it to the back and help.

"Hay?" Adeline turned an inquiring look to Maude.

"Aye. To cushion your piano. It makes good traction for a stuck tire, too. You've got to be ready for the weather out here."

"That's very clever. Well, shall we go to the kitchen?"

"You start ahead, Miss Adeline. Tavish and I will do the cleaning up here first."

"Thank you." Adeline left the foyer and started down the long hallway to the kitchen. The cat was clinging to her left shoulder and purring loudly.

Thomas appeared beside her. He rubbed the cat's cheek and head. "Well, we've got our cat. And our first houseguests. Though I hope they'll be our last."

"It's just for tonight." Adeline entered the kitchen and turned on the light. The lorry was just pulling up outside the back of the house.

Watching from the window, Adeline understood clearly how Thomas must feel, watching and waiting: a part of the world around him and yet apart from it, too. Feeling disappointed, she looked up at him. "You'll have to disappear again."

"I will." He bent to give her a kiss and met the cat's face instead.

The back door opened and Thomas disappeared.

152

"Here we are, miss," Ham announced. Tavish was just behind him. "This here's Molly." The big mare poked her head through the doorway and whinnied. She was brown with a black mane and tail, but her face was brightened with a broad blaze of white. White hairs about her muzzle showed she wasn't a young horse.

"Hello, Molly." Adeline went to pat the mare's neck. The cat jumped down from Adeline's shoulder and went to inspect the mare. They touched noses.

Adeline smiled. Unusual and unexpected circumstances were familiar to her now. She told the men they could have a beer after they'd looked after the mare. "Tavish? Would you take one to Owen, too, please? It may be a bit of a wait for dinner."

"I will, miss. And thank you." He bobbed his head and went to help Ham. Several minutes later, with the lorry parked and Molly in her temporary stall, the men entered the back door. This time they removed their boots and hung their raincoats on the hooks by the door.

Adeline had three beers ready on a tray with a bowl of pretzels. It didn't look like much to her, but the men smiled and thanked her. Ham led the way to the Great Room.

Before she could speak to Thomas, Maude walked into the kitchen. She was wearing a red sweater tucked into loose trousers that looked like they might have once belonged to her husband. Thick wool socks protected her feet from the cold floor. "Right then. All's clean. Let's see what we have to work with."

The five of them ate in the dining room. Ham had brought a cooked roast of beef and Maude, with Adeline assisting as best she could, prepared hot roast beef sandwiches with potatoes and peas.

"The gravy disguises that the peas are good for them," Maude had told Adeline, winking at her.

When the plates were almost too clean to need washing, Maude instructed her 'boys' to tidy up while she tuned the piano. "Don't worry, Miss Adeline. They know their way around a kitchen."

Adeline followed Maude into the Great Room and stood by as the woman expertly ran her thick fingers up and down the keys, listening intently with only the occasional adjustment.

Again Adeline found herself empathizing with Thomas. He was right beside her and she felt almost as invisible as he was. "We'll have cold beef later," she whispered to him.

"No peas," he said.

Maude looked up. She seemed to be assessing Adeline. "The piano's made the trip well. You can play it now."

"Thank you, Maude." Adeline hesitated. "I think I'll wait until tomorrow. I'm out of practice and it's getting late."

"Go on," Thomas said, his eyes on Maude's face. "Play something for me."

Maude smiled a little. "I'll play something for you then." Her fingers lightly caressed the keys and she played a short, happy tune that made Adeline want to dance.

"That's lovely! Thank you, Maude."

Maude nodded. "Does he like it, too?"

"I beg your pardon?"

"Him. Lord Éclair. I've always had 'a good ear,' Harold would say. I could never see what I heard, but I knew and he knew I heard the sounds of life lingering. Magic is not always evil, you know. And magic was here long before the house. Don't ask me where it's from or even how I know.

"But I can tell you this: don't be letting anyone disturb the magic. Lord Éclair belongs in this house. As do you. The magic is strong enough to be felt, but fragile too. Take care of it."

"I . . .I will."

Maude pushed back the piano bench and stood up. "I'll help you with the rooms. The boys and I get up early. The rain will stop in the night. No storm."

"All right." Adeline turned away, glad that Thomas was near. He made no comment.

Tavish, Owen and Ham were waiting for them at the bottom of the stairs. The orange cat, too. He went to Adeline and rubbed against her legs, purring, and the little group agreed that he liked his new mistress.

They climbed the stairs, the cat running and jumping ahead of them. Two rooms opposite Adeline's bedroom were made up. One of them had two beds and Tavish and Owen would share that one. Ham would take the other.

Looking around the beautiful bedroom that Adeline had recently vacated, Maude said she doubted she could sleep with so many flowers. "I'll be gardening in my dreams."

"I think you'll sleep. I find the flowers restful," Adeline said.

"And you? Where will you spend the night?"

"Oh. I have another room. On the other side of the house. I love the view of the lake."

"'Course you do. And it's no business of mine. Will you be down for breakfast?"

"Yes." Adeline turned to leave, then stopped in the doorway. "Does everyone know about Lord Éclair?"

"Only a few. Others guess, others like the stories. But me and Aggie know. And I think we know the most."

"Aggie?"

"Your housekeeper, Mrs. Folly. Agatha and I play cards once a month at a pub in town. A good friend she is, but she does like to talk. Don't be worrying that I'll say anything."

"I'm sure you won't need to. Like you, she senses things."

"That's a sweet way of putting it. Nothing fancy or fearful, just plain and accepting. It's a good sign that you know the truth when you hear it. Or see it."

"Thank you," was all Adeline could think of as a response. Then she said good night and closed the door behind her. She walked the length of the hallway, turning left before reaching the stairs. She resisted speaking to Thomas as she followed the now familiar route to their bedroom. Once there, she closed the door firmly behind her, leaned back against it, and spoke.

"Where are you?"

"Right here." Thomas appeared in front of her and Adeline went to him, looping her arms about his neck and kissing him. "That was a strange and curious end to the evening. An odd day too. What do you think?"

"I think we have another visitor."

"What?"

Adeline turned to the door. A faint meow of protest came from the other side. She went to the door and opened it. The orange cat ran into the room and jumped onto the armchair. After a few licks of one shoulder, he curled up, tail tucked around him.

"At least he left us the bed," Thomas said. He went to turn down the covers.

"We should give him a name." Pulling off her shirt, Adeline went to the bathroom and started a bath. In a few minutes she was soaking in the tub and letting her thoughts drift.

"You should have some bubbles," Thomas remarked. He leaned against the frame of the door, arms folded across his chest, a smile on his face and in his eyes.

"That would be nice. Maybe Mrs. Folly can purchase some for me. I'll have to get in touch with her and ask her to shop for more groceries. And beer." Adeline looked up as Thomas came and sat down on the side of the bathtub. "Do you think Maude is right? I mean, about the house? And the weather? Will it only rain tonight and not storm?"

"Yes. I think Maude is right."

"Why?"

"Even when I was a boy, there were rumors and stories about the house. The lake, too. And the wind. Stories about magic. Fanciful tales, ghost stories, depending on the source."

"Like the story your nanny told you."

"Well, she was as close as she could be about the history of the house. I do remember once she took me for a walk beside the lake.

She pointed out to sea and warned me never to cross the water. I thought at the time she meant not to go out in a boat to the other shore. But perhaps she was referring to something else."

"Like magic?"

Thomas splashed a little water between Adeline's breasts. "You don't give up once you've got an idea, do you?"

"It's more than an idea. And it's not only mine, but Mrs. Folly's and Maude's too. I think they're proof that we're looking in the right direction." Adeline stood up and reached for the towel Thomas held out to her. "We've successfully contacted Lady Moorhouse. I think we should try again. Once we've found the treasure."

"You make it sound easy."

"It was. It will be." Adeline kissed him quickly on his right cheek and laughed as Thomas made a grab for her towel. She dashed for the bed, flinging the towel at him and snuggling under the bedding.

Thomas imagined the room lit only by the light from the fire, and then it was. Then he undressed and got into bed next to Adeline. He put his left arm about her shoulders and kissed the top of her head. "You've forgotten something rather important."

Adeline pressed against his body and ran her left hand over his chest. "And what's that?"

"A name for the cat."

———————◆———————

The 'goodbyes' in the morning were done early, after breakfast in the kitchen, and before the sun had completely cleared away the clouds.

Adeline motioned to Maude and the two women walked a little away from the group of men.

"I was wondering," said Adeline in a low voice, "when you hear Thomas, I mean, Lord Éclair, what do you hear? His words? His voice?"

"I don't hear words. 'Tis more a soft sound like a breeze through long grass. Positive, it is; nothing to fear. Happy, too, or so it seemed to me."

Maude looked up at Adeline, her gaze piercing. "But you hear him, don't you? His words, his voice."

Adeline looked away, watching the waves on the lake for a moment. "Yes," she whispered. "I hear him. I can see him, too. I only wondered if he will be safe with all the restorations and, with me being here."

"You care about him." It was a statement.

"Yes. Very much."

"You'll be fine. The restoration of the house is a good thing. You can tell by Ham's horse. She's not frightened. And no storm last night." Maude paused, her eyes narrowed. "It's the storms that cause trouble; the wind and the rain bring the magic from the water. Powerful and old it is; dangerous, too."

"What can I do to prevent it?"

Maude shook her head. "I don't know the answer. I only know you and he are right together. How or why is a mystery of the magic that's in this house."

She put one hand on Adeline's left shoulder. "Embrace the magic. Don't fight it."

Maude turned and called to her boys. They got into the cab of the lorry and, joining them, Maude started the engine. A minute later, the lorry backed up and made a turn around the driveway. Then it lurched and bounced down the road into the distance.

"I'll be going now, too, miss," said Ham. "Unless you need me for something before tomorrow."

"Thank you, Ham. I'll be fine." Adeline went to pat Molly. "She seems to like the house now, don't you think?"

"Aye. You're doing a great thing. All will be right again, soon enough." Ham touched his right hand to his cap. "I'll see you tomorrow morning then, miss."

"Yes."

Adeline stood back and waited as Ham and Molly rode away. For an instant, she felt lonely, then Thomas appeared. "What did Maude say?"

"I thought you heard."

"You seemed to want a bit of privacy."

"Let's go back inside."

"Don't tell me it's another mystery."

Adeline laughed. "Maybe. In a way." They entered the house together. "It's ours again. At least until tomorrow morning. And the restorations will be done soon." She told him about her conversation with Maude.

Thomas listened carefully, not interrupting. He stopped at the door to the Great Room. "Let's go to the tree now before I lose my nerve."

"Lose your nerve? Are you afraid of what we'll find?"

"No. I'm afraid we might not find anything." He held up one hand as Adeline started to object. "Don't argue yet. Let's just go and examine my tree."

"All right."

The orange cat walked casually out of the Great Room. He paused and looked up at Thomas, then meowed and went to Adeline. Picking him up, she stroked his head. "He doesn't seem afraid. I think he thinks he belongs here."

"He can come with us. Perhaps he'll smell something."

Adeline set the cat on the floor. "He's not a dog, Thomas."

"I know that. But I don't think he thinks he's a cat, either. He's already made himself at home in our room and now he's heading down the hallway as if he owns the house."

"Maybe he does." Adeline took Thomas's left hand. "Come on. Did you have breakfast?"

"I had a piece of toast when no one was looking."

"We'll have a big lunch."

The cat meowed and they hurried after it.

"He's got us trained already," said Thomas.

159

They stopped to get a flashlight and then went out the back door. The cat romped away across the damp ground. Thomas and Adeline continued along the back of the house, enjoying the crisp air and the absence of other people. As they approached the tree, the cat returned and raced for the tree trunk. He jumped up, then clawed his way to the first branch. Stretching out, he licked one paw and then meowed.

Thomas and Adeline went to the tree. The trunk was thick with knots, graying in color, but its branches still curved up and were beginning to leaf.

"What kind of tree is this?" asked Adeline, touching the trunk with her fingertips.

"I've no idea. My mother liked to garden. She tried many times to plant flowers and plants all around the house. But none survived except this tree."

"And your garden."

"That was here before."

"That's interesting." Adeline walked around the tree. Her hand slipped a little into a small groove in the trunk. "Thomas? I think I've found your hiding place."

He joined her and they pulled back a few vines that had somehow managed to make their way from the side of the house to the tree. A dark opening revealed itself, about three feet high and two feet wide.

Adeline shone the flashlight and Thomas stretched his right arm inside and felt about. The floor of the hole was covered with moss and dead vine leaves; the sides were smooth with lines like wrinkles. It was depressingly empty.

Standing back, Thomas shrugged. "Nothing."

Undeterred, Adeline crouched down and examined the little cleft carefully. The flashlight showed a furry clump directly across from her. It had eyes. She fell back with a shriek.

Thomas grabbed her and pulled her away and behind him. They waited. A minute later a little fox poked its head out of the hiding place. On the branch above, the cat meowed and the fox dashed away, disappearing around the front corner of the house. The cat did not take up pursuit; instead it jumped down and went inside the tree.

"That's odd behavior even for a cat," Thomas observed. "He might not be inclined to chase a mouse after all, let alone a rat."

"Maybe he's just curious."

They knelt down together and Adeline again shone the flashlight. The cat wasn't there.

"Hold onto me," she said to Thomas and stuck her head inside the hiding place. "I think our cat's a detective. He's found some sort of hole beneath the leaves. I can see his tail."

She set the flashlight down and reached for the cat. He sat up a little and she wriggled her fingers in front of his face. "Come on, boy. Let me see what you've found. Just move over a bit."

The cat stood up and went to the flashlight. Adeline managed to move a little further into the small hole. She felt Thomas tighten his grip about her waist.

"I'm all right," she called over her shoulder. She felt along the bed of leaves. There was mud beneath instead of moss and she scraped at it.

The mud caught beneath her fingernails as she began to dig. She was about to give up when she felt something cold and hard. Spreading her fingers apart, she pushed her right hand back and forth across a rough metal surface. The flashlight showed a thick box. It was square with a thin handle, stiff with rust and age. Working faster, she managed to lift the handle just enough to drag the box toward her. It was heavier than it looked and she told Thomas to pull her back while she hung onto the box.

"Keep your head down," Thomas said as he pulled her free.

They fell back together and Adeline released her grip on the handle. Her fingers hurt. She looked up at Thomas. "I think we found the treasure."

He helped her up, noticing that she was cradling her right hand. "What happened? Let me see." He took her hand and gently turned it over, palm up. "We'll have to disinfect that. Does it hurt?"

"A little; I'll be fine."

Thomas bent to pick up the box and Adeline warned him of its weight. He picked it up with both hands, almost staggering. "Wait here. I'll be right back." He disappeared.

In an instant he returned. "Sorry. That was just quicker and easier than carrying it back to the kitchen."

"You could have taken me with you."

"Not with both hands holding that box. Anyway, you're hurt and we don't know what whisking will do to an injury."

Adeline looked at her right hand. The fingers and palm were scratched from the tight grip she had applied to the handle of the box. "All right. We'll walk." She looked around. "Where's the cat?"

"Don't worry about him. Let's get you back to the kitchen. There's a First Aid Kit there. Somewhere."

"We really have to give that cat a name."

"King?" Thomas suggested as they walked back to the kitchen door. "He's already made himself the king of the castle."

Adeline laughed. Entering the kitchen, they saw the cat sitting on the table next to the box. "Now how did he do that?"

"Perhaps he was next to me a minute ago. I didn't notice him. I was hurrying."

"He seems fine." Adeline went to the cat. His paws and tummy were damp and muddy but his green eyes gazed up at her as if to say, "What took you so long?"

"He doesn't look like a 'King,' but he does act like one. What's another word for king?"

"Rex," Thomas answered. "Early 17th century Latin." He checked the contents of a couple of drawers. Finding what he sought, he went to the table and set down a small First Aid Kit. He stared sternly at the cat. "Excuse me, your majesty, but get off the table. Please."

The cat jumped to the floor, sat down and began to clean his paws.

"Rex it is," said Adeline.

"You'd better sit down, too," Thomas said. "I doubt I'm good at this."

162

Adeline sat down and held up her hand. "I trust you." She bit her lower lip as Thomas cleaned her fingers and the palm of her hand with disinfectant, then she smiled up at him. "See? I'm all better now."

"Do you want a bandage?"

"I don't think I need one. The skin's scraped but not broken."

"I think I might faint."

"Ghosts don't faint. They make other people faint."

"Do you feel faint? Do you want to lie down?"

"I do not. I want to look at the treasure."

The box was covered in dirt and mud with a single latch behind the rusted handle. Thomas got a screwdriver and pried it open.

Adeline eagerly lifted the lid. "Oh, my god."

Chapter Fourteen

Adeline reached into the box and picked up the large rock that rested there. It was heavy and dotted with gold spots. "Thomas? What is this?"

"I think it's gold." He leaned over her right shoulder and picked up several letter-size pieces of paper that had been underneath the rock. He read to himself for a minute, then said, "This is a land title for the mountain across the lake; it includes all mineral rights. It's in my name only." He looked through the rest of the papers. "And these are stocks and bonds in my mother's name and mine. I was aware my mother worried that my father would gamble away our family fortune.

"I remember that sometimes he would threaten to sell the house and the land, but she would argue with him. She knew I loved the house."

"And she didn't want you to lose it," Adeline said softly. "You never told me how she died. Have you forgotten?"

Thomas straightened. He set the papers on the table. "No. That I remember too clearly."

"You don't have to tell me if you don't want to."

Thomas walked around the kitchen, paused to pet Rex, then returned to stand beside Adeline. "I told you my mother liked to garden. She was going to have several trees planted near the edge of the cliff to keep it safe. She said trees would be prettier than a fence.

"One day, after lunch, she told me to go to my room for my nap. She said she had decided on a place for the trees and that we'd go and have a look together when it stopped raining. I remember it was raining very hard that day.

"Naturally, I didn't stay in my room. I was about to climb out the window when I saw her walking near the cliff's edge. She stumbled in the mud, slipped and fell. She couldn't get up. I wasn't there to help her. A torrent of mud loosened by the rain, rushed at her, struck her. She disappeared over the edge. I never saw her again."

"Oh, Thomas." Adeline stood up and hugged him, pressing her head against his right shoulder. "How terrible for you. I'm so sorry."

He held her close. "I never climbed down the tree again. I just did as I was told until my father died. Then I inherited the house, the land, and my father's gambling debts.

"My mother had insisted on buying some stocks for me. They were in my name only. I never asked why; I just lived off that income. I never tried for more. It was enough money to let me live here and have a wife and family one day."

Lifting her head, Adeline looked into his eyes. She touched his right cheek. "You've got me. And Rex. Is that enough?"

"More than enough."

They kissed. Adeline felt the sadness seep from Thomas's body. She leaned into his embrace.

A loud clunking noise made the couple step apart. Rex jumped down from the table before he could be scolded. He pawed at the rock he had knocked to the floor.

Picking up the rock, Thomas was about to put it back in the box when he noticed an envelope. It was yellow with age and sealed with a wax stamp. He broke the seal and pulled out a piece of paper.

"What is it?"

"It's a letter from my mother." He gave it to Adeline.

She sat down and looked at the elegant handwriting, faded but still readable.

"My dearest, Thomas," she read aloud. "This is your inheritance. Do not tell your father should he still be alive. It was some time after we married that I realized he did not marry me for love, but for my money. True, he was already very wealthy, but the acquisition of wealth can become an addiction. He always wanted more. Power too. I had no suspicion of this when I accepted his proposal. He was a man of the world and I was young. I believed his words of love. I believed him when he said we would be happy. We were not."

Adeline shivered. The story was very much like hers. She continued.

"I did become happy when you were born. And I tried to give you a happy life here. You always loved this house.

"In secret, I had the mountain across the lake surveyed. Veins of gold were detected. I arranged its purchase. These papers give you sole title to the mountain and whatever you may find there. It is my hope that, unlike your father, you will choose love over money.

"Love cannot be bought or sold, its value cannot be counted, but it can fill your life in ways wealth and possessions never will. Do not forget this.

"And do not forget that I loved you. And that you deserve to be loved. Remember that words of love are not enough. Protestations of love can be like promises in politics: empty or full of lies to please your ear. Listen instead to your heart.

"If, as you grow older, you think you will not find love, wait. It will find you. Mother."

Adeline carefully refolded the letter and returned it to its envelope. She set it on the table. "I think I'm going to cry."

"Please don't. I haven't a handkerchief."

Stifling a sniffle, Adeline tried to smile. "A house and its land, a lake, a mountain of gold and you don't have a handkerchief?"

"I was never very good at looking after myself. I was busy waiting."

"I'm so glad you waited, Thomas. There must have been dozens of beautiful girls who wanted to marry you."

"At the time, I hoped that would be true. But they were, as my mother wrote, more interested in my money than me. And they only pretended to like the house."

Adeline stood up. "Let's put all this away and make lunch."

"Where shall we hide it now?"

She turned to him with a look of surprise. "Where no one will find it, of course."

"Ah." Thomas nodded. "Under the bed."

They spent the day talking about the house. Inevitably that included what to do about the dancers. Adeline wanted to contact Lady Moorhouse again. Thomas said he was beginning to suspect, based on what Mrs. Folly and Maude and even Lady Moorhouse had said, that the dancers could simply be part of the magic of the house.

His only explanation for why he resembled the man in the portrait remained the same: Sebastian Éclair was Thomas's ancestor. He had won the title of 'Lord' in a poker game. "Remember?"

"Yes. And it makes sense." Adeline looked out at the lake. They stood hand in hand well back from the edge of the cliff. She had suggested that they go forward with the idea to have trees planted with perhaps a low but sturdy fence in between the trunks.

The tragedy of the death of Thomas's mother weighed on her. While she had no great affection for her mother and father, they were still her parents and loved her in their own 'socially acceptable' way.

When she asked Thomas if he had a picture of his mother or a scrapbook containing pictures and memorabilia from his childhood he answered no. He didn't pause to think and she didn't press the matter. She was beginning to understand how important it was to him that he leave the past at rest. In peace, if possible, so that he could enjoy the present. *Our present. And our future.*

It was the future, more than solving a mystery, which now occupied Adeline's thoughts.

Yes, they were re-creating a sanctuary for themselves, but how to keep it safe? She would have to contact her solicitor and it would likely be best if she gave him the deeds and papers they had found. Thomas agreed that everything should be in her name now. He pulled her back from where they stood and they continued around the house. Before they went to the garden, Adeline pointed at the stables below.

"We could keep it as a garage but it's useless when it rains. The road, if you can call it that, is too steep and dangerous."

Thomas suggested that the men knock it down and build a smaller building nearer to the main road and the house.

Adeline squeezed his right hand. "I like that idea. And I have an idea that might assist us and even Lady Moorhouse."

"Oh, not her again."

"Yes." Adeline pulled him with her and they headed to the garden. "I thought that once the restorations are completed we could have a picnic. A sort of thank you to everyone who has helped me, I mean, us. The people have been so accepting of my presence here, even welcoming and kind. And we need to maintain their goodwill to protect the house."

"I hadn't thought of that. I've been . . . preoccupied." Thomas opened the garden gate and they entered. Inside it seemed a world apart from the house. The flowers were blooming; the trees were green with leaves and noisy with small birds. The path beckoned.

"Where's the third tree? The one that matches the one in the courtyard and your talking tree? And what do you think about an atrium in the courtyard? Do you like it?"

"It's just over there."

"What's over where?"

"The tree. And yes, I think if that young man—"

"Robert."

"Yes. Well, if he can build a glass roof and make the courtyard into an atrium, then we could have the outside inside all year round."

Adeline stopped in front of the tree. It was small and its leaves were only starting to leaf. Its branches were thin and delicate as if it were nothing more than a sketch. She touched it gently, like a caress.

"This one might be a cherry blossom tree," she said, her voice thoughtful.

Thomas didn't answer. He had been standing with his hands in his pockets. Suddenly he pulled his right hand out with an accompanying word of annoyance.

"What's wrong?"

"It's the locket we found." Thomas looked sheepish. "I thought I'd just hang on to it for a while. I don't know why. I never saw my mother wear this piece of jewelry."

Adeline lifted the locket, sliding one thumbnail along its edge to open it. The front lifted, but this time it looked thicker. "There's a second divider behind the first," she said. "Thomas? Do you know this person?"

Thomas looked at the picture, tainted with time until it looked more like a reflection in water. "That's my mother. It looks like the other picture was scraped away."

"Did your mother have a brother?"

"No."

"She was very beautiful. But why destroy the other picture? And why hide the locket?"

"Perhaps she just didn't care for it anymore."

"Will you whisk us to the kitchen, please? The light there is better."

"Is your hand all right?"

"Yes." She held it up. "Not even a bruise."

Thomas whisked them to the kitchen and they sat down side by side at the table. Sunlight mixed with the kitchen light and the photograph was easier to examine.

"Maybe the other picture was of your father."

169

"That I doubt. I never got the impression that my mother liked him. Certainly not enough to keep a picture of him in a locket."

"I'm sure she must have liked him when they married." Adeline studied the locket. "There is another possibility."

Thomas waited. Finally Adeline spoke. "It could have been a picture of a lover. He must have been important enough that she wanted to keep his picture and then, worried that your father might discover it, destroyed the picture and hid the locket."

Thomas sat back. "Do you mean to say, my mother had an affair?"

"Maybe. She was unhappy and young. She might have fallen in love and had a desperate affair of the heart. It would explain why she didn't divorce your father; so that you could keep the house, your inheritance, and your title."

Thomas looked depressed. He stood up then sat back down again. "Assuming you're right, as you usually are, do you think my father knew about the affair?"

"I don't think so. According to what your mother wrote, he was obsessed with money and power. That means social standing, too. His marriage to your mother was probably for status. When she realized that, you noticed her feelings for him were . . . less than loving.

"I'm sorry, Thomas. If it's any consolation, affairs of the heart are rarely consummated, except with tokens of love, like this locket."

Thomas closed the locket. "No wonder she kept it hidden. We'll put it back in her jewelry box tonight. Unless it bothers you."

"Not at all. We'll keep it safe, the locket and your mother's secret."

Adeline went to the refrigerator and took out two bottles of beer. She turned to Thomas. He was still holding the locket. "Does it make you sad? That your mother loved someone other than your father? She loved you very much."

"No. It only makes me sad that she gave up that love for me. She gave up happiness."

"She didn't give up happiness, Thomas; you were her happiness. Just as you are mine."

She handed him a beer. "Come on. Let's go look at the tree in the courtyard."

Opening the beer, Thomas took a long swallow. "I'd much rather look at the piano. I didn't have much chance when it was delivered."

"Let's go then. Whisk or walk?"

"Let's walk. I love to walk with you. Stroll, amble, skip if I could."

Leaving the kitchen, they held hands and started down the hallway. When they reached the Great Room, Adeline asked, "Will you dance with me?"

"Yes. Unfortunately, we don't have music."

"Oh, but we do. I have CDs—" She explained. "They're recordings of music. We could play those while we dance."

Thomas stood still a moment and kissed her. "You think of everything, don't you?"

"Not everything. Sometimes I think too much. But I do have a portable CD player. It's like a modern phonograph." She changed the subject. "I love waltzes, Thomas. Do you?"

In answer, Thomas went to the piano. He lifted the top and propped it open, then sat down on the bench. "Waltzes were always my favorite, but it has been a long time since I played one." He started to play. "Do you like this?"

"Oh, it's lovely." Adeline danced a few steps, did a twirl, then stopped abruptly. She looked at the open dining room doors.

Thomas stopped playing and looked up. "What's wrong?"

"I think there's something in the dining room."

He rose and went to stand beside her. "It must be Rex."

Adeline called to the cat.

"You don't really expect him to answer, do you? He's not a dog," Thomas teased.

"Well, he acts like one. Come on." She started toward the doors.

Thomas grabbed her left hand to slow her down. "We'll investigate together."

They went into the dining room and Thomas turned on the light. Rex was on the floor by the fireplace. He was pawing at something near the corner of the fireplace screen.

Releasing Thomas's hand, Adeline went to the cat and knelt beside him. "What have you got there, Rex?"

Rex batted at his find, then tried to pick it up with his teeth.

Adeline plucked it quickly from the cat. She stood up. It was a piece of paper, worn and folded many times. "It must have been tucked near the base of the fireplace screen." She turned it over in her hands. "I think it's a note." She gave it to Thomas.

He unfolded the paper carefully.

"What does it say?"

"'I must speak to you again. Meet me here tonight. I need your help.'"

"Who do you suppose it's from?"

Thomas showed the note to Adeline.

She read the signature aloud. "Anne, the Lady Moorhouse."

Chapter Fifteen

"Why do you think the note is meant for me?" Adeline asked Thomas. They were sitting at the kitchen table. "I didn't tell her my name."

"Because she signed it formally. And because she wrote 'speak' not 'see.' She would have written something more personal for one of her lovers, particularly Sebastian, and signed only her first name or perhaps just her initial."

"She sounds so desperate. We have to help her."

"We will."

A small frown drew Adeline's eyebrows together. "But how can I speak with her tonight?" She went to the kitchen window and looked out. "I know the weather changes quickly, but it doesn't look like there'll be a storm tonight."

Thomas rose and looked about the kitchen. "Mrs. Folly isn't the only one who can predict the weather." He crossed to a little table near the kitchen door. On it sat an old radio. He fiddled with a dial until a man's voice entered the room. After several minutes, the man said, "And now, the Weather Forecast."

They listened: clear with little or no chance of rain.

"How depressing," said Adeline.

Smiling, Thomas went to the refrigerator and took out a beer. He opened it and took it to Adeline. "You're forgetting something."

"What am I forgetting?"

"Time. It's on our side, remember? We don't know when she wrote the note only that, for Lady Moorhouse, tonight will be during the next storm that happens for us."

Adeline took a sip of beer and passed the bottle back to Thomas. "But why didn't the men discover the note when they were doing the restorations?"

"Because she hadn't written it yet." He drank some beer and changed the subject. "Now, let's make a cold lunch and take it back to our room. I want to see this small phonograph you mentioned."

"And dance?"

"And dance."

"But first I have to phone Mrs. Folly. I hope she won't be alarmed by such a large order. Including cat food and kitty litter."

"Personally I doubt Mrs. Folly is ever alarmed by anything."

Outside the house, where the lake waters met the sea, a small waterspout appeared. It hovered over the surface of the lake for several minutes then disappeared again.

Inside the house, in their bedroom, Thomas and Adeline danced, unaware of something dangerous nearby.

"May I say, Lord Éclair, you dance divinely?"

Thomas swirled Adeline around once more then stopped and kissed her. "I'm only as good as my partner."

Adeline liked the sound of that. "Thomas?"

"Yes."

"We will always be together, won't we?"

"Always."

"How?"

He led her to the bed and they lay down together. As he stroked her hair he told her that he had put some thought to that matter. She could live with him as they were doing now, and then, when she died, she would become a ghost like him.

"But what if I don't become a ghost? Especially a magical one, like you?"

"I think the magic of the house will make certain that you do."

"Why?'

"Because that's the only way we can stay together. It's just as Maude said: we're 'right' together."

Adeline thought for a minute. "Do you think I'll have to get myself murdered?"

Thomas rolled her onto her back. "I think you have a decidedly gruesome side."

"Not gruesome, just practical. Part of thinking too much, I guess."

He kissed her right shoulder, beginning to undress her. "Then think about this: the magic in the house is ancient. It probably existed long before the time of the knight and his lady. It won't fail us."

"But it failed them."

"Because they left the house. They could have taken shelter in the fireplace and stayed. Even in the storm, the magic of the house would have protected them."

"Okay." Adeline still felt worried. "But what about Lady Moorhouse and the dancers?"

He propped himself up on one arm. "I've had years to wonder about that and now, with you, I've a theory, of sorts."

"Go on."

"If we think of the dancers as her party guests, then it's possible that her party was taking place at the same time as mine. Well, in a different century, but still, in this house, in the Great Room. Both during a storm." He paused. "Now don't think me ridiculous for what I'm about to say next."

"Never."

"Isn't it possible that some kind of overlap of time occurred? Allowing some, or at least one, of her party guests to mingle with mine?"

"And that guest thought you were Sebastian Éclair and murdered you." Adeline pulled back from Thomas a little. "I think that's more than possible. I think it's exactly right. And it includes the one element of mystery we've continually overlooked."

"And what is that?"

"Magic." She leaned forward and kissed him quickly. "You're very clever and not at all ridiculous. When I speak to Lady Moorhouse again, I'll ask what Romanivich said that upset her. We thought he insulted her, but if he threatened her or, threatened Sebastian—"

"Threatened to kill him if she didn't give him 'the treasure,'" Thomas suggested.

"Of course! Why didn't I think of this before?" Adeline started to sit up but Thomas gently pulled her back. "Slow down. We have to think this through more thoroughly."

"But it's so exciting. He murders you, she murders him."

"I promise you, being murdered isn't exciting."

"You know what I mean."

"And remember, her party guests—the dancers—were here long before me and whatever plan Romanivich had, he would have come prepared, as he was with his magic tricks. Isn't that how murderers work? Conceive a plan, prepare for various outcomes and then . . . finish the job. Isn't that what they say in the movies?"

"Then we'll simply have to conceive our own plan and outwit him." Adeline thought for a minute. "Maybe there's another clue, more magic; we find it first and maybe Romanivich just vanishes. Poof! Then Lady Moorhouse and her guests are safe."

"It's possible." Thomas drew Adeline close against him. "You know, in a curious way, the villain of our little murder mystery did us both a favor."

"Why do you say that?"

"Because, except for being murdered, our villain's plot never affected me. It kept me here in this magical existence, to wait for you.

"At any rate, we'll have to wait until you can speak with Lady Moorhouse again."

Adeline flopped back on the bed. "I hate waiting."

Thomas leaned over her. "Even with me?"

Adeline ran one finger along his lips. "No. I don't hate waiting when I'm with you, Thomas. Besides, we'll win in the end."

"I have no doubt we will."

"Tell me again what you told me the first time in the kitchen. It feels so long ago and I can never hear it enough."

"You're very beautiful."

They kissed, oblivious to the changing weather far out to sea.

———————•◦•———————

Morning sunlight woke Adeline and she hurried to get ready before the men arrived. She went downstairs to the kitchen. Mrs. Folly was already there, unloading groceries.

Knowing she would only be in the way, Adeline sat down at the table and waited while Mrs. Folly went about the kitchen, putting away food and beer.

Mrs. Folly paused when she looked at the three boxes of cookies Adeline had asked her to purchase. "Not many people care for these old recipes anymore."

"Oh, I love them. And of course all the work around the house makes me hungry."

Rex came into the kitchen and jumped on a counter. Mrs. Folly turned to him at once and shook a finger at him. "None of that now. You'll mind your manners. If you have any."

Rex immediately jumped down from the counter.

"Do you know this cat?" Adeline asked. "I thought he was a stray."

"Indeed he was. The town has assorted litters every spring. But this fellow slipped away before the vet could catch him. He stops at shops for milk and snacks and then leaps off across the moors. I'm not surprised to find him here. This house suits him. If he suits you."

"Oh, yes. We, I mean, I like him very much. And he's good company."

Mrs. Folly paused to straighten her apron. "And I'm supposing Lord Éclair likes him, too?"

"Here's your chance to get her to talk more," Thomas said to Adeline. He had been standing near, invisible.

Casually, Adeline poured a cup of coffee. "Mrs. Folly? Do you know anything about a woman named Lady Moorhouse? She owned this house long ago. Maybe there's a book about her? Although, I'm sure it wouldn't be as accurate as anything you might know."

Mrs. Folly turned to Adeline, a small cloud of flour making her appear almost unreal. "Ask me straight and I'll answer, but I've no patience for manipulation."

"I apologize. I didn't mean to insult you. I just feel . . . desperate, I suppose."

"Desperate. Now there's a word and a fine story that can be told with that." She turned back to her baking and Adeline sat quietly and waited.

"I can tell you this much," Mrs. Folly said. "There's a story about a grand lady long ago. She had many lovers, but only one had her heart. He was murdered, it's said, on the night of a great dance right here in the house. Or it may be they both escaped the murderer. Out on the waters. Or it may be it was the murderer who escaped. Everyone has their own idea of what might have become of the three.

"All any know for certain is, they disappeared that very night never to be seen again."

Adeline considered this new information. "What do you think happened, Mrs. Folly?"

There was no answer for a minute, then Mrs. Folly said quietly, "I think the murderer tried to escape and drowned. It's treacherous where the waters meet, especially during a storm and at night. The magic is stirred up. You'd have to be desperate to face it. Now there's desperate for you."

"Yes." Adeline stood up. "Well, thank you, Mrs. Folly. I'd better get back to the men. They're working upstairs this morning in the Music Room. Making it larger."

Mrs. Folly set down her spoon and bowl and turned again to Adeline. "Are they now?"

Adeline nodded. "Yes. And the room above it and the room beyond."

Mrs. Folly nodded. "There's a wardrobe in the room beyond. Tell them not to knock it about. I'll have a bit of coffee and cake ready soon enough." She turned back to her work.

Adeline waited, but Mrs. Folly had retreated into her unusual silence.

Leaving the kitchen, Adeline walked halfway down the hallway, then whispered to Thomas. "What do you think of that?"

He appeared at her side. "I think you should give Mrs. Folly the wardrobe."

"What? Why?"

"I'm remembering it now. I used to hide in it when I was a boy. The door sticks."

"And you got stuck."

"I did. It was some time before my mother found me or perhaps it was my nanny. Anyway, give it away. We don't need old memories like that."

Adeline knew Thomas meant he didn't need those memories. She understood. "Of course I'll let Mrs. Folly have it. But I want to keep the paintings of the house."

"Why?"

"I suspect somewhere in one of those paintings is our final clue. They all look magical and I didn't really have time to look at all of them before you interrupted me."

"I didn't interrupt you. I merely took advantage of the opportunity to introduce myself."

They reached the stairs. "You'd better turn invisible again," Adeline said. "And you still didn't answer my question," she continued as she walked up the stairs.

Invisible, Thomas lowered his voice a little. "I think Mrs. Folly is right. The villain drowned trying to escape, after murdering his victim."

"Morning, miss." Ham's voice startled Adeline as she entered the Music Room. "We've a good start here today. But there's a stack of paintings in the room above. I wanted to ask if you knew about them and, if so, what you'd like done."

Drawing herself back to the reality of Lady of the Manor instead of woman in love with a ghost, Adeline smiled at Ham. "I know about them, Ham. They're paintings of the house. I'd like the paintings brought downstairs please. To the Great Room for now, so I can have a better look at them. Then I can choose which one I might want to hang in the new gallery."

"No problem at all, miss. We'll get it done as soon as we move the wardrobe. We found it when we broke through that wall over there." Ham pointed at the where the wall had been and explained that they had found another room behind the wall just as Samuel had suspected.

Robert thought it was once a ladies' dressing room from the size of it and because there was a full mirror attached to one wall. No other furniture now, but no doubt it would have had a chair for sitting. "Robert knows these things, miss."

Ham went on to show Adeline some of the work they were doing to ready the Music Room for the French doors she wanted. Suddenly he stopped his tour and for a moment Adeline worried he had noticed Thomas's footprints in the dust on the floor. She quickly stepped on them herself and Thomas objected that she had stepped on his foot.

"You've more than one," Adeline whispered then, seeing Ham's face, she said, "You wanted to tell me something more, Ham?"

"Oh, yes, miss. I'm sorry I forgot earlier this morning, but I've the painting you wanted reframed. Picked it up late last night. A chandelier, too. For the dining room."

At this news Adeline momentarily lost her composure and clapped her hands together with delight. "That's wonderful. Are they still in your truck?"

Ham seemed pleased at Adeline's obvious happiness. "Samuel and I can bring them in right after lunch, unless you want us to stop and do it for you right away."

Adeline smoothed her hair unconsciously, reminding herself to play her part. "After lunch will be just fine, Ham. And please thank Old Boy for me, will you?"

"Yes, miss."

Rex came into the room and thoroughly inspected the dust all over the floors, covering Thomas's footprints with paw prints. Adeline picked him up. "I'd better let you get back to work. Mrs. Folly said she'll have coffee and cake ready soon."

"Thank you, miss." Ham reached out one hand and gave Rex a friendly rub on his head. "He seems happy. I'm glad you like him."

"Very much."

Rex purred loudly as Adeline held him. She smiled and left the men to their work.

"I think you need a bit of fresh air, Rex," she said and took him to the front doors. She noticed how lovely it was to have both doors open and welcoming. She set Rex down and he hurried off into the sunshine.

"It's going to be a lovely day, isn't it, Thomas?"

He didn't answer.

"Thomas?" Adeline stretched out her right hand, then her left, trying to feel Thomas in the air around her. He wasn't there. She was about to hurry inside when he appeared.

Fear made her cross. "Where were you?"

"I wanted to look upstairs at that little room one last time before it changes."

"But you agreed to the changes. Have you changed your mind?"

"Not at all. I was just remembering a morning when I met a beautiful young woman who was nosing through some old paintings."

"I wasn't nosing through the paintings," she whispered as she heard Mrs. Folly coming down the hallway.

Thomas made himself invisible.

"Come on," Adeline said quietly. "And please don't wander off without me again. I was frightened when you didn't answer."

She heard him whisper an apology in her right ear and felt a light kiss on her right cheek. She smiled and entered the house, ready for more excitement.

The men continued their work throughout the morning, stopping only long enough for a cup of coffee and a piece of Mrs. Folly's cake. By lunchtime, the Music Room was spacious, the wardrobe had been brought downstairs and set near the front doors, and the paintings of the house were in the Great Room.

Adeline could hardly wait to look at them. She insisted that the men eat their lunch in the dining room while she looked through the paintings. When Mrs. Folly brought the lunch, she told her she could have the wardrobe if she wished.

"I hear you have a daughter that's getting married," Adeline explained.

Thomas had told her he'd overheard Mrs. Folly talking to Ham about the upcoming wedding.

"I thought the wardrobe might make a nice wedding present. Once it's repaired and polished up, of course."

If Mrs. Folly was surprised, she didn't show it. She only thanked Adeline and asked what price she wanted for the wardrobe. Adeline insisted it was a gift and that perhaps Ham, when he could spare the time, would fix it up for Mrs. Folly.

"But you can work out the details with him as you like."

"Aye. I'll do that." Mrs. Folly gave each waiting man their one beer and Adeline went into the Great Room to organize the paintings.

Even though they were unframed, they were heavy and she struggled to pull each one to a wall. Thomas helped by pushing. They arranged the paintings in a long line and then looked at them carefully.

"I don't notice anything out of the ordinary," Thomas said.

Adeline moved slowly back and forth in front of the paintings of the house, pausing thoughtfully in front of the last one. "There's something different about this one," she said aloud.

"It's the angle," Robert said, coming up behind her.

"Oh!" Adeline turned around quickly. "Robert. You startled me."

"I'm sorry, miss." He bobbed his head in apology.

"It's all right. Um, what were you were saying about this particular painting? Something about the angle?"

Robert knelt down on one knee and pointed out how, in this one painting only, the lake could be seen. "Where it meets the sea, miss. In all the other paintings you just see the house in different weather with the mountain behind it. But in this one here, you can see that the artist wasn't really concentrating on the house, if you know what I mean. He was looking at the water." He stood up, towering over Adeline and smiling, waiting for his marks.

She peered at the painting again and stifled a gasp. That was it; she could see it now in the sunlight of the Great Room: a strange swirl in the water with a slight mist above it. She told Robert he had a good eye and, if he had finished lunch, would he please put that one painting upstairs in the new gallery for her.

"Certainly, miss." He paused as he easily picked up the painting. "I was wondering, if it isn't being rude of me, if I might have one of the other paintings? Or are you wanting to keep them all?"

Adeline tilted her head to one side, unconsciously mimicking Thomas. "What would you want it for, Robert?"

"My studies, miss. The architecture of this house is very unique; the different levels and that sunroom on the other side facing out to sea. Beautiful."

Adeline smiled, appreciating the young man's interest. Beside her, Thomas coughed and she could tell he was feeling jealous again.

"Choose whichever one you like best, Robert," she said firmly. "You deserve it. The work you've done on the gallery and balcony alone shows what a fine architect you're going to be. Is there a scholarship for your studies?"

"No, miss. But I'm saving up." Still holding her painting, he looked carefully at the others and chose one. "Might I have this one?"

"Yes."

Robert gave her a happy grin like his grandfather's and hurried off to take her painting upstairs.

"You're spoiling the boy," Thomas grumbled.

"I am not. And I'm going to make certain he gets to go to school."

"How?"

Adeline shrugged. "I'll think of something. What's more important is I've seen the last clue we need. It's in the painting I chose."

Samuel and Ham came into the room. Ham held the reframed painting of Thomas's garden and Samuel held a beautiful antique chandelier. They both proudly showed their possessions to Adeline.

She admired Samuel's choice of chandelier and thanked Ham for getting Old Boy to work so quickly and beautifully on the new frame for the painting of the garden. Pleased, the men took their work into the dining room and she followed. Thomas was right behind her.

By the time the men were ready to leave at five, the house was taking on a new charm. It had always felt special to Adeline but now she could see and touch what she had only before imagined.

She waited until everyone had left for the day then turned to Thomas. "Well? What do you think?"

"I think you're very beautiful. And now you've made the house beautiful, too."

Adeline gave him a happy hug and they went upstairs to the gallery to inspect the painting.

Chapter Sixteen

"There. See the whirlpool on the water?" Adeline pointed at the painting and Thomas examined it closely.

He told her that he had been watching something on the television one day and came across a channel that appeared to broadcast only weather news and not accurately. But they had mentioned something that had stuck with him: a waterspout. "Some sort of swirl of water and air, powerful and destructive."

"And maybe magical?"

He stood back and nodded. "It could be construed as magical. Especially around here where ghosts and magic houses are considered quite normal, even expected."

"Then why do you keep hiding from everyone? They obviously believe or at least suspect that you're here."

He thought about her question. "I was afraid at first, waking up dead is a bit hard on one's self-confidence. For some time I didn't know how to make myself heard or visible. I used to practice in front of a mirror." He laughed. "At any rate, by the time I had got the hang of that, I thought I was forgotten and I didn't want to frighten anyone.

"Being 'the ghost of the house on the moor' became a habit, I suppose. It's surprisingly easy to drift through the years when you're alone."

"You're not alone now."

He put one arm about her shoulders. "No. Now I like to be alone, with you. And I like our privacy. Also, I don't seem to be a 'proper' ghost, whatever that may be. I think the magic of the house made me different. What do you think?"

"I think you may have been caught in the overlap of time when you were murdered and that's why you're not a 'proper' ghost. You're so very much more, Thomas." She turned to face him and they kissed.

"It makes me afraid of our future," Adeline confessed. "That I won't become a ghost when I die."

Thomas held her close to him. "Don't be afraid. Over the years that I've waited for you, I've come to find the magic of the house comforting. Let's trust in the magic. And let's not talk about it again for many years. You're still a young woman, you know. And we have time for all this nonsense later.

"For now, let's go and have a look at the painting of my garden. And we can talk about other things you enjoy."

"For instance?"

"Mystery! And what shall you ask Lady Moorhouse? And whatever will we do with that old barn?"

He whisked them to the dining room and Adeline asked him if he liked where she had told the men to hang the painting. Over the fireplace. And where should they hang the other painting of Lady Moorhouse? And did he like the new chandelier? But she knew he was only trying to distract her.

"When I told Mrs. Folly I was going to have the barn taken down, she said 'it's bad luck to knock down a barn.'"

"Yes. I heard. We can just leave it standing. It's your choice."

"All right." Taking his left hand, Adeline led him from the dining room and headed for the kitchen. "Mrs. Folly also said she'd left me something for dinner."

Thomas chuckled. "I thought you were going to learn how to cook."

"Eventually. We're rather busy right now, don't you think?" She went to the stove and lifted the lid off a soup pot. "Thomas?"

"Yes." He stood behind her and put his arms about her waist.

"I think Mrs. Folly's right."

"I wouldn't be at all surprised. What is she right about this time?"

"The murderer tried to escape across the lake. He headed into the waterspout and was drowned." She looked up at him with a slight smile of satisfaction. "The soup's ready."

They sat at the kitchen table to have dinner. "But why would anyone head deliberately into something as dangerous as a waterspout?" Thomas asked.

"Maybe he didn't know it was dangerous. Or maybe . . ."

Thomas waited. He knew the look on Adeline's face; she was thinking about how to solve a mystery again. And she was having fun. More importantly, she wasn't thinking about dying. She was happy. "Well?" Thomas ate some soup.

Adeline leaned forward. "Maybe he saw the magic, too. Maybe that's the treasure he had been looking for. And maybe he thought he could control it or take some of it with him." She paused to take a bite of bread. "What do you think of that?"

"Brilliant theory as usual."

"Thank you." Completely distracted now, Adeline gave Rex a gentle shove as he jumped up on the table. "Mind your manners, Rex, or I'll tell Mrs. Folly you're not being well-behaved."

Rex meowed and jumped down on the floor. He went to his dish of cat food, scratched the floor around it, then returned to the table and meowed again.

Thomas got up and went to the stove. He got a small saucer, poured a little soup on it and set it down on the floor. Rex immediately went to the saucer and lapped up the soup.

187

Adeline watched, amused. It seemed her life was beginning to take shape at last. In the mornings she rose early and met the men at the front doors. Mrs. Folly was already in the kitchen cooking and baking and readying lunch, counting the number of beer they had. Then Adeline would discuss what the men were doing that day and she and Thomas would watch or just wander off together. Often they went to the sunroom and waited until lunch.

Changes to original plans were approved by Adeline with Thomas telling her what he wanted. Yes, taking out the old stairs and rotting floor in the room above the Music Room would be better—Robert's suggestion—and then the Music Room would have a high ceiling and a skylight. No, she didn't want any more people in the house. If that meant the atrium wouldn't be ready for another three weeks, that was fine.

When Robert said he was very sorry but he would need a specialist for the atrium's new roof, she agreed only because she knew he wanted to do the best work possible. She had just finished making arrangements with her solicitor: Robert was going to be receiving an unexpected notice in the mail soon. He had won a scholarship for architectural school in the city.

She had changed her mind about the barn; they would leave it standing, but she would still need some sort of smaller, discreet building for her car.

After everyone had left, she and Thomas would stroll about the house, discussing the changes. And the day would end with a long bath, a beer for Adeline and a brandy for Thomas.

And cookies. And lovemaking that made them both feel alive.

As the weather stayed sunny and became warmer, Adeline worried less about murder and more about where were the books she'd ordered for the new library.

Thomas didn't' worry at all. Or so it seemed. He loved Adeline and sometimes, after dinner, he would play the piano for her.

"You said you could play," he told her one evening.

Adeline made a fist with her right hand and rolled it over a few of the black keys. Then she played a child's song with two fingers. "What do you think?"

"I think you should stick to cooking."

"But I haven't learned how yet. Mrs. Folly won't let me."

Thomas laughed, kissed her and whisked them to their bedroom. Rex was usually already there, asleep in the armchair.

The rhythm of her new life was wonderful to Adeline, but one night she felt restless. She got up, put on Thomas's housecoat, and went to the sunroom. She looked out at the lake.

"The moon's out tonight," said Thomas, coming up behind her.

She jumped and pretended to be annoyed. But she always felt happier, safer, knowing he was near.

They looked at the water together. "The books are supposed to arrive tomorrow," Adeline said absently, as Thomas wrapped his arms about her waist and held her against him. "We can unpack them together."

"All right."

"And the atrium is almost finished."

"I know."

"Thomas?"

"Yes."

"I'm feeling afraid again."

"I know that, too. But we're together and we will, as you said, win." He kissed the top of her head. "Anyway, you still have your picnic to plan."

"Mrs. Folly is organizing that."

"What about the guest list?"

"I told her to invite everybody. After all, everybody's been so kind. It's as if they feel the house is theirs, too."

Thomas had told her how, for many years, people from the town would take turns looking after the house when it stood empty. No one from the city wanted to live there for long. They complained the house was too cold; too much wind and too near the lake.

"I think we should go out on the lake," Adeline said suddenly.

"Whatever for?"

"To have a closer look at where the waters meet. We can do it on a day when the lake is calm. Ham has a boat. I'm sure he'll take me, us. And then we might get a closer look at the magic."

"That sounds dangerous."

"Do you really think so? I thought we should be as prepared as our villain."

"Ah, yes. Our villain. I'd quite forgotten about him. Well, I trust Ham. And I'll go with you to look after you."

Adeline leaned back into Thomas's warm embrace. "Yes. I know you will. I love how you look after me, Thomas. And I love you."

⸻

Waiting for the books to arrive in the morning proved frustrating and Adeline took advantage of the time to ask Ham when he might be bringing his boat to the lake.

"It's already moored at the dock, miss. I've been doing that for years. I hope you don't mind."

"Not at all. In fact, I wanted to ask a favor of you."

"Yes, miss?"

"I'd very much like to go out on the lake. Close to where the lake waters meet the sea."

"You've a wish to go fishing, have you, miss?"

"No. It's more of a sight-seeing tour."

"Well I don't see the harm of it as long this good weather holds. The lake waters are calm at this time of year; it'll be safe enough. But I must insist you wear a life-jacket, miss."

"Certainly, Ham. And thank you very much." Adeline tried to sound casual. "When do you think we might make the trip?"

He thought about that. "The trip doesn't take more than twenty minutes. We could go in the late afternoon today seeing as you're in a hurry. Although I'm thinking tomorrow might be better."

Adeline was disappointed that she hadn't been able to fool Ham and conceal her excitement. "Of course I'd like to go today because the weather has been so nice. But I have to wait until the books are delivered," she said, trying to maintain her role as Lady of the Manor. "There isn't a rush and you're the expert."

"Tomorrow late afternoon might do fine then, miss."

"That's suits me just right, Ham. And thank you again."

There was the sound of rumbling outside the open front doors. It was a large van with the books Adeline had ordered. She gave up hiding her excitement and hurried to the doors. A stout man with the end of a cigar in his mouth stepped down from the cab of the van. He held a clipboard in one chubby hand.

"Lady Moorhouse?" he asked.

For a moment, Adeline's excitement left her. She couldn't answer.

Ham stepped forward and took charge. "That's Miss Parker to you, Mister—" he peered at a faded name label on the man's jacket— "Green." He pointed at the cigar. "And there's no smoking in this house. And you're late as well. Miss Parker has been kept waiting a week longer than she should have had to wait."

Mr. Green quickly rid himself of his cigar, accepting Ham's admonishment and saying between the weather and the bad roads he had been slowed down.

"The weather's been fine. And the roads are good enough. Now let's open up your vehicle and see how many boxes you'll be unloading." He looked over his shoulder at Adeline for her approval.

She stepped forward. "There should be twelve boxes," she said, smoothing her hair. "A total of seventy books. Oh, and a globe with a stand."

Mr. Green looked at his clipboard and nodded. "Yes, Miss Parker. Where would you like me to unload the boxes?"

Confidence restored, Adeline said she wanted the boxes taken upstairs to the library. The globe and its stand as well.

Mrs. Folly had come from her domain of the kitchen, wiping her hands on her apron. "Here now. What's the commotion, Ham? Why is my morning being interrupted?"

He explained and Mrs. Folly scowled at Mr. Green. "You'd best get started unloading right away and not waste more time just standing around. And don't be banging into the walls or dropping anything or leaving a mess behind. I keep this house nice and clean and you'll be leaving it that way."

Mr. Green looked from Mrs. Folly to Ham to Adeline and then back to Mrs. Folly. He seemed to reach the decision that it was Mrs. Folly he had better listen to and gave her a quick nod of his bald head. "I'll get started right away."

Mrs. Folly ignored Mr. Green now and spoke to Adeline. "I've a good pot of coffee wasting on the stove and lunch to make so I'll be getting back to my kitchen now."

"Thank you, Mrs. Folly," Adeline said with sincerity.

Not answering, Mrs. Folly paused long enough to issue orders to Ham to get the 'boys' to help with the unloading.

Ham nodded and hurried up the stairs to get Samuel and Robert.

Adeline stood back and waited and watched with Thomas beside her. The unloading went quickly and in an orderly manner. Adeline managed to hide her happiness when she saw the globe and its stand being unloaded.

"I still don't see why we need that," Thomas commented.

"Because I've always wanted one," Adeline whispered back to him. Facing her workers, Adeline announced that she'd wait in the library and, once the boxes were open for inspection, she wanted to take out the books herself. She headed for the stairs, aware that at least one of the men was following her with a heavy box. It turned out to be Robert. He asked where she would like the globe set and she told him she thought by the window would do nicely.

"You're really enjoying being the Lady of the Manor," Thomas commented.

Adeline said nothing, not wanting to be caught talking to herself or so it would appear to the men working around her. What she was really enjoying was being looked after by everyone, and knowing they did so because they liked her. She had spent too many years being unloved not to recognize when she was liked and appreciated.

An hour later, Mr. Green was carefully cutting open each box and Adeline was looking inside to make certain the books had been properly wrapped and packed. When that was done, she signed the invoice and Mr. Green, not daring to shake such an important woman's hand, thanked her and said if that was all then he'd be going.

"That will be all. Thank you."

Mr. Green departed. Ham, Samuel and Robert went back to work, and Adeline felt momentarily alone as she stood among the open boxes in the library.

"I'm right here," Thomas said quietly. "You were marvelous."

She turned to him. "Was I? Mr. Green caught me off guard when he called me Lady Moorhouse."

"I saw that. But you recovered nicely. Now, where's the book I ordered?" Thomas started poking through the boxes, but Adeline stopped him. "We have to wait until this evening, Thomas."

He drooped. "All right. I know you're right. It's just—"

"You've waited such a long time," Adeline finished his sentence. Understanding, she asked which book in particular he wanted to find. He said he didn't remember the title but it was an older book that had to be special ordered. She looked at the packing list Mr. Green had given her. "It should be in that box over there." She pointed.

Thomas smiled and kissed her quickly on her right cheek before becoming invisible. Mrs. Folly was coming down the hall. She entered the library and said that she'd be serving lunch early and leaving early too.

"Oh? Something special to attend?"

"My daughter's wedding."

"You shouldn't have come at all today, Mrs. Folly."

"I'm not one to shirk my hours, but a woman's got only one daughter to marry off."

Biting back a smile, Adeline agreed and told Mrs. Folly there was a card for her daughter on the kitchen table.

Mrs. Folly thanked her and left the library. Adeline waited for a minute and then faced the room. She knew Thomas was standing nearby somewhere.

"Maybe we can take our boat trip this afternoon after all?"

Thomas became visible. "Ham said tomorrow."

"Oh, but I've waited, too, Thomas."

"To go out on the lake?"

"No. To start solving our mystery again."

"But . . . but you've been busy with the house. Why worry about it now?"

Adeline walked toward him, puzzled. "Don't you want to solve the mystery anymore?"

Thomas glanced away then, stuffing his hands into his pockets, he faced her. "It's just that it's starting to look like it might be dangerous. I love you, Adeline. I don't want to risk your life for a silly mystery that no one has cared about for centuries."

Adeline understood but she persisted. "I care about the mystery, Thomas, and I won't be in any danger because you'll be with me. And I love you too. Don't you know that by now? Don't you understand how right I feel when I'm with you?"

He gave in. If Ham agreed, Thomas would agree.

Satisfied, Adeline left the library to look for Ham. Invisible, Thomas was by her side.

Ham was sweeping up the floor in the Music Room. The French doors had been installed and he had cleaned each window pane carefully. Then he had taken the time to clean the small window again. The new skylight poured sunlight into the room, but Ham wanted everything to be extra nice. He knew Miss Parker really cared about the house and he was glad of that and happy to help her in any way he could. He looked up as she entered the room.

Adeline stopped and gazed about her in appreciation. "It's beautiful, Ham."

"You should be telling Robert, miss, seeing as how it was your idea and his. I'm just the handyman of the projects."

"You're much more than that, Hamlet. Don't think for a minute that I don't notice how much attention you pay to details and helping me find just the right person to do a special job; like Old Boy. The painting looks lovely now. In fact, the entire house is so much more than I could have hoped for or imagined."

"Thank you, miss." Ham wiped his hands on the cleaning cloth he had been using. "It's been a pleasure working on this house. I always hoped someone like you would come along and appreciate what it once was and make it possible to be that way again.

"It's almost done now. Just a few details left to attend."

"Yes." Adeline went to look out the window, then turned to Ham. "Do you think we could go out in your boat this afternoon and not wait until tomorrow? Mrs. Folly's leaving early."

Ham considered his employer. *Something is troubling the lady. She's more than sightseeing on her mind.* "We could give it a try, miss. I can go down to the docks now and look at the lake. Check the waves. I wouldn't want to give you a bumpy tour."

Adeline smiled. "After lunch will be soon enough, Ham. Mrs. Folly will be serving it now. You should go and eat before she takes away the beer."

He chuckled. "Aye. She's a tight-fisted one is our Mrs. Folly. But she loves this house as much as I do, maybe more."

He set down the cloth on a table and went to the door. "I'll check the lake for you right after lunch."

"Thank you, Ham."

He left and Thomas became visible again. He couldn't shake a feeling of anxiety. "Are you certain you want to do this? Is it really necessary?"

"I'm not certain it's necessary, but yes, I really want to go out on the lake and have a closer look at that spooky spot."

Thomas rolled his eyes. "Must you say 'spooky?'"

"Yes." She waited for more objections but Thomas had already decided to be more supportive. They had started out to solve the mystery of his murder and found themselves in the middle of something much bigger, possibly worse. And still Adeline remained almost fearless and, he had not failed to notice, determined.

"Don't eat too much," he said. "Or you'll be hanging your head over the side of the boat and miss the view."

Adeline laughed. "The same goes for you. I'm going to get us a plate of food and a beer to share. We can whisk it to the sunroom. Then we'll go and hear what Ham has to say about the waves. All right?"

Hiding his reluctance, Thomas smiled and agreed. He stood for a minute looking out the window at the lake and wondering why it made him feel uncomfortable. Then he hurried after Adeline.

Chapter Seventeen

Thomas sat in the boat beside Adeline. When he had first stepped onto the boat, it had rocked and he had been concerned that Ham might notice. But Ham was making certain Adeline was comfortable and wearing her lifejacket properly.

Thomas looked at Adeline. She was smiling and happy. She wasn't just investigating their mystery, she was enjoying being out on the lake, feeling the wind as it came up off the water. Thomas tried to relax.

"You're not worried at all, are you?" he said.

"No, I'm not worried. I'm having fun. I've never been on a boat like this before. I've been on a yacht but that doesn't count."

"Why not?"

"Too big. Too fancy. Not like this. This is wonderful."

The ride in the boat was bumpy, but Ham did his best as he steered his small boat toward the place where the waters met.

Adeline heard the sound of the engine change and Ham shout to her that they had arrived. She stood up and looked at the surface of the lake. It was strange to see it so close; the water slapped the sides of the boat. It also seemed to slap against itself in a single spot just ahead of the boat. She lifted her right hand to shield her eyes from the late afternoon sunlight.

"What do you think?" she asked Thomas.

"I think I feel sick."

"Really? You didn't eat much lunch."

She felt him clutch her left hand, not realizing he had got up and moved around her to look at the water.

Ham came up beside Adeline. "What's that you said, miss?"

"I said, I think I must have eaten too much at lunch. I guess I'm feeling a little seasick. I'll be fine. It's very beautiful here." She barely heard Ham as he pointed at the water, the land and then out to sea, telling her something that she couldn't pay attention to because the grip Thomas had on her hand had tightened.

"Get me back to the house," Thomas said in her left ear.

She was about to repeat his words to Ham when Thomas slowly began to become visible.

"Thomas. You're becoming visible," she whispered.

"I can't stop it. I feel like something horrible is happening to me. Adeline. Get me back to the house. Now."

She turned to Ham. He was staring at Thomas. "Bless me. It's Lord Éclair himself."

"Yes it is," Adeline spoke fast; now she was worried. "Take us back to the house, Ham. Immediately. Something's terribly wrong. Please. Help."

Not bothering to ask questions, Ham hurried to the wheel and began turning the boat around.

Thomas was now completely visible and audible. He gasped as if he couldn't breathe. Adeline grabbed him about the waist with one arm and put his right arm over her shoulders. "Hold onto me! Thomas! Thomas!"

Feeling desperate, she called to Ham. "Hurry! Please! Go faster."

Ham increased the boat's speed to maximum and it leapt across the waves, heading for the dock in the distance.

"Can you sit down?" Adeline asked Thomas.

"I don't know." His voice was strange: strangled and weak. "I'll try." He leaned against Adeline and she struggled to help him sit down.

"What's happening? Thomas, talk to me. Keep talking to me."

"I don't know. I think it's the magic. It doesn't seem to agree with me." He tried to laugh but coughed instead.

Adeline's worry escalated to fear. She called to Ham again. "Can we go any faster?"

"I'm sorry, miss. I'm pushing the motor for all she's worth. We're well away from that place now if that's the cause of the trouble for his lordship. He should be feeling better soon."

Adeline looked at Thomas. He was pale but seemed a little steadier. "We're away from the magic, Thomas. We're heading back to the house as fast as we can. You'll feel better any minute now, darling. Talk to me. How are you feeling now?"

"Better." Thomas tried to smile, but he still held onto Adeline's shoulders and leaned his weight against her.

"Oh, god. I'm so sorry, Thomas. This was so stupid of me. Please be all right."

After a few minutes, he straightened a little. "I'm all right. But I can still feel the magic. We'd better get me into the house. And I don't think I can make myself invisible."

"You don't have to. There's no one there but Rex. And no one here but Ham and me."

"You've never called me, darling, before," Thomas said and gave her one of his lopsided smiles.

Tears streamed down Adeline's cheeks. She kissed him quickly. "I'll call you darling every day of my life if that's what you want. And I'll give up all this nonsense about solving a mystery that's centuries old. I promise."

"Oh no you won't. We'll solve it together, remember?" Thomas managed to look up. They were getting near the dock and he could breathe again.

"Is his lordship feeling better, miss?" Ham asked. "We're just nearing the dock now."

"Are you feeling better, darling?" Fear colored Adeline's voice.

"Yes. Much. But I need to get inside the house."

Ham was docking the boat. He tied it fast and hurried back to where Adeline sat with Thomas. "We're here, miss. Let me help you and his lordship now."

"Yes. Please."

Ham put one arm about Thomas's waist and helped him to stand up. Thomas, still unsteady, leaned a little forward, stumbling as they climbed from the boat and onto the dock.

"It's just a little further now." Adeline tried to smile. "We're almost at the house. Then I'll get you a beer."

"Brandy," Thomas mumbled.

"You're feeling worse again." Alarmed, Adeline looked at Ham. "We have to get him inside the house, to his side of the house."

"I understand, miss. It's just a few more steps, your lordship. You're doing fine. You just don't have any sea legs."

Thomas didn't answer, saving his strength to make it up the slope to the house. He could see the front door. "Perhaps I should try to whisk us there," he said to Adeline.

"No! Don't! Please, Thomas. Give yourself time to recover. Stay with me." She looked at Ham beseechingly. "We're just about there, aren't we?"

"Yes, miss. I'll support his lordship while you get the door."

"I can't let go of him. I'll hold him, you get the door."

"Would somebody just get the bloody door open?" Thomas's voice was stronger.

"I will." Ham unlocked the door on the right and quickly pushed both doors open for Thomas and Adeline to enter together.

"We're home!" Adeline started to cry again. "I'm sorry, Ham. Please help me get him upstairs to his room."

"I will, miss." Ham put Thomas's left arm over his shoulders and he and Adeline helped Thomas up the stairs.

With each step Thomas straightened until, at the top of the stairs, he stopped and took a deep breath. "Thank you, Hamlet. You're a good man."

"Thank you, your lordship. May I say it's a pleasure meeting you?"

Thomas smiled and Adeline hoped he was feeling better at last.

"I think I should sit down," Thomas said suddenly.

"Here." Adeline, with Ham's assistance, steered Thomas to a chair by the wall. "It's a good thing I haven't bothered to have this old chair moved yet."

"We'll keep it right here always." Thomas sat down. "For my old age, as it were."

"Definitely for mine," Adeline said. She sat down beside him and wiped at her face.

Ham gave her a handkerchief.

"Thank you, Ham." She looked steadily into his eyes. "You must never, never speak of this to anyone. Never. Promise me."

Ham touched one hand to his cap. "Not to worry, miss. I promise you that I will never speak a word of this to anyone. On my life, I swear."

"Where's the damned brandy?" Thomas asked, looking about. "We need a table here."

"I'll pour you your damned brandy when we get you to our room you sweet fool. Come on." Adeline stood up and Ham helped her walk Thomas slowly down the hallways that led to their bedroom. She opened the door with one hand and they took Thomas straight to the bed.

He lay down, then grabbed for Adeline's right hand as she started to turn away. "Adeline. Don't go."

"I'm not going anywhere except to the table to get you a brandy. Or do you want the whole bottle?"

"No sympathy at all," Thomas teased her.

"None." Adeline waited until he let go of her hand, then went quickly to the table and poured a large brandy for him. Returning to the bed, she saw that Ham had helped Thomas to sit up and lean back against the pillows, adding an extra one for support. She handed Thomas his glass of brandy and he drank it down.

"Now I feel better," he announced. "Thank you, Hamlet."

"You're most welcome, your lordship." He turned to Adeline. "Is there anything else I can do for you, miss? Perhaps you'd like a brandy yourself?"

"I'm fine," Adeline lied.

"Bring her a beer, Ham, there's a good chap. And some of those cookies she likes so she can get crumbs everywhere."

"Yes, your lordship. I'll be right back, miss." Touching his cap, Ham hurried from the bedroom. As he left, Rex trotted in and jumped up on the bed.

"Oh no you don't," said Adeline. "You have the chair, remember?" She gave the cat a gentle shove and Rex jumped from the bed and went to his armchair.

"Thomas?"

"Yes."

"Are you really feeling better now? Would you like another brandy?"

"Yes to both. And Adeline?"

"Yes, darling?"

"Thank you for taking care of me."

She smiled and bit her lower lip to stop from crying again. "It's my pleasure, your lordship."

"No sympathy at all," Thomas said.

"None," she answered, then added, "I love you, Thomas Éclair."

———————◆———————

It was sometime in the middle of the night. Thomas had drifted off to sleep while Adeline sat next to him. She was keeping a vigil, making certain that the man she loved with all her heart was going to live.

"It's not easy having a brush with death," Thomas had commented earlier after Ham had left. "Especially when one is already dead."

"You're not dead," Adeline insisted, brushing his hair off his forehead with the fingers of her right hand.

"Then what am I?"

"The man I love. My knight in shining armor. And whatever else you might be, we won't worry about it. Not now, not ever. And we'll never go out on the lake again."

"I wonder what happened to me out there?" Thomas had turned his head a little, as if he could see the lake in his mind.

"You said you could feel the magic. It must have interfered with the magic that holds you here. I don't know." She had looked down, feeling ashamed that she had rushed to do what she wanted and not waited and thought it through more.

"I think that's a very good theory," Thomas said. "Now kiss me. I'm tired. After all this time, I'm feeling very tired."

She had leaned over him and given him a kiss on the lips. "Of course you're tired. It's not every day you almost die. Go to sleep."

His eyes were already closed. Adeline knew she couldn't check for a pulse. She decided to watch him, watch him sleep and breathe and, in some magical way, be alive.

Thomas opened his eyes a few hours later. He sat up a bit. "What time is it? Is it morning?"

"No. And I don't wear a watch. And we don't have a clock in here. I think it must be about two in the morning."

Sitting up more, Thomas reached for her right hand and held it gently in his. "Have you been awake all this time? Looking after me?"

"Yes."

Thomas lay back down, moving over a little. "Lie down next to me. I don't need sleep, but you do."

For a change, Adeline didn't argue. She lay down next to Thomas, putting her head on his right shoulder and her right arm across his chest. She closed her eyes, but she didn't sleep.

After a little while, she lifted her head. "Thomas?"

"Yes."

"Why do you think Mr. Green called me Lady Moorhouse? It was quite a shock."

"I could see that it was. I'm sorry. It was my fault. That's another mystery I can solve for you right now."

"How?"

"When you were placing the order for some of the books, I added one that was listed in the back of the library book. I think I accidentally put the name on the order list because it was in my mind at the time."

"What's the book about?"

"Lady Moorhouse."

At that, Adeline sat up straight. "I'll go and get it now."

"We'll go together. Tomorrow."

Again, Adeline didn't argue. She had learned a frightening lesson: Thomas could leave her. It would be against his will but the magic outside the house was dangerous and, just as Thomas had warned her, their mystery was dangerous, too. She had to be more careful. Lying down again, she closed her eyes, still awake and wondering what they were to do next.

"I know you're awake," Thomas said quietly. "And you're thinking about the book. It's the one I was looking for. I was going to unpack it earlier, remember?"

"Yes. And I was a fool and we went out on the lake and risked your life." She almost sat up again, but Thomas held her next to him, his chin resting on top of her head.

"You're anything but a fool. You are, in fact, very clever. It's just a book that tells a bit of history about Lady Moorhouse. I thought it might be helpful, perhaps give us some sort of advantage, before you speak to her again."

"Then you still want me to do that?"

"I told you, we're going to solve our little mystery together."

Adeline tried to relax but her curiosity made her restless. Finally she drew away from Thomas and got up from their bed.

"Where are you going?"

"To get that book from the library."

"I'll whisk us there."

"Oh, no. No whisking until tomorrow. After all, you wouldn't do that with me when my hand was injured."

"Is it injured again?"

"No, but—"

"Then I can whisk us to the library or go by myself and be back before you have time to miss me."

"Please don't, Thomas. We'll go together in the morning. I mean, later this morning. Oh, you know what I mean."

"Yes. Then come lie down with me again."

Adeline did so, feeling a little better. They were together and in agreement again. Together, they would solve their mystery of the house and maybe even learn more about the magic out on the lake. But from a distance. And carefully. She closed her eyes again.

"Thomas?"

"Yes."

"I'm sorry about today. I was wrong."

"I'm not sorry. And I don't think you were wrong. We had to find out more and we did. And now we're safe again and everything is going to be fine."

"Is it really?"

"Yes."

"How do you know?"

"Because I happen to be very clever, too. Now go to sleep."

Adeline snuggled closer to him. Eyes closed, she listened to him breathe and finally drifted into a light sleep. It was Rex who brought her wide awake. He was meowing at the door, wanting to be let out.

That was when Adeline realized she was alone in the bed. "Thomas!"

"I'm right here." He was standing at the window. "It's going to be sunny again today, but it might rain before the picnic."

Adeline went to him and he hugged her. They looked out the window together.

"We'll let Mrs. Folly worry about the weather," Adeline said.

Rex meowed again and she went to open the door. He hurried away and she recalled that Mrs. Folly left the kitchen window open a bit for him.

Thomas came up behind her. "Do you want to go to the library now?"

"No. Not yet." She ran her fingers through her hair. "I have to freshen up. Change my clothes. Maybe eat something." She smiled up at him. "You're feeling better, aren't you?"

"Much."

"Do you feel well enough to whisk us to my old room? I need to shower and wash my hair. We can walk instead. I don't mind."

Thomas reached for her right hand, clasping it with his left. A second later, they were in her old room, standing together by the window. "There. See? I'm all better."

"And we didn't even end up in the shower."

"That's because you didn't rush me."

Adeline started to undress. "I don't rush. I just . . ."

"Charge ahead?"

Adeline tossed him a look of annoyance, not really feeling annoyed and knowing what he said was true. "I may be a little impulsive."

Thomas laughed. He sat down on the window seat, intending to wait while Adeline showered. But the view of the lake was disquieting. He tried to think of a distraction and remembered that Adeline had left a few clothes in the closet, still pretending that she used the room. He got up and chose a dress that he thought was pretty and put it on the bed.

A very wet Adeline came into the bedroom, a towel wrapped about her. "I can't wear that," she objected.

"Why not? It's a perfectly pretty dress. You wear trousers far too often."

"I do not. Anyway I can't unpack books in a dress."

And their day began.

It was just before lunch. Mrs. Folly was in the kitchen and the men were working in the atrium. Thomas and Adeline were unpacking books in the library. She stopped abruptly when she heard her name called.

"Disappear," she whispered to Thomas.

"I will not disappear. I'll just become invisible to the casual eye." Thomas disappeared.

Adeline smoothed her hair and her skirt. It was a compromise from the dress Thomas had picked out: a skirt and blouse. It was pretty but practical.

"Miss Adeline?" It was Ham. He knocked on the frame of the library's open door.

She looked up and gave him a big smile. "Yes, Ham. Come in. What is it?"

He looked over his shoulder, then entered the library. "I was just wondering, if it's not being too bold of me, if his lordship is feeling better today?"

"Yes. He's quite himself now, Ham."

"That's grand." He fidgeted. "Begging your pardon, miss, but might I have the rest of the afternoon off? We've made great progress in the atrium this morning. It's ready for you to have a look at."

"Of course you can, Ham. Are you all right?"

"He's worried about his boat," Thomas said. "He must have pushed the engine too hard to get me back so quickly. Tell him I want to buy him a new one." He nudged her with one elbow.

"I'm fine, miss," Ham answered, not hearing Thomas. "But my boat needs a bit of work before I can use it again for fishing. The engine's not sounding good."

"Yes. You did have to push it hard yesterday." She took a step forward as Thomas gave her another nudge. "His lordship would like to buy you a new boat."

"He's had his eye on a bigger boat for years now," Thomas remarked.

"A bigger one," Adeline clarified. "He knows you've had your eye on a new boat for a few years now."

"That's very generous of his lordship, miss. Please thank him for me, but it's not at all necessary. I just did what needed to be done to help his lordship and you. You needn't pay me for such a thing as that."

"Then we'll just give you a bonus. Samuel and Robert, too."

"It's called a boon," Thomas said.

"Do you mean a boon, miss?"

"Yes. Exactly. A boon. But do take the afternoon off. In fact, I'll come with you now and you can show me the atrium."

"That would be fine, miss." Ham looked very happy.

"I still haven't found my book," Thomas complained.

"We'll find it this afternoon," Adeline whispered.

"What's that, miss?" Ham paused in the doorway.

"Oh, I was just talking to myself. Again."

Ham looked at the empty library and touched one hand to his head. Then he looked at Adeline. "Of course, miss. I do it all the time meself."

He entered the hallway and Adeline and Thomas followed him.

Hamlet's tour centered on the plants and flowers he had chosen for the atrium, explaining that the little tree had been dying and he thought it best to replant it in the outside garden. Adeline agreed and then Robert took over the tour. He pointed up at the new double-glass domed roof, describing its structure. Most of that was lost on her, but not Robert's enthusiasm.

The enthusiasm of his grandfather, Samuel, was also apparent when he proudly told her that Robert had won a scholarship to go to architectural school in the city. "Of course he'll be studying hard through the summer, miss," he said, then he showed her the new doors they'd installed, the floor, too. "With a drain for the water sprays. We only installed two, but we can do more if you wish."

"Mrs. Folly didn't want your new table and chairs getting wet," Ham put in.

Adeline looked at the table for two almost in the center of the atrium. It was almost identical to the few tables she had ordered for the gallery: small and round with two chairs that were designed to be comfortable but pleasing to look at as well.

She felt overwhelmed to see more of her dreams come true. She included Thomas by repeating what he said and told the men how pleased she was with all they'd accomplished. And that she wanted them to take the afternoon off. "Tomorrow is soon enough for any details left to be done. And I hope to see all of you at Mrs. Folly's picnic on Saturday."

"We'll be there, miss," Samuel assured her. "It's me that'll be making the fire for the salmon."

"If I can catch you a big enough one," Ham said.

Samuel slapped him on the back and said they'd use his boat while Ham's was being repaired. When he asked him what had happened to the engine, Ham shrugged and said it was just old and time maybe to get the new boat he'd been saving for.

"That's the spirit," Samuel said.

Robert agreed. He looked shyly at Adeline and asked if he could have a minute of her time to explain why he'd chosen a particular design and place for the switches that would operate the special lights and water sprays. "Of course it was Ham that installed them," he said.

"I know. But you designed it; remember that."

They walked away from the other two men and Robert began talking about the wall and the waterproof cover that protected the switches and controls. Then he dropped his voice to a whisper. "It was you that entered my name for the scholarship, wasn't it, miss? I thank you for it with all my heart."

"I might have mentioned your name to a friend, Robert. There's no need to thank me. You'll have hard work ahead of you. But you're very talented and I know you'll make your grandfather proud."

"That I will, miss. And you as well."

Ham and Samuel joined them; the men went into the dining room to have their lunch and Adeline left. She walked slowly along the hallway. It still needed 'one more lick of paint' as Ham said, but she thought the brighter color lovely. She went into the kitchen to get a tray from Mrs. Folly, telling her she was going to eat lunch in the gallery, then continue unpacking the books.

Mrs. Folly seemed to have little interest in books, and she had already told Adeline that morning how much her daughter appreciated the wedding boon and the wardrobe and that the wedding had been 'fine enough.'

"You do know you'll have to be joining your guests at the picnic. Eating with them, too. None of this hiding yourself away as you've been doing all these weeks."

"I haven't been hiding. I've been . . . staying out of the way."

Mrs. Folly straightened her apron and gave Adeline her lunch tray. "I'll be taking the afternoon off, if you don't have a need for me."

"That'll be fine. Still working hard on the picnic?"

Mrs. Folly nodded and went to take the men their beer.

As Adeline passed the dining room, she heard the men laughing and joking with each other. "I hope they enjoy the picnic," she said to Thomas.

"Of course they will. Why are you nervous?"

"I'm not good at social events, small talk and pretending I'm interested when I'm not. And I'm shy, too."

"Shy? Don't be ridiculous. Anyway, you'll be interested because the subject will be our home and the renovations. The talk will be anything but small and it's not an event, it's a picnic. I promise you, you'll have fun."

He gave her a nudge in the back. "Now come on. I'm hungry."

They went up the stairs to the gallery. "Mrs. Folly must think I have an enormous appetite," Adeline said, noticing the tray held one plate with two sandwiches, a plate with fresh slices of melon and cucumber, and two bottles of beer with a small plate of cookies beside them.

"She knows I'm here," Thomas said.

"How? I've kept up our masquerade, haven't I? I'm sure Maude wouldn't have said anything."

"Don't worry. I think Mrs. Folly has always suspected I'm here somewhere even though I've always stayed out of her way. And until you arrived, she's never said a word about me. At least, not that I know of."

"You can't end a sentence with a preposition," Adeline teased.

"I'm allowed."

"Why?"

"Because I'm the ghost. Remember?"

"Not with me, you're not. Remember?"

Thomas smiled. "Let's have our lunch. Then we can look for that book."

After lunch, when the men and Mrs. Folly had left and the house was quiet once again, Adeline and Thomas went to the library. They found the book.

Chapter Eighteen

Thomas sat on a chair in the library and read the book. Adeline was having fun unpacking books. Each one she unwrapped felt like a present. She ran her fingers over the title, then set the book carefully on the new bookshelves. She decided to arrange them according to the color of the books' spines and dustcovers instead of alphabetically.

"If you do it like that, we'll never find what we want when we want it," Thomas said, looking up from his reading. "And I told you I would help."

"Oh, don't spoil it for me; keep reading. Just be sure to read aloud when you come across something important." She looked at the spine of a book that was gold and pretty, deciding to put it at an angle. "As for the rest of the books, I like them this way. It's artistic."

Thomas smiled and returned to his reading. "There's not as much here as I'd hoped." He flipped through the pages a little, then stopped and read silently for several minutes.

Turning a page more slowly, he started to read aloud.

"On the night of her Art Party, when the paintings were to be given to her guests—"

Adeline paused, a book in one hand. She turned to Thomas. "Given to her guests? She meant to give the paintings away?"

"To her guests," Thomas repeated and continued reading aloud. "One of her guests, Lord Sebastian Éclair, became noticeably absent from the party shortly before midnight. After a search of the house, he was found dead in a guest room. It was thought he was murdered, perhaps poisoned, by one of the lady's jealous lovers.

"When the body was discovered, Lady Moorhouse was missing. She had last been seen on the edge of the cliff and thought to have thrown herself into the lake in a fit of despair.

"Good lord." Thomas looked at the book as if he'd never seen it before. "Whatever you paid for this, it seems well worth it now."

"Keep reading, please."

"The man suspected to be the murderer, the artist who painted the portraits, escaped in a boat and was drowned. His body was never found.

"However, the body of his assistant was found," Thomas paused, "in the garden!" He slammed the book shut. "In the bloody garden. That can't be right. Ham tends my garden regularly and he's never found a body."

"Of course not. It would have been taken away by the authorities." Adeline put one more book on a shelf and stood back to admire her work, then she went to sit beside Thomas. "I have an idea."

"I've no doubt you do."

"Well, we know we have to stop Lady Moorhouse from throwing herself into the lake. We have to make certain she runs away with Sebastian. I think we should give the paintings away as she intended."

"To whom and why?"

"To our guests at the picnic. Because then, any possible spell of magic will be broken."

"And what do we do with our villain who has now committed more than one murder?"

"Oh, we let him get away."

"We what?" Thomas stood up and slammed the book down on a table beside him.

"I mean, we let him think he's getting away. In murder mysteries, the murderer always thinks he's gotten away with murder and gets careless at the last minute.

"In this case, desperate and reckless, he sails a boat out onto the lake, probably heading for the waterspout. In his arrogance, he probably thinks he can control the magic. He can't and . . ." She looked at the book on the table. "And what almost happened to you happens to Romanivich instead. The magic gets him; he dies. We win. I know it's awful of me to be relieved, but I can't help it, Thomas. He's cruel and a murderer."

Thomas stared at her. "Brilliant. That's absolutely brilliant. Tell me, love of my life and death, how did you become so wonderfully clever?"

"Watching lots of mystery movies on television when my husband left me alone to see his mistress."

"Lucky for me the man was such an idiot."

Adeline stood up and went to the balcony. She looked down at the Great Room. "You know, I don't think I ever loved him. I wanted to get away from the cloying stuffiness of my family, doing everything that was 'proper' and all that. I wanted more."

Thomas went to stand beside her. "What more did you want?"

"Love, attention, excitement; everything he promised. But I only ended up lonely and unhappy and unloved."

"I love you, Adeline."

She smiled. "And I love you, Thomas."

He kissed her lightly. "Come on. Let's go get our supper."

She laughed, then stepped back, suddenly serious. "Thomas?"

"Yes."

"Do you think that, because I'm being exposed to this overlap in time, I'll be like you when I die?"

He nodded. "I do think that very thing. Yes. It's all mixed up with the magic that's in the house. The more we restore the house, the stronger the magic becomes. Can't you feel it?"

"Sometimes I think I can."

Thomas reached to hold her right hand and whisked them to the kitchen. After dinner, he studied Adeline, leaning back in his chair, arms folded across his chest. "You still haven't told me all of your idea. I'm guessing it involves aiding Lady Moorhouse in her escape."

Adeline stood up and started clearing the dishes from the kitchen table. "It does. But it depends on you."

"On me? How?"

"Did you really mean to give me your mother's jewelry?"

"I did. It's yours." He tilted his head to one side. "You want to give it to Lady Moorhouse, don't you?"

"Not all of it. Just a necklace and a pair of earrings. They'll have to be very valuable, of course."

"Of course."

"Something I could wear when I meet with her again. Then, at the right moment, I'll give them to Lady Moorhouse so that she and Sebastian can run away. They'll have to be secretive for a long time, perhaps the rest of their lives. She can't publicly divorce her husband for being unfaithful when she's been the same; she'd lose everything."

"What about Sebastian's money?"

"I doubt he has much, if any. Just a title. What's it say in the book?"

"Only that he was the murder victim. Or rather, the first body to be discovered the night of the party."

Returning to the table, Adeline sat down. "What do you think of my idea?"

"I think it's very good. And very likely to work, as well." He leaned across the table. "You are a romantic, Adeline."

"Yes. But only where you and I are concerned. As for Lady Moorhouse," she shrugged her shoulders, "I'm just being practical."

"Come on." Thomas stood up. "Get your beer and don't forget the cookies."

"Where are we going?"

"To our bedroom. I didn't make love to you last night. I want to make up for that tonight."

"Isn't it a bit early?" she teased as she put several assorted cookies on a plate.

Taking the plate, Thomas held onto her right hand. "It's never too early for lovemaking, or too late for that matter. You are preoccupied with time."

"I'm not preoccupied with time," Adeline feigned objection as Thomas led her to their bed. "Maybe a little preoccupied with our mystery. Maybe a little impulsive."

"Be impulsive then. With me. Now."

She kissed him and they fell back on the bed together.

***

For Thomas, the morning came too soon. After decades of drifting through the days and nights, he had found not only love, but sleep. He decided he had missed it very much and did not enjoy waking up early. Watching Adeline as she went about getting ready, he relaxed in their bed, Rex beside him.

"You're spoiling that cat," Adeline said as she pulled on a pair of pants.

"And you are wearing trousers again." He looked at Rex. "Didn't I tell her that she wore trousers too often?"

"Well, I'll be wearing a dress tomorrow at the picnic. Today, I have to be not only the Lady of the Manor but the foreman, too."

Late at night the two of them had discussed what Robert had suggested for Adeline's car: a one car garage with a cement floor. It would provide her car with the necessary protection from the weather and, if it was built on one side of the road just before the house, it would allow Adeline to access it easily and safely. He had said he could even paint the outside green and brown to blend with the color of the moor. Or a bit of grey and pink to accent the house.

"He's sounding more like a designer than an architect," Thomas had complained.

"I think design is part of architecture, isn't it? Anyway, I like the idea. What about you?"

Thomas agreed he liked the idea, but when was Robert, due to leave at the end of summer, going to accomplish the task?

"He said he would help with the general design and structure, then Ham and Samuel could easily take over and finish the job. Weren't you eavesdropping, I mean, listening in?"

Thomas admitted he had been doing just that, but he still wanted a work schedule. Robert had said he would be studying through the summer before going to the city to attend school.

Brushing a few cookie crumbs from the bed, Adeline reminded him that Robert had also said he would still have time to stop by and help as needed.

"I have to write the checks this morning," she was saying now. "And the checks for the boons." She did up her blouse and then went to kneel beside the bed, reaching underneath it for the jewelry box.

Thomas told her to wait a minute. He got up from the comfort of their sanctuary and was almost instantly dressed. "A little trick I've managed and no, I don't know how I make it happen. Now, let me help you."

He lifted the box for Adeline and set it on the bed.

"I think I know how you make that happen. And other things, too."

"How?"

Adeline opened the jewelry box and lifted the top tray, setting it aside as she told him what she had figured out so far. "When you really want something to happen like whisking or making love, the magic of the house makes it possible."

"Sounds rather like making a wish."

"Then let's wish it lasts forever. Adeline lifted the emerald and diamond necklace from the jewelry box and then the matching earrings. She held up the jewelry. "Is there any more to this set?"

"I think what you have there will be more than enough."

"Too much?"

"Not at all."

They heard a few loud bangs from the new door knocker Adeline had asked Ham to install on the right front door.

"Why ever did you want such a noisy thing?"

"Because it's noisy and that warns us someone's at the door."

She set the jewelry on the bedside table and let Thomas put the box away. Going to the door of the bedroom, she said they should whisk to the front doors to save time.

"If it can only happen when I really want something, then what do you think will happen when I don't?"

"Don't you want the house finished? And the plans for the garage? And—"

"All right, all right. Point taken." Thomas whisked them to the front doors and Adeline opened them. She stood back as the men entered, greeting each one of them and asking what they were going to do that day.

As they answered, Thomas listened and watched. But he was thinking about what he had read in the book. He wondered briefly if the magic really was getting stronger because of the restoration. The book, A History of the House at the Edge of the Moor, had said the house had always been considered to have magic.

Lost in thought, he realized he was counting on that magic very much; more than he had admitted to Adeline. He was counting on it to make it possible, when the time came, for her to stay with him and, like him, exist and live a magical sort of life.

"A magical sort of life," he said aloud, without thinking.

"Beg your pardon, miss?" Samuel asked.

"Oh." Adeline covered for Thomas. "I said I'd like to see exactly where the garage will be built. Maybe after lunch?"

"That'll be just fine, miss. Happy to do so. Ham is going to go and get your car from the barn now, if you're ready. The road is dried out but rough and rutted."

"I have the keys right here." Adeline went to the table under the mirror. She gave her car keys to Ham and, with a touch of one hand to his cap, he left to get her car.

She turned to see Robert and Samuel discussing something and said she'd just go to the kitchen now and speak to Mrs. Folly. The men nodded and she started down the hallway, feeling she was missing something. *Thomas must feel like that every day*, she thought, *even though he's always with me.*

"Are you there?" she whispered.

"Yes."

"Are you happy?"

"Very much so."

"Good. Good morning, Mrs. Folly," Adeline said, entering the kitchen.

Mrs. Folly had, as usual, already started her baking for the day and whatever she had decided to prepare and leave for Adeline's dinner. Lunch was always large sandwiches and beer.

Rex trotted in and Mrs. Folly ordered him out the back door. "No need for you to be using your litter box on a nice morning like this. Out you go."

Adeline sat down at the kitchen table and Mrs. Folly gave her a glass of orange juice. "I noticed you don't seem to much care for coffee. I made a pot for the men. They don't need it yet though."

"I'd like a coffee," Thomas said.

"I'd like a coffee," Adeline automatically repeated. "I've started to get a taste for it."

Mrs. Folly turned to her. "Have you now?" She poured a cup of coffee and set it down in front of Adeline. "Milk?"

"Yes, please."

"I like it black," said Thomas.

"I'll just take it with me. I've got to go to the study to write the checks."

"You'd best sit here and eat your breakfast first," Mrs. Folly told her, preparing eggs and toast. "You've got a big day today and an even bigger one tomorrow."

Knowing she would only lose any argument, Adeline stayed and listened to Mrs. Folly as she prattled about the picnic details. After breakfast, Adeline thanked her for all her careful organizing. Then she left the kitchen.

She went to the small study. She and Thomas had agreed they liked it as it was. She had told Robert not to restore the study unless something needed to be done to keep it in good condition. He had examined the room carefully, pointing out the cornices and original wood and saying that the room appeared to have been untouched and the walls were sound.

"You might want Ham to paint it for you. Strange that this room was never wallpapered," Robert said. "Lucky, too. It's not good for the old paint. Lifts it right off the walls sometimes."

He had waited for Adeline's opinion and she told him as Thomas told her: the room was to be left alone for now. She was using it regularly and didn't want anything to be disturbed.

She had asked Thomas later if the study held a special importance to him or something sentimental. He said that he wanted one room on this side of the house left untouched. That it was one of the few rooms that felt familiar the way it was.

Adeline now sat down at the antique desk and pulled open a drawer.

She started writing the checks and noting them in a ledger. Thomas became visible and relaxed in an old armchair he liked, stretching out his legs and setting his feet on one end of the desk. Adeline smiled and kept to her work. When she was finished, she closed the door and went to stand beside Thomas.

"When I took out the jewelry earlier this morning, I felt a sudden rush, like a blast of air going through me. Did you notice? Did you feel it too?"

"I did. Both."

"What do you think it means?"

"I think it means we're on the right track."

They heard Ham driving Adeline's car to the front of the house. Thomas made himself invisible and then said he didn't understand why she wanted to keep the thing in the first place. "You don't have to go shopping for groceries or any other sort of supplies."

"True. I don't."

"Then why keep the car?"

"I might need it at some time. Besides, it's only proper that a Lady of the Manor have a car. And an expensive one at that. I made certain it cost my ex-husband a lot of money. It has all the extras."

"Vengeful woman." Thomas smiled at her.

"Maybe a bit. But now we have a car for, I don't know, Christmas shopping?"

"But that's months away."

Adeline heard Ham call to her and she went to the door. "Years of Christmas shopping to come," she said before opening the door, checks in one hand. She went to meet Ham and they discussed the best place to park the car for the summer. It had to be near the front of the house but well out of the way of any delivery trucks still to arrive.

Thomas could see the day was getting organized without him again, but he no longer let that bother him. He stayed near Adeline, enjoying how she almost always repeated anything he wanted said and how she would pause, and try not to laugh, when he whispered something not to be repeated.

By the end of the day, the house was ready for Adeline's inspection again. All three men proudly gave her the full tour starting in the Great Room. She didn't need Thomas to prompt her; it was all glorious. "You've all done excellent work; everything is exactly what I wanted."

The men thanked her and she gave them their checks. When she gave them the boons, they beamed at her and didn't seem to know what to say.

"Tell them you appreciate how much they care about the house," said Thomas.

Adeline repeated his words to the men as they stood in the freshly painted foyer, a new chandelier above them. The little table had been polished and the mirror cleaned. The tapestry had been taken to town where it had been cleaned and then put in storage. The front doors had been restored and properly hung and the wood rubbed until it shined. The lock was new and Ham gave her the new set of keys.

"Did you keep one for yourself and give one to Mrs. Folly?" she asked him.

"Yes, miss." He touched his cap and Adeline suddenly remembered the first time he had been introduced to her. It seemed years and not months, not because of the restorations but because she knew she could trust Ham.

"Thank you, Hamlet. I'll see you at the picnic?"

"Yes, miss. I caught a fine salmon for you."

"That sounds wonderful." She gave him a smile and waved as the men departed. Standing in the doorway, she looked up at the sky. "Do you think the weather will hold?"

"The wind is the weather," said Mrs. Folly, coming up behind her. She looked up at the sky. "And the wind is going to change soon enough. But tomorrow will be a fine day. Well, I'll say good night."

"Yes. Good night, Mrs. Folly."

Mrs. Folly started to walk away then stopped. "You might want to be calling me Agatha now and again. When it's just us two. It's not appropriate in front of the men."

Adeline was startled. "Agatha," she repeated. "Thank you."

Agatha took off her apron. "The Mrs. is long past now and the folly was in marrying the man. But I've a daughter to show for my troubles; she's my pride."

"Will she be at the picnic?"

"No. She wanted to be, but her husband is taking her on a honeymoon in France. He said something about how she had to see a tower there."

Agatha headed down the hallway and Adeline remembered when she had first met the stern looking woman. It felt like she was saying her final goodbyes and she had to remind herself that it was only because she was now looking past the day of the picnic to the meeting with Lady Moorhouse. And that made her feel afraid.

"Thomas? Why do I suddenly miss them all?"

"I don't know." He became visible. "They'll be back tomorrow and Mrs. Folly and Ham will always be about whenever you need them. And there's the garage still to be done."

Adeline noticed he was drooping a little.

"So you miss them, too."

222

"Maybe just a little. But soon we're going to have the house all to ourselves."

"Yes. Soon enough." She closed the doors and started toward the kitchen. "It's our home, Thomas, isn't it?"

"Yes."

———————

Late at night, sitting in bed with a plate of cookies, Adeline talked to Thomas about the meeting with Lady Moorhouse. She glanced at the jewelry on the bedside table. "Do you think she'll accept the jewelry?"

"Yes."

"What about running away? Do you think I'll be able to convince her?"

"Yes." He leaned over and kissed her left shoulder. "You've convinced me."

"Of what?"

"That you're almost always annoyingly right."

She laughed and relaxed. "Everything's going to be fine."

"Yes. Now put the plate of cookies on the table."

———————

The weather in the morning was sunny and warm, but there were clouds behind the mountain. Turning away from the bedroom window, Adeline continued dressing. She put on a pair of small diamond earrings.

Admiring her, Thomas said she looked beautiful. She gave him a smile and pulled a dress over her head, waiting as he did up the zipper for her. Then she hurried to the kitchen, heart beating a little too fast. She couldn't tell if she was excited or nervous. Deciding she felt both, she sat down at the kitchen table and listened as Agatha worked. Agatha said she had told Ham and Samuel to borrow tables and chairs from the town hall.

Adeline realized the many details she would have overlooked if she hadn't let Agatha take charge.

"Now you'll not need to be greeting everyone as they arrive because they'll all be expecting a speech before they stuff themselves. Samuel will look after the salmon and Ham will . . ." Agatha continued but Adeline was stuck on the word 'speech.'

Finally she rose and went to the kitchen window. "I can't give a speech. I'm not good at things like that."

"Things like what? Doing a courtesy to the people who have been looking after you and this house? Thanking them for their help and kindness?" Agatha straightened her apron and folded her arms across her chest. She waited for Adeline to answer.

"Well, I . . . I could do that, I think. For I do very much appreciate everything you just said. And more. The townspeople have made me feel welcome. I didn't expect that. I thought I'd be all by myself up here; alone."

"Tell them that." Agatha went to the oven to check on her pies. "Sincerity is all they're wanting. A good meal. And beer. I ordered a few bottles of whiskey, too. They're already in the pantry. But I'll not be putting them out until the dancing starts."

"Dancing?"

"Yes. First the welcome, then the lunch, then your speech—keep it short—then the music and the dancing." Agatha paused. "And haven't you been saying how you were going to give away those paintings?"

"Oh, yes. I'd forgotten."

"Well, Samuel will set them outside, lean them against a wall of the house and let the people have their pick."

"That sounds fine. In fact, I think I'm looking forward to the picnic now. I was feeling nervous."

"Nothing to be nervous about, except the wind. A gust or two would spoil the day. But I'm thinking it will stay away for another day. Then we'll be having a storm. Meanwhile, you'll have a bit of fun."

Agatha was right. The wind stayed away, the picnic was fun and Adeline's brief speech was accepted with a round of applause and raised mugs of beer. All the paintings had been given away and as each one was admired and accepted, Adeline's heart felt lighter. She had quietly said her 'goodnights' not long after the dancing started.

Samuel had started a bonfire and a friend of Ham's was playing the bagpipes. Another friend had brought a violin and a friend of his a drum. Suddenly they had a band for the dancing. It was fun, but Adeline missed sharing it with Thomas, even though he was beside her throughout the long day and evening.

It was after midnight before they were sitting on their bed with a plate of cookies between them. "Did you get anything to eat at all?" Adeline asked.

"Of course I did." Thomas took a cookie and washed it down with a swallow of beer. "It's amazing they didn't drink all the beer."

"I hid these in the kitchen." She lifted her bottle of beer to Thomas. "Here's to you, Lord Éclair."

"And to you, Lady Éclair." Thomas raised his bottle. "You do know I'd marry you if I could, don't you?"

"I know." Adeline stretched out her left arm, admiring the ring Thomas had given to her that morning. He had done it so casually, saying he wanted her to wear it always.

She had put it on without thinking about its meaning at the time. Now she sat back against the pillows, a smile lifting her lips. "It's beautiful." As the diamonds sparkled in the light, she remembered what still needed to be done.

"Don't you think the house feels better, lighter somehow, as if the paintings had been a weight?"

Thomas drank more of his beer. He leaned back against his pillows and they sat side by side, listening to the distant laughter and music. "It does," he answered after a minute.

"Did you want to stay at the picnic?"

"Not at all. I am, in fact, relieved it's over. But you did have fun and I love to see you happy. You should have danced more."

"Well, I think one dance with Ham, then Samuel, and then Robert was enough. I didn't even know the steps. And I danced with Tavish and Owen, too. But I felt . . . worried."

"Why? I wasn't jealous."

"I know. I was worried the dancing might start the magic out on the lake. Wake it up or connect with it somehow."

"If it did, I doubt it was the dancing."

"Oh. Why not?"

"It's more likely to have been the music, perhaps coupled with the dancing."

"I don't understand."

"Music often plays a part in magic, dancing as well. But I wasn't worried."

"You knew that and you didn't tell me? And why weren't you worried?'

"I didn't tell you because I knew there wasn't anything to worry about. The magic isn't evil, only some people.

"You and your guests were having fun and laughing with sincerity and joy. Not at all like Lady Moorhouse and her guests, full of pretense and self-indulgence."

Adeline was silent. She hadn't thought about any details or consequences of the picnic, including the most important: the magic.

They heard the sound of engines starting; the guests were beginning to leave. As they listened, Adeline realized how right it felt to be upstairs with Thomas and not downstairs with the guests. Agatha would see them off and Samuel would make certain the fire was 'well out' as he put it. It was proper for her to leave first, and she was fine with 'doing the proper thing' at last because it was the right thing for her and Thomas.

Thunder rolled over the mountain.

"Will the storm come tonight, Thomas?"

"No. But it's building up. It's going to be a big one when it does get here." He turned his head and smiled. "But we're ready for any storm now. It's about time the weather changed; the wind, too."

"The wind is the weather," Adeline reminded him.

They listened to the wind as it rattled the windows.

The front doors held firm and the wind went away. It would return to stir the magic of the house the next night.

Chapter Nineteen

"How do I look?" Adeline did a turn for Thomas. She wore a mint green gown. It was strapless with a tight fitting bodice and a wide, floor length skirt. She thought it nicely displayed the emerald and diamond necklace and earrings.

"Beautiful as always."

"I have a present for you." She went to her dressing table and pulled open the center drawer.

"Whatever for? It isn't Christmas yet, is it?"

"Don't be ridiculous. It's just a present." She turned and handed Thomas a flat box wrapped in gold paper. A white ribbon was tied about its center.

He stared at the box.

"Open it."

"All right." Frowning a little, Thomas pulled the ribbon apart, then slowly unwrapped the paper. He lifted the lid and smiled. "Very funny. Thoughtful, too."

"May I?" Adeline took one of the handkerchiefs from the box and tucked it into the bodice of her gown. "Now you have everything, Thomas."

"I do indeed." He went to stand beside her, turning her to face the mirror and slipping his right arm about her waist. They looked at their reflections. "Is there an ulterior motive for my present?"

Adeline scowled at Thomas's reflection. "If you must know, I thought a handkerchief would be the best thing to put the jewelry in when I give it to Lady Moorhouse." She turned her head to look up at Thomas. "I really did want to give you a box of handkerchiefs. I asked Agatha if there was a linen shop in town. I said I wanted something classic. For me."

Smiling, Thomas held up a handkerchief. "That would explain this lovely lace trim."

"That happens to be the style for men now, as well as centuries ago."

"Ah. Well, it's still thoughtful. Thank you very much."

"You're welcome." Adeline kissed him on his right cheek. "Shall we go?"

"I suppose so."

The storm had hurried across the lake in the early evening and now, at just past ten o'clock, it was roaring outside. The wind struck the windows of the house like fists and the rain beat the ground, creating muddy streams of water.

They had decided to go after the hour, hoping that would allow enough of an interval for the overlap of time. Adeline would have met Lady Moorhouse earlier and then later the note would have been written and left behind for Adeline to discover. Now they could speak again.

"We really have to get a clock," Adeline said.

Thomas took her right hand in his. "Why don't you wear a watch?"

"They make me nervous. I'm always glancing at the time and noticing how long I've been waiting."

He whisked them to the dining room. They were by the windows. The drapes were drawn open but the room was dark. "Hide behind the drapes again," he whispered.

As she did so, the double doors opened. But it wasn't Lady Moorhouse. It was Romanivich.

Thomas put one hand over Adeline's mouth, stifling her gasp. They watched Romanivich enter the room. He moved around the perimeter, passing within an inch of where they were hiding. He didn't look up until he reached the painting. He stared at it for several minutes, eyes narrowed. Then he lifted one side of his coat and searched a pocket.

Finding what he wanted, he held up a vial. A satisfied, sinister smile cracked his lips apart. "If she will not tell me where the treasure is, I will make her feel pain as she has never imagined possible." He hid the vial away inside the pocket.

Adeline almost stepped forward, but Thomas still had one hand over her mouth. His other hand was holding her right arm tightly. She waited.

Romanivich looked again at the painting, studying it. "I think I shall kill him anyway. No one will ever suspect me. They've yet to find the body of that impertinent painter I hired. What a fool he was to tell me his plans. Threatening my position, my power." His voice rose in pitch on the last word. He spun away and strode from the room.

After a minute, Thomas released Adeline. She took a deep breath. "Oh, no. We're too late."

"Only to save Peter. We can't be everywhere at once. The poor boy must have confronted Romanivich, perhaps wanting to take credit for his work after all."

"I think he just wanted to get away from him. Peter was in love with Lady Moorhouse, remember? Hopelessly."

"Quiet," Thomas whispered. "Someone's at the doors again."

The double doors opened. This time it was Lady Moorhouse. She signaled to one of the servants. He went to light a twin set of candles that stood in a silver holder on the table. Then he bowed and left, closing the doors behind him.

Lady Moorhouse locked the doors. She walked toward the candles and sat down at the head of the table. A small sound of despair escaped her.

Adeline couldn't wait any longer. She stepped from behind the heavy drapes. "Lady Moorhouse." She made it more a greeting than a question. "Your note said you needed my help."

Lady Moorhouse stood up quickly, one hand to her chest. "You quite frightened me. Must you always hide your presence? It's very rude."

"I think it discreet."

"Yes. Yes, of course. That's what I meant to say." She looked around the room. "Is anyone with you?"

"No." Adeline went to the table. She let the fingers of her right hand slide over the tops of the chairs. "What sort of help do you require?" The formal speech solidified her part in her mind, making Adeline feel at ease as she moved slowly around the table, returning to face Lady Moorhouse, stopping just a foot away.

"I wanted to know if you're prescient in some way. Tonight, after we spoke earlier, Romanivich threatened me again. He said if I wouldn't tell him where the treasure is, he would kill Sebastian."

"And what did you tell him?"

Lady Moorhouse lost her composure for a moment. Her eyes widened and she reached to grasp Adeline's left arm. "Nothing. I couldn't. I don't know where it is."

"Stay calm," Thomas said. He spoke to Adeline, invisible beside her, but this time Lady Moorhouse looked around the room again. "There is someone with you, isn't there? I've a gypsy fortune teller here tonight, for the entertainment of my guests. When she looks at a person's palm, she always speaks of a bright future. But when she looked at my palm, she seemed anxious and uncomfortable."

"What did she say?"

"She said tonight there would be someone uninvited here. Someone who would 'know my most secret of secrets.' I thought, after we first spoke, she meant you."

"What makes you think she didn't? I wasn't invited. And I do know your secret. You're in love with Lord Sebastian Éclair."

Lady Moorhouse released Adeline's arm and regained her composure. She flipped her fan open. "And what do you think I should do about it?"

"I think you should leave here tonight, immediately. Find Sebastian and tell him you'll run away with him."

"Impossible. My husband will divorce me for the scandal. I'll have nothing."

"You'll have Sebastian. Isn't your love for him worth everything? And what's a scandal but more gossip among people you don't even like? People you call friends but cannot trust. People who eat your food and drink your wine and then talk about you behind your back. Do you think they do not mock you right now? That they think your open flirting and your lovers are an acceptable game?

"If that is what you think, I promise you, you're wrong."

Lady Moorhouse looked down at the floor and stood silent for a long minute. "But how can I leave? I have no money of my own and Sebastian has only his title." She looked up at Adeline. "How will we live? And where?"

Adeline went to the table. She took the handkerchief from the bodice of her gown and spread it flat on the tablecloth. Then she removed her necklace and her earrings. She put them in the center of the handkerchief, folded it over the jewelry and tied it tight. She held the makeshift bag out to Lady Moorhouse. "Take these. I am told they are worth a small fortune. It will be enough."

Taking the handkerchief from Adeline, Lady Moorhouse looked into her eyes. "Why such kindness? I'm no more than a discourteous stranger to you; vain and silly."

"Because . . ." Adeline faltered. She waited for Thomas to tell her what to say. "Because I do know what's about to happen next. Now, we must hurry. Where is Sebastian?"

"He wasn't feeling well. He was going to his room upstairs and lie down for a few minutes. He said he wouldn't be long."

"We have to go to him right away." Adeline went to the side door of the dining room. Opening it a little, she looked out and then motioned to Lady Moorhouse to follow her. The two women moved quietly into the hallway. Music and laughter could be heard in the Great Room. They quickly passed the open doors and went up the stairs.

"This way," said Lady Moorhouse. She took the lead and they went to one of the guest rooms. Opening the door, she stepped inside the room and called to Sebastian. He didn't answer. She went to the interior door and opened it.

"Sebastian!"

She hurried to the bed where Thomas's body lay. She hovered over it, trying to rouse him. "Sebastian? Sebastian!" She shook the body.

"He's dead! Romanivich has killed him." Her voice broke and she wept.

"That's not Sebastian." Adeline moved swiftly to the bed and pulled Lady Moorhouse away from the body. "That's not Sebastian," she repeated. "Look again. Look!"

Lady Moorhouse obeyed. She frowned. "No. It isn't him." She looked at Adeline. "Who is he?"

"It hardly matters now," Adeline said.

"Oh, thank you very much," Thomas grumbled, not enjoying having to relive his death.

"Where else would Sebastian be? If he felt better, would he be in the gallery?"

"Yes. Yes!"

"We'll go there now."

"But what about—?"

"Leave that man alone. Someone will be checking the rooms soon. You and Sebastian have to get away now. Do you understand?" Adeline grabbed Lady Moorhouse by one hand and pulled her away from the bed and out of the room. They hurried to the gallery. Adeline stopped before they were noticed. She drew Lady Moorhouse to a door across from the room. "What's in here?"

"I think it's a closet."

"That will do very nicely. Wait here. And give me your fan."

"You want me to wait in the closet? Why?"

"If you want my help, you will do as you are told."

Lady Moorhouse stepped reluctantly into the closet and relinquished her fan.

Taking it, Adeline closed the door. She turned, entered the gallery and took a few steps into the room. "Has anyone seen Sebastian Éclair? He promised me a waltz." She snapped the fan open and fluttered it a little.

"I think he's over by the balcony," said a woman.

"No doubt watching for Lady Moorhouse." Her companion sniggered.

"No doubt." Adeline gave them both a thin smile and glided to the balcony.

A man was standing there. He turned to her. "Who are you?"

Adeline stood still. She felt dizzy. Time rushed at her from every side. The man who stood before her looked almost exactly like Thomas. She found her voice. "You promised me a dance, Lord Éclair. Don't you remember?" She forced herself to walk forward and put her left arm about Sebastian's right arm. "Come with me," she whispered. "Anne is waiting."

"Ah." He covered his surprise. "Yes. I did promise you a dance. We must hurry before the musicians tire." They left the gallery together and Adeline led Sebastian to the closet. She pulled the door open.

Lady Moorhouse gasped, afraid she'd been discovered, then she rushed forward and embraced Sebastian. She tried to explain to him what had happened, what they must do. He didn't argue but said he didn't know how they could leave without being seen.

"I think I know," said Thomas.

When he didn't say more, Adeline looked up and down the hallway. "Tell me!"

Watching her, Lady Moorhouse asked, "To whom are you speaking? Is it a spirit?"

"Tell her, yes. Tell her the spirit of the dead man is about to appear and aid their escape. Tell her he's going to touch her arm. Tell her she must remain quiet and calm."

Adeline would have argued but she knew they had little time. She repeated what Thomas said and Lady Moorhouse held onto one of Sebastian's hands. "I'm ready."

Thomas became visible; he raised one hand and touched Lady Moorhouse so she could see him.

She flinched and bit her lower lip, but she stood still.

It was Sebastian who paled and took a step back. "How is it that you look like me?"

"Be glad that I do. Now, have you a horse outside?"

"A small carriage, yes."

"Where? Tell me precisely where."

Sebastian thought a moment. He cleared his throat. "Beside the front doors, to the right."

"That will have to be enough." Thomas held out his right hand. "Take my hand, sir. Release your lady. I promise I will bring her to you."

Sebastian looked at Anne. He kissed her, then stepped away from her side and grasped Thomas's proffered hand. The two men disappeared.

Lady Moorhouse put one hand across her mouth. She looked at Adeline, eyes full of fear.

"It's too late to fear now." Adeline kept her voice calm. "You'll be safe soon enough."

Thomas appeared. "He's at his carriage and getting it ready. Let's go." He extended one hand to Lady Moorhouse and one to Adeline. Before Adeline could object, before Anne could protest, they were outside by Sebastian's horse and carriage.

Sebastian turned quickly and then lifted Anne up, holding her in his arms. "At last we're going to be together, my love."

"Yes, my only love. Yes."

Sebastian set her down and opened the door of the carriage.

Anne, the Lady Moorhouse, turned to her rescuers. "I don't know the words to thank you. I don't even know your names."

"My lady's name is Adeline," said Thomas.

"And his name is Thomas," said Adeline.

"We are in your debt. Thank you both." Anne turned to Sebastian and he helped her into the carriage. Then he climbed into the driver's seat. "I'm leaving my driver behind," he said to Thomas. "What of you? Will you be safe?"

"Yes," Adeline answered. "Now go. Hurry and never think on this again."

Sebastian nodded. "You have our eternal gratitude."

He touched the whip to the horse and the carriage pulled away from the house. It was swallowed in the dark of the storm.

Adeline shielded her eyes from the rain. "We did it."

She was about to ask Thomas to whisk them to their room when he grabbed her right hand and made them invisible. "Stand against the wall of the house."

The music inside had stopped. The voices were no longer laughing. Someone inside was shouting. The front door opened and a man in a cloak appeared. It was Romanivich. He glanced behind him and then hurried from the doorway, disappearing into the night.

"He's heading for the dock," Adeline said. "We have to follow him."

"No. I think we should wait here."

"I need to watch him, Thomas. Please. I need to know for certain that's he's gone away."

Thomas looked at the anxiety in her eyes. "All right." He whisked them to the dock.

A small boat was tied to the dock and Romanivich was running toward its safety. Voices were shouting behind him. They watched as he stepped into the boat and freed it from its mooring. Then he sat down and began to row away from the dock and out onto the lake.

"Do you think he'll make it, Thomas?"

"No. Not if he's headed where we think he's headed. The magic will get him."

"Then he really is gone. We're safe."

236

Several men arrived on the dock. They all looked out at the lake.

"The man has escaped," one of the men announced.

"He'll be drowned," said another.

"That boat will capsize in the storm," another man said.

The group of men stood in the rain and discussed various possibilities and ideas. They agreed to return to the house. One of them would go to the authorities in the morning. For now, they would search the house again for Lady Moorhouse and Lord Sebastian.

Listening, soaked with rain and feeling exhausted, Adeline looked at Thomas. "Whisk us away, please, Thomas. I can't take any more of mysteries and magic. Not tonight."

She felt the familiar tickle of whisking. Then they were in their bedroom.

Adeline turned to Thomas. "How long do you think the storm will last?"

"Not long. It's almost over." He put his arms around her, hugging her, and she rested her head against his right shoulder, her hands pressed against his chest.

They stood together for a minute, each knowing they were listening, waiting. A mist spread across the floor, the room tilted then went dark. The thunder stopped and the roaring of the wind turned to the softer sound of light rain. The storm was over.

"What do we do next?" Adeline asked as Thomas helped her out of her wet dress.

"We get you into a hot bath."

"I mean after that. How do we confirm that we've solved the mystery? How do we make certain we've won?"

"Wait for another storm, of course. Now get into the bath."

An hour later they were in bed with their plate of cookies and their beers.

"Are you sure you don't want a brandy?" Adeline asked again.

"Yes."

She wriggled closer to him. "Are you sure you love me?"

"Yes."

"Are you ever going to say more than 'yes'?"

"Yes." He turned to face her and kissed her lips. "You taste of beer and a chocolate cookie. Maybe I should have a brandy after all."

"No." She put the plate of cookies and her beer on the bedside table. Then she took Thomas's beer from his hand and set it beside hers. "Don't have a brandy just yet."

"Why not?"

"Don't you want to make love?"

"Yes."

The next day was Sunday and they had the house to themselves. After breakfast, Thomas whisked them to the garden. Protected from the storm, the garden seemed to gleam in the sunlight. They checked on the tree that Ham had replanted there. He had placed it next to the first.

Looking at the two trees, Adeline said she thought they looked different; healthier, happier even.

Then Thomas whisked them to every room that had been restored. When they reached the Great Room, he went to sit at the piano and played a pretty melody for Adeline. She sat beside him on the piano bench and Rex trotted into the room, sat down, and appeared to listen.

"And where have you been?" Adeline asked the cat. "So much excitement last night and you probably slept through it all."

Thomas finished playing and looked at the cat. "I think he found some quiet place to curl up and sleep through all the excitement. Isn't that exactly what you did, Rex?"

Rex trotted over and walked back and forth between Thomas's legs, rubbing against them and purring.

After a dinner of leftovers from the picnic, they walked back to their room.

"Thomas?"

"Yes."

"When do you think there will be another storm?"

"Tonight."

"But it's been such a pleasant day. Sunny and warm; the wind just a breeze. Even the lake is calm."

"Thank you for the weather report."

"You're welcome." She stopped walking. They stood at the end of the hallway where they could turn either right to the sunroom or left to their bedroom. "Let's go to the sunroom."

"Why?"

"Because I want to look at the lake."

"You want to watch for a storm."

"Yes."

They walked toward the sunroom. The sky was starting to darken with clouds. The lake that had been calm all day looked rough and wild now. Wind lifted the water into waves that slapped each other and Adeline remembered the terrible day they had been out on Ham's boat.

"Maybe we shouldn't watch."

"Don't be afraid." Thomas pointed out to sea. "There's our storm coming. We'll go to the gallery." He whisked them there. "We can watch from here."

"But I'm not dressed for a party."

"If we've won, if we've solved the mystery, there won't be a party."

"Okay." Adeline paced up and down along the railing of the gallery. She stopped occasionally to admire the room and then looked down at the Great Room. It was beautiful and still. She listened, but the wind couldn't find a weak place against the new windows or the front doors. It did manage to blow down the fireplace a little, but there wasn't a fire burning and the sound of the wind was soon replaced by the drumming of rain.

Thomas was walking around the library, looking at all the books, and smiling. The books were like old friends; there were some from his childhood and more from when he was a young man at school. He had often brought them back to the house, knowing his father didn't care, and Thomas began a collection of his favorites. He pulled one

239

from the shelf and sat down to flip through the pages, stopping at a fairytale he remembered.

Looking up as Adeline walked toward him, he closed the book. "How does the story end?"

"Happily, of course."

"Of course." She went to the balcony. "I don't think there's going to be a party tonight, Thomas."

Joining her, he looked down at the Great Room. "I don't think there will ever be one again. Unless you want one."

"Not me." Unconsciously, Adeline smoothed her hair. "One almost endless party was more than enough."

"You won't miss our mysteries?"

"We'll watch them on TV." She turned and went to the wall of bookshelves. "And there are more mysteries in these books. We can solve those instead."

"Will you be happy, Adeline?"

"I am already. Call me what you told Lady Moorhouse."

Thomas thought for a minute. "My lady?"

"Yes. I'm not just the Lady of the Manor anymore; I'm Adeline, the Lady Thomas Éclair."

"So you are. But you still have to play your part," Thomas reminded her. "The men will be back in the morning to start the garage. And I heard Ham talking about the trees and the small fence you want along the cliff's edge."

"I'm not playing a part now." Adeline kissed him. "Not now that you've called me your lady. It's like a vow of marriage."

"Is it? Well, then. We'd better start our honeymoon."

The days began to blend into one another as Adeline and Thomas relaxed into a new and gentler routine. Agatha shared her opinions about what trees Ham should plant along the side of the cliff, warning Adeline to 'stay well away from there always.'

Ham and Samuel worked on the garage together. Whenever Robert came to help, Ham took time off to work on the trees.

One afternoon, Thomas said he was going to inspect Ham's work. "I think he'll be finished soon."

"I'll come with you."

"No you won't. Remember what Agatha said. Anyway, you can't do a proper inspection until the fence is up. It's only been a few weeks. Wait a little longer."

"All right."

He smiled. "I'll be right back."

He disappeared, and Adeline went to the front doors. Rex was lying on the step, enjoying the summer weather. "You lazy cat," she chided him gently and bent down to stroke his head. "I bet you haven't caught one rat, let alone a mouse. Fortunately, I haven't seen either."

She stood up and crossed the pavement to where Samuel and Robert were working. They greeted her and she waved, then continued to walk along the side of the house. She turned the corner, realizing she was heading toward the 'tree that talked.'

She stopped there and noticed Rex had followed her. He jumped and climbed the tree until he reached a comfortable branch. Together they watched Ham work for several minutes.

The fence was low but strong. It stood between the trunks of mature trees. "Young ones will break in the wind," Ham had said. "It will cost you more, but trees that are little older will stand a better chance of getting their roots well into the earth. I'll plant them deep and they'll be ready for any change in the weather. The weather being so unpredictable once it changes after summer, miss."

"When is that?" Adeline had asked.

He pursed his lips. "First day of October, miss. The lake gets cold and the wind seems to change direction. The visitors stop their fishing and sailing long before then. The days and nights get cold fast and before you know, it's winter, and the storms are bringing you snow."

She had asked him how long the winter lasted.

He had considered that, looking thoughtful. "Till spring."

Adeline had smiled and thanked him.

Now, not wanting to disturb Ham while he was working, Adeline returned to the front doors and went inside. Thomas was waiting for her.

"What do you think?" he asked, remaining invisible.

"Of the trees or the fence?"

"The garage."

"I like it."

Agatha was coming down the hallway with a tray of beers. She nodded to Adeline and went outside to give the men their beer. She shouted to Ham to come and get his share.

"It must be the end of the day," Adeline said.

"She's more accurate than a clock," Thomas remarked.

Adeline laughed. "You're right."

Late one afternoon, a truck bounced along the road to the house and parked near the front doors. Adeline was in the kitchen with Agatha. Hearing the truck's engine, the two women went to investigate.

"And what do you have for us today?" Ham asked the delivery man.

The younger man was shorter than Ham, with a crop of ginger hair and freckles sprinkled across the bridge of his nose.

"Don't know," he said. "I was told to handle it carefully. It's fragile. I was told to ask for Ham and he's to help me put it in the house. I don't know where. Just in the house and ask for Ham. That's what I was told." The young man looked at Ham. "Name's Tosh."

"I'm Ham. Let's get that crate down from your truck. I know where it goes."

Adeline and Agatha stood back from the front doors as the two men unloaded a very tall crate. They set it on a dolly and rolled it inside the house. Ham paused inside the doors and touched his cap. "It's for you, miss. A special delivery."

Before Adeline could ask, Agatha stepped forward. "Special delivery, is it? And what is it you have that's so special?"

Thomas whispered into Adeline's right ear, invisible to everyone and audible only to her.

"It's a clock!" Adeline wished she could give Thomas a hug. She went to touch the crate. "Do open it up, please, Ham."

"I will, miss. Just tell me where you'd like it placed." He gave her a steady gaze, then his eyes shifted a little to an empty wall to the right of the doors of the Great Room.

Adeline turned and walked to the wall. "Put it here, please. This will be perfect. I'll be able to hear the time all over the house—" Thomas continued to whisper to her—"because it's a grandfather clock. Oh! The chimes will be lovely."

Ham and Tosh rolled the crate near the wall and started opening it. They carefully removed the clock and put it in place. Ham wound it and set the time. He waited until the clock chimed five times. "Five of the clock it is, miss."

Adeline felt like jumping up and down. She smoothed her hair. "Thank you, Ham."

She signed the invoice Tosh presented to her, thanked him, and then waited as he put the crate on the dolly and left.

She waited again until Agatha had finished her inspection of the clock and left for the kitchen, calling back to her that she was leaving for the day. "Your supper's on the stove."

When Agatha was no longer in hearing range, Adeline looked at Ham. He smiled. "It's a present, miss. From his lordship. He said you wouldn't mind paying for it seeing as he no longer has credit anywhere. He asked me to order it for you. Found a picture of it in a magazine and told me that you had been wanting a clock and had admired this one."

Samuel called to Ham and he touched his cap and left, leaving the doors open for Rex to enter. Rex went up to Adeline, meowing until she picked him up. She hugged him and then set him down on the floor. She felt Thomas put his arms around her waist.

"Do you like your clock?"

"Yes, I do." She reached her right hand to touch the wood. It was light oak and carved at the top and down its sides. The scrollwork framed the glass front that protected the weights, the pendulum, and the face of the clock. "It's beautiful." She looked over her right shoulder. "Thank you, Thomas. However did you manage it?"

"I just waited until Ham was alone one day and then made myself visible. I had the magazine with me, showed him the picture, and asked him to purchase it using your name. Just as he said. Ham did all the work."

"But you thought of it. And me."

The clock chimed once at half past five.

"Let's go and see what Agatha has left us for dinner," Thomas said.

"All right." Adeline touched the clock again. "I don't mind waiting as long we're together."

It took many years and many chimes of her clock before Adeline realized she did mind waiting. Waiting for the time, the day, the moment when she would be with Thomas forever and share his magical existence.

The magic in the house became stronger. The garage kept the car she never drove safe from the rain and snow. The little trees grew bigger and blossomed each spring, their branches waving in a gentler wind.

Adeline grew older. She stood before the mirror in the foyer and smoothed her hair, frowning at her reflection.

Agatha came up beside her. She had been standing at the foot of the stairs, calling to Adeline that her breakfast was ready. She was about to ascend when she noticed Adeline standing, not in front of her clock, as had become her habit lately, but in front of the mirror.

"It won't help to watch," she said.

"Watch what?"

"Your hair change from gray to white. It won't help to watch. It'll change, soon enough."

"I'm not watching."

244

"You might try listening. You're getting deaf." Agatha started down the hallway. "Your breakfast is ready. I won't be trying to keep it warm for you. I've bread to bake. And that cake you like so much.

"Come along, then. Your breakfast is likely to be cold by now." She continued down the hallway to the kitchen.

Adeline sighed. She started down the hallway, then stopped. "Thomas? Are you there?"

"Yes. Always."

"I don't like getting old, Thomas. I want to stay young and beautiful." She looked around her. "Where are you?"

"Here." He became visible and held his arms out to her.

She walked into his embrace and hugged him tightly, then she looked up at him. "Will I be old after I die? I don't want to be old forever, Thomas."

He held her, resting his chin on her head. "Don't worry. When you die, you'll be young again. Restored, just like the house and the magic in the house. It protects me and you."

"Promise?"

"Yes."

Epilogue

The house stood alone near the cliffs, but it was not empty. Its occupants numbered two. Two lovers together because of the magic of the house.

"How old was I when I died?" Adeline asked Thomas one day. They stood in the sunroom, looking out at the lake. She leaned back against his chest; his arms were about her waist. She was young and beautiful. He was young and handsome. And they were dead.

"Let me think." He remembered the day when she hadn't felt well and gone to bed early. When he lay down beside her, she had whispered, "I love you, Thomas," then she stopped breathing. He had held her all night, waiting for the magic of the house to work.

"You were eighty-five," he said at last and kissed the top of her head. "Why? Does it matter?"

"Not really. It only mattered then. I hated getting old while you remained young. And I hated waiting, too."

"At least we waited together. And, as I recall, we did much more than just wait."

Adeline smiled. "Oh, yes. We did much more." She lifted a hand to shield her eyes from the sunlight. "Everything's all right now, isn't it?"

"Yes."

She watched the gentle waves on the lake. "We haven't seen the waterspout since the night Romanivich died. Do you think it was the source of the overlap of time? That somehow it connected with the magic of the house? We never solved that mystery."

"Some mysteries are never solved. Anyway, we're still here; safe and together."

She turned in his embrace, looking up into his eyes. "You're my knight in shining armor, Thomas Éclair." She kissed him. "Let's go to the garden."

"Ham's grandson might still be there. It's spring again."

"He won't see us."

"Ah, but you'll see him."

"Now you're just being silly. And jealous, too, I think."

"Of that boy? I'm not jealous."

"Oh, yes you are. Remember when I started having the house restored and you were jealous of Robert?"

"I remember you once said that a little jealousy could be a good thing."

"Then I'm right. You are jealous."

"You do always have to be right, don't you?"

"Not always." Adeline hugged Thomas. "But I usually am."

"You can't end a sentence with a preposition."

"Yes, I can. I'm a ghost and I'm magical too."

"If you're so magical, why is it that you never learned to cook?"

"Do you want to know a secret?"

"Of course."

"I never really wanted to learn how to cook."

Thomas laughed.

Together, the lovers walked through an outside wall and into the air.

Manufactured by Amazon.ca
Bolton, ON